CLAIMING THE WHITE BEAR

WHITE BEAR SERIES
BOOK 2

TERRY SPEAR

ISBN-13: 978-1-63311-044-1

Thanks so much to Lola Faber for loving my bears and books and pictures and always being such a fun-loving lassie on my blog and Facebook.

SYNOPSIS

A Romeo-Juliet type family feud, polar bear style, tore them apart; can they find true love again?

It's nearly Christmas, no tours on the schedule for Edward MacMathan and his brother and so they're working in their uncle and aunt's tavern when the love of Edward's life returns with two young boys in tow, and they look a lot like him when he and Rob were that age. Robyn Conibear is in trouble and she's fled her deceased mate's sleuth to keep his parents from taking custody of her and Edward's sons.

Can she and Edward renew the love they had for each other despite the six years that have passed? Or will her return only cause more grief between her family and his as the hostilities renew?

But Edward is the boys' true father and she wants to be with him no matter what. Likewise, Edward is determined to protect her and the boys, both from her former mate's sleuth and her own, and take up where the two of them had left off.

PROLOGUE

Six years earlier, Alaska

Hoping the weather would hold out, Edward MacMathan was eager to pop the most important question of his life to Robyn Conibear, the love of his existence, as he stocked kitchen cabinets with food for a three-day weekend at his family's cabin getaway. In his hometown of White Bear where his polar bear sleuth had settled centuries earlier, Robyn was finishing up her finals on her summer marketing classes before her fall courses began. Her own sleuth lived in Anchorage and they had been the reason for Edward's sleuth relocating and settling White Bear all those years before, but the territorial disputes had been ancient history between the sleuths and it didn't mean anything to Edward and Robyn.

She would join him in a few hours, courtesy of his cousin Craig, who flew a seaplane for rescues, taking tourists on tours, and ferrying people and supplies all over the state.

Even though Edward had wanted the marriage proposal to be a surprise, he figured she already knew what he was up to. He was so excited, he could barely think straight. He started a fire in the fireplace, set the table, having even had the foresight to bring a vase of red roses with him, and surveyed the cabin.

Blankets folded and stacked on a shelf in the corner of the cabin, puzzle boxes and books, DVDs on more shelves, all with earthquake proofing, the warm fire crackling in the fireplace. And smore's for some nighttime fixings.

The canoe was ready for some long paddling and short portages. They would have to be prepared for moose and bear encounters on their treks. Not the polar bear kind out here though. Unless they were shifters like them. He glanced at the clock and sighed. Three more hours before she arrived. He hoped she would do well on her test, though he was certain she would. And he was hoping she would say yes to a proposal of marriage. He prayed she wouldn't decline his offer and return to Anchorage after her fall and winter classes were done and she had earned her marketing degree.

Edward had adored her ever since Robyn had arrived at his aunt and uncle's White Bear Tavern with a couple of classmates, human variety, to have lunch and he'd first seen her. He'd dropped by the tavern with the tour group he and his brother and their friend operated. Their fledgling business was just getting started and they were having lunch before they headed out into the wilderness to show the group members the beauty of Alaska.

Robyn had even signed up for one of his tours because she thought *he* looked like he would be fun to be with, not to mention they were both polar bears. From then on, he and she had been an item and he'd been totally sold on her. He had fallen in love with her cheerful smile and lighthearted humor, her adventurous spirit, and enthusiasm to try new things. Snowball fights, running and swimming as bears, playfighting, paddling, making wild and passionate love, she was the only one for him.

He kept envisioning how he was going to propose to her—on a paddling trip as the sun set, sitting on the deck as the sun's last rays colored the sky and water with their magical colors, or before he fixed them a grilled steak dinner. He wanted to ask her as soon as she got off the seaplane. He wanted to scoop her up and carry her across the threshold and tell her just how much he loved her and wanted her to be his mate forever. But that was the impulsive side of him and he really wanted to make this memorable for her.

He glanced outside at the gray skies. Maybe they wouldn't have any spectacular sunsets while they stayed here.

Well, if it rained the three days they were here, they would still find a way to have a great time. He just hoped she would say yes to his proposal of marriage!

FEAR MIXED with excitement at the prospect of having Edward's baby, maybe twins, since so many polar bear shifters had twins, Robyn was trying to concentrate on her final exam in her last summer marketing course. The baby wasn't planned. She sure hoped Edward was going to propose to her sometime during the stay at the cabin and that he wouldn't change his mind when he heard they were going to have a baby. But after she took the pregnancy test this morning before her last final, she'd been anxious too. What if he wasn't ready to be a father? Not that he had much of a choice.

She worried how he would take the news. She just had to finish the exam and quit thinking about being with Edward and of telling him what she'd learned. She was sure it would be as much of a shock to him as it had been for her.

As soon as she was finished and turned in her final exam, she drove to the place where Edward's cousin Craig would fly her out to the wilderness. She called her parents on the Blue-tooth to let them know she wouldn't be home until Christmas break. Though if she was married by then, she might be just staying in White Bear with her mate.

"Hey, Mom, I just finished my summer finals."

"You know we don't approve of you being there."

White Bear, living in the MacMathan bear territory, her mom meant.

Robyn ground her teeth. "Yes, well, they have the best busi-ness marketing degree and that's why I came here. Which I've mentioned to you before." Like a hundred times.

"You've been seeing Edward MacMathan."

Robyn clenched her teeth. How the hell had her mom known that? Someone her family knew must have been in town and had seen her and Edward together at some time and reported it back to the family. She was certain her own family wouldn't visit here. If they had, they sure hadn't come to see her.

"I'm dating him. So?" And mating him, if things worked out about the baby.

"You'd better knock off that nonsense right now before it's too late."

It was already too late. She loved Edward and she was certain he loved her. "It's not happening. Unless things don't work out, of course." She wasn't naïve enough to think that Edward would be totally thrilled about being a father so all of a sudden. But no matter what, she was keeping the baby.

"You won't be seeing him any longer."

"Uhm, Mom, I'm twenty-four and living on my own, which means we're beyond you telling me what to do." Though if Robyn didn't end up mating Edward, she was going to have a tough time of it getting her degree, a job, and raising a baby or more. But she would do whatever it took.

"You're pregnant, aren't you? Damn it, Robyn. You know we're mortal enemies."

"*No. We. Aren't.* Our *ancestors* were. Just get over it." She couldn't believe her family could hold a grudge against people they'd never known. She hadn't told her mom that she was pregnant. Robyn figured her mother had just guessed at it. Robyn had no plans to reveal to anyone that she was pregnant until after she told Edward. Suddenly, her bright outlook on a future with Edward was overshadowed by a black cloud—her family's insistence that everyone hate the MacMathan family for all eternity, and now she was carrying a MacMathan's child.

It would take an hour to fly to the location where the cabin was, and the whole time, all she would think about was the baby she was carrying and if Edward was ready for it, or if her family would ever accept their decision to mate, if this was where this was going. So much for taking a mate home to see them for Christmas ever, if Edward and she tied the knot.

"The weather's going to get socked in." Craig loaded her bags into the seaplane. He smiled at her like he was ready for her to be part of the family and he knew what Edward had planned.

They'd all been lovely to her: Edward's brother, Rob, his cousins, Trooper Andy, pilot Craig, and Ben, who worked with his parents at the tavern, and of course, Edward's aunt and uncle who owned the tavern. They were like the parents Edward and Rob had lost when they were younger, due to an avalanche. Miraculously, Edward had rescued his brother from being buried in the snow, but he and Rob had been too late to save their parents. All because a teen polar bear with a grudge against their law enforcement parents had caused their deaths.

At least the MacMathans didn't have any issue with her being a Conibear, and for that, she was grateful.

"We'll have a...uhm, good time, no matter the weather," she finally said, strapping herself into the seaplane. As long as

Edward wasn't upset about the unplanned baby or two...or three.

ONLY AN HOUR TO go now and Edward couldn't believe how anxious he was to see Robyn and propose to her. He went outside to cut up more wood for the fire and saw a man approaching, six-foot-four, tall like Edward was, his hair blonder, and his eyes dark, and he was wearing a growly expression.

"Howdy. Are you looking for someone or something?" Edward didn't like the way the man was stalking toward him. His posture was aggressive, and from the way the breeze was blowing, Edward smelled he was a polar bear, his scent indicating he was riled up about something. He wasn't anyone Edward knew. All that came to mind was that the man could be one of Robyn's kin. Maybe a brother and somehow, he'd learned that Edward was dating Robyn and he didn't like it.

"Are you Edward MacMathan?" the man practically growled.

"Yeah." Edward refrained from adding, "What's it to you?" But if the man was related to Robyn, Edward wanted to smooth things over between them, not add to the friction. Not that his family had anything to do with hers. Not until now when he'd fallen hard for Robyn.

"You're the one seeing Robyn." The man stated it like he knew it for a fact.

"Yeah." Edward wasn't going to hide the fact. Robyn must have finally told them that she was and mentioned she was coming here. How else would anyone who wasn't with their sleuth know?

"If you know what's good for you, you'll stay away from her."

That wasn't going to happen. "Why? Who are you?"

"Her brother Butch, and I've come here to tell you to call this off now."

"It's not happening. I'm proposing marriage to her as soon as she arrives here." Edward had planned a slow seduction, but now he wasn't. If her family was going to get involved, he was going to flat out ask her as soon as she left the seaplane and before he grabbed her luggage.

"After what you did to her—I'm going to kill you." The man began stripping off his clothes.

Hell, Butch was going to shift and fight him? Edward hadn't expected this. Some bad weather. Sure. Not a fight with one of Robyn's four brothers. He suspected the guy wasn't offering idle threats either. And Butch could kill him with one bite if he didn't hurry to strip and shift to battle the bear.

Damn it anyway. This could screw up everything between him and Robyn.

Tossing his shirt last, Edward shifted just as the bear charged him, not waiting for Edward to prepare himself for the onslaught.

Half a ton of bear slammed into him, both growling, their teeth biting, sparring, trying to take down each other. Edward finally tackled Butch to the ground, but the bear was ruthless and not giving up. Butch managed to wriggle free and came in for another vicious attack. It wasn't just a warning bout, meant to tell Edward to stay away from his sister. Edward wondered how in the hell Butch thought he'd wronged Robyn in some way.

Blood trickled from both Edward and Butch's wounds as they continued the onslaught. Edward kept trying to break off the fight, but Butch wasn't having it. Every time Edward would part from him and put some distance between them, Butch would just come barreling in to attack him again. Each time, Edward tried to break off the fight, it was giving Butch the advantage and wearing Edward down. Yet, he would do anything to stop the fight before either of them had to die over some perceived wrong.

They heard a seaplane coming and Edward's heart sank. Robyn would see him and her brother fighting. What if she didn't want to be the cause of the trouble between them and left Edward for good? Hearing the seaplane seemed to spur Butch on, as if he was worried Robyn would choose being with Edward over returning home with her brother. Once again, Butch tore into Edward with the intent to kill.

Edward continued to spar with the bear, continued to get his bites in, continued to try and wrestle him onto his back, and he finally pinned him down again. But he couldn't kill her brother with a clear conscience, though he had every right to protect himself from the bear who was trying to kill *him*.

Edward released him and backed off. With narrowed eyes, Butch stared at Edward for a moment, and then full of rage, rolled to his feet and charged him again. Edward couldn't keep this up. He was going to make a grave error and Butch would finally get the best of him.

Butch tore into him again, and Edward could barely last the assault. Badly wounded, feeling his strength ebbing, Edward had no choice but to try and stop Butch from killing him. That's all that mattered. He hated what he had to do, *if* he could even do it now as bad a shape as he was in.

Butch managed to tackle Edward to the ground and he tried to fight back, the bear's teeth sinking into his shoulder instead of Edward's throat where Butch had aimed his large snout and deadly teeth.

The seaplane landed on the water, and Edward knew Butch had to kill him now before anyone could stop him.

"No!" Robyn screamed, sounding horrified as she rushed to leave the seaplane. "Butch, no!"

Butch wasn't stopping for anything and tried again for Edward's throat, but Edward called on more of his strength to pull free from the bear. Robyn and Craig were running from the shore, trying to reach them. To stop them.

Edward tried one last time to end the fight and backed off, but Butch tore into him again, and this time it was the end—his or Butch's. In his heart and his mind, Edward told Robyn he was sorry for what he had tried to prevent all along, but this time, he couldn't hold back.

He fought with all the dwindling strength he had left and managed with one last ditch effort to kill the aggressor bear. Butch crumpled on the ground and Edward collapsed next to him.

"No!" Robyn screamed.

But Edward wasn't sure if he'd killed her brother or if he would even live himself. All he cared was that he loved Robyn with all his heart, and he was certain he'd lost her because of some damn feud that had occurred between their families, way before they were even born.

1

Six years later, Yellowknife, Northwest Territories, Canada

When polar bear shifter Robyn Conibear lost her husband, Callahan Gardner, in a hunting incident five months earlier, she never thought she might lose custody of her twin sons—if his parents had their way—unless she ran away from Yellowknife and the polar bear shifter sleuth that she belonged to there. Even so, Robyn had known she would have to leave and had to tell Edward in person that her sons were also his.

She worried that if she had any trouble with Callahan's sleuth, she might not get some help from Edward MacMathan and his family when she drove into White Bear. She had always wished Edward and she could have been together.

She didn't even know if Edward was mated or not, or if he was seeing another woman by now. After Robyn had left him so suddenly and never had another thing to do with him, he might not even want to see her again. His family might be on the outs with her too.

What if he already had a mate, and once he learned the boys were his, he wanted custody of them? She would be in the same situation she was now, except she was certain that he wouldn't want to keep the boys from her like she thought her former in-laws did. And they *were* his sons. She couldn't blame him if he wanted full custody after she hadn't told him about them all these years. If her in-laws managed to get full custody, she was certain they would try to brainwash her sons into believing she was a bad mother and never let them see her again.

"Momma, Grandma and Grandpa said we gotta live with them," Bryan said to Robyn when he and his twin brother, Garrett, hurried to pack up their last-minute belongings in the truck.

Robyn couldn't believe they would actually told the boys that! She'd thought her in-laws were trying to hide the truth from her until it was too late. She wondered if that meant they were making the move to take them from her sooner than later. She'd been desperate to pack up and just leave, but she'd had to do this right, for fear the sleuth would stop her before she got very far.

She tucked the fire safe with all her important documents, like the boys' birth certificates, title on her truck, her birth certificate, marriage certificate, and her husband's death certificate, in the back seat on the floor.

She had been urgently attempting to make ends meet ever since she'd lost her mate and was trying to keep her company, Bear Necessities Marketing, going. Callahan had wanted her to stay home with the boys while he was off on his trucking job. But once he was dead, she'd created the company to support her family. Callahan had been a good mate and father to the boys, protecting them on a vacation when they were running as polar bears in the Northwest Territories, and she knew, if he'd still been alive, he would have been furious with his parents over this.

She packed up her business cards and tucked them in the

console because at least her email address and phone number would still be the same when they moved.

For some time now, she'd heard the rumors that her in-laws were making waves with the leaders of their bear sleuth that she didn't have the time to properly take care of her sons, and *they* needed to raise the boys. They could offer them more stability and the boys would only have to follow one set of rules. *Theirs.* That had been disturbing news to her. Her in-laws had been so nice to her about keeping them when she'd joined the Canadian Marketing Association and had needed to travel. When she was busy trying to secure business clients, and then working to continue to make her business thrive, she left the boys with them. Her in-laws had encouraged her to do whatever she could to get her business off to a good start, and she was doing better so she could support herself and her kids. But now?

She packed up her camera and the rest of her gear into the front seat of the truck.

Had their insistence that she leave the boys with them all been a scheme to win over the boys and the bears in their sleuth to show that Robyn couldn't manage both taking care of the boys and running her business? She had to work, or they would lose their home. But the home, the business, none of it mattered if Martha and Arnold Gardner were able to take the boys away from her.

She packed the rest of the food she planned to take with them, mostly just items they would consume for the few days' trip they had to make.

No way was she going to allow her in-laws to take the kids from her. If they ever learned the truth of who their real father was? She didn't even want to consider what might happen then. Create a nice fatal accident for her, she could just imagine, so the secret would die with her.

The tallest of the twins, Garrett, stuffed some more books

underneath the driver's seat, turned to her, and lifted his chin. "I'm not staying with them."

"No, you're not," Robyn adamantly said, rushing around the house to ensure everything looked just right, nothing out of place, no clue as to where they'd gone. She'd even left fake wrapped Christmas packages under the tree, some of the kids' older toys they had agreed to leave behind, and books she promised to replace when they got settled.

Of the two boys, Garrett was the most independent and stubborn. He took after both her and their real father. Bryan was more laid back and flexible. She wasn't sure where he got that from.

Neither her own parents, nor her brothers, had been reasonable concerning her and Edward. Of course, if they had been reasonable, she believed she would have been with Edward in White Bear all along.

"We've been doing this forever," Garrett complained.

For a couple of months, true. Robyn had known her in-laws would have had a fit if they'd learned she planned to take the boys to see Edward too.

"Yes, but this is the last time." For weeks now, Robyn had been packing and getting ready to leave, knowing the influence Arnold had over the town and their sleuth as their former mayor. And Martha was such a social butterfly, when she wasn't taking care of the boys, she was socializing with her many friends. Robyn couldn't trust that the bear council would side in her favor as the boys' mother over her in-laws.

She hadn't been able to tell the boys what they were doing until now, knowing Garrett would have told her in-laws that they were leaving, *so there.*

It would take them forty-one hours to reach home, and she was certain the bear sleuth would try to stop her before she got very far. Which was why she was leaving at four that morning. It was a Friday, so it wouldn't be unusual for her to take a drive somewhere, except she never drove off *that* early. She'd been taking the kids for short trips for several weeks, driving them out in the wilderness to shift and run, so she wouldn't arouse any suspicions when they left for good. She'd wanted to leave last night, but she was afraid that would seem suspect if anyone checked on her and found they weren't at home.

"We're really going away this time?" Bryan asked, sounding hopeful.

"Yes." She always took off the whole three-day weekend to be with her kids. And she'd already told her in-laws that she needed to be at work longer on Tuesday, so she was taking off from work on Monday to make up for it. With any luck, that would give her four full days to travel to White Bear, hopefully, before anyone became suspicious. It was still a horribly long drive, and if she ran into any trouble along the way... She just prayed they wouldn't.

"Okay, kiddoes, have you got everything you want to take with you?" she asked them one last time. She'd packed bedding, clothes, toys, some food they could eat along the way, and her computer. Other than stopping for gas, bathroom breaks, and a few hot meals to go and a couple of overnight stops that they would have to make, she didn't want to rest, afraid someone in the sleuth would catch up to her and force her to return with the kids.

"Yeah," Bryan said, looking at his made-up room.

"I am!" Garrett said with enthusiasm.

She had to leave everything looking the same, so they'd had to forsake some things to make it appear as though they were still living there—clothes in the closet and drawers, food in the fridge and in the cabinets, toys the kids didn't want any longer. The bedding she'd taken with her was brand new and her in-laws had never seen it. She hated leaving the bear community behind like this when she wouldn't have a bear sleuth to help her out when she needed it. She didn't know if her family would even take her back, or how Edward and his family would react to her arriving in White Bear. But she was sure how this was going to turn out *if* she stayed in Yellowknife and she lost custody of her boys to her mate's parents. Once she felt safe and protected, wherever they ended up, she would put her house in Yellowknife on the market to sell.

"Yay," Garrett said. "We're off on another adventure."

"We sure are." That's what she'd called all their trips away, so if they'd let it slip, they were just going on another adventure, like they always did. But this time it was a really *big* adventure.

They piled into the truck with their picnic lunches that they would eat in a few hours. Though they each had apple slices for a snack. They'd gone to bed especially early last night, mainly so she could be well-rested enough for the long, tedious drive. Despite the early hour this morning, she fed them a hearty breakfast of ham and eggs and hash browns before they left.

She pulled out of her driveway, glad she had a top for her pickup bed so no would know it was packed to the roof with their treasured belongings.

She suspected her in-laws were worried that she would find another mate, and they wouldn't approve of him and how he would treat her kids or that they wouldn't see them again. Especially, if she left Yellowknife to find a mate.

She couldn't even tell her best friend, Becky Whitestone, that she was leaving and never coming back. That was the worst part.

But she wasn't about to allow her in-laws to dictate who she could date, if she ever chose a mate again. They'd already suggested she mate one of their other sons. She would worry enough about whether another mate could love her *and* her kids just as much. But she would only mate a bear she was truly in love with. Certainly, not one of Callahan's brothers. As soon as she learned her in-laws planned to force the issue of taking her sons from her, stating they took care of the boys more than she did, she knew she had to run. She would be forever grateful to Becky for clueing her in after she'd overheard some of the conversations Martha had with her friends.

For some time, Robyn drove on the dark, snow-cleared road, and everything was fine, though she couldn't slow her beating heart.

She'd been driving on the road for about three hours when her cell phone rang. Her heart took a dive. She hesitated to look at the caller ID on the Bluetooth. When she did, she saw it was her mother-in-law, and she didn't want her to suspect anything since Martha knew they were all early risers. She answered the call. "Hello, Martha?"

"We want to keep the boys overnight on Tuesday night."

"They only stay with you when I have to be away." Robyn thought of telling her that was fine, just so she could end the call and not have any hassle with her. She didn't want her voice to give her away either. She wouldn't normally have just let it go and she didn't want to sound like she was deviating from their usual routine or her in-laws could become suspicious. One problem she hadn't thought of, not that she'd expected Martha to call, her mother-in-law would know they were in the car, using the Bluetooth, driving somewhere.

"We thought we could do it then because we're not going to see them on Monday."

"Maybe some other time. Not this coming week. I'm taking the kids to fish as polar bears. We'll talk later. See you on Tuesday."

"Alright. See you then." Martha sounded disgruntled that she couldn't have her way.

Robyn hoped she hadn't given herself away. She would have

to start up her business again in a new location, but at least a lot of the work she did was online. Still, she loved to solicit local businesses too, taking videos of them while they were creating their products or providing a service, and turning them into marketing videos to help promote them. She had to be there in person for that.

The kids were quiet, and she glanced back at them. Both were sound asleep. Even though they'd gone to bed early last night, she'd overheard them whispering about leaving and they were so excited, as if it were going to be Christmas. She suspected they hadn't slept all that long. She hadn't. She had been too anxious about leaving and she had an awful time waking the kids at first this morning. Not her. She'd been ready to go first thing.

She hoped the boys wouldn't miss the only grandparents they had ever known, if she could even stay free of them. Even though she was heading to White Bear to tell Edward the truth, going there could open up a whole new can of worms since she'd broken Edward MacMathan's heart after leaving him nearly six years ago. And never told him about his sons. Everyone in the sleuth liked him, so she wasn't sure she would even be welcome there.

Her family was a whole other story. She really wasn't sure they would accept her back either. And if they learned the boys were Edward's? No way could she return home. Not unless they could accept the situation now. No matter what, she wasn't keeping it secret from Edward any longer. The problem was, as polar bear shifters, she didn't have a lot of choices about where she and her sons could live either.

So far, so good. No sign of her late mate's family.

After three days of driving, she made it most of way through the Yukon Territory, but then had to stop again for the night. She thought they might just make it to White Bear, without getting caught, though she had one problem. She had only one more day to reach White Bear before her in-laws would discover she and the boys were gone. The day after that, they would probably be out for her blood. They still had a way to go before they could catch up to her. If they weren't already hot on her trail.

2

Edward MacMathan and his twin brother, Rob, were serving meals and drinks to help their aunt and uncle out at the White Bear Tavern in the small Alaskan town of White Bear while *White Christmas* was playing overhead. Family was too important to not spend it with them, and the MacMathan brothers always closed down their White Bear Wilderness Adventure Tours to work at the tavern during the holiday season.

They'd all helped to trim the tavern in Christmas garlands, wreaths, and an eight-foot, evergreen tree standing in one corner was decorated in tons of little polar bears and red bows, balls, and multi-colored lights. The reflection of Christmas lights sparkled in the smoky mirrors behind the long bar. Red-cinnamon candles sat on each of the tables, and the aroma of steaks broiling, cinnamon, and wassail filled the air.

They were all busy serving patrons at this joyous time of year, everyone's spirits bright. Even Rob's new mate, Alicia, a photojournalist, wanted to assist them this Christmas. But she had been turned into one of their bear kind two years earlier, and their babies were three-month-old twins: a boy, Daniel, and a girl, Jenny—and they suspected they might have psychic talents like Rob and Alicia did. Instead of helping at the tavern, Alicia had brought the babies into the place to enjoy a late lunch with Rob. That meant their Aunt Genevieve, her white-hair tucked in a bun, and wearing a Mrs. Santa apron, had to stop supervising the kitchen staff and come out to cuddle the babies for a few minutes while Alicia ate before she had to take care of the babies again.

Knowing about their psychic abilities, Edward didn't know if he felt left out now, or relieved that he didn't have a psychic gift. He met up with their cousin Ben, who was getting another tray of fish and chips platters. Ben worked here for his parents on a regular basis, and he still swore he'd matched up Rob and Alicia, but they knew he hadn't had anything to do with it. Now, Ben was targeting Edward. Every cute bear shifter who dropped into the tavern, he made sure to give out the tour guide brochures to, stating Edward was one of the best tour guides around. Which amused his brother, Rob.

"Hey, it's going to happen," Ben said to Edward. "I just need to see the right woman, and know she's the one for you."

Edward snorted. "Make sure she doesn't have a significant other first, the next time, will you?" At least the black eye he'd received from the last mistake was starting to fade. How would he look when Alicia began taking all the family Christmas photos this year, the first time for her and the babies? Though she said if he didn't really want to have a black eye for the pictures—which would give him more character—she would Photoshop it out.

The door opened and three male snow leopards, the Wright brothers who frequented the tavern, entered and found a seat near the fireplace and waved at the MacMathans gathered at the counter.

"If I could see what was going to happen to anyone in the

family, I would tell you who was going to be in your future," Rob said. "If it was something that was going to happen soon, I should say." Though Rob couldn't see anything that would happen to family members—being that he was too close to them, Edward suspected. Rob was serving the meal for his mate and himself so no one else had to do it.

"I was surprised you would leave Alicia at home taking care of the babies for most of the day so you could help out here," Edward said.

They'd all tried to talk Rob out of coming in this year, so he could be home with his family.

"She had a couple of women friends come over who were assisting with the babies while she got some rest," Rob said. "She just wanted to say hi and eat lunch with me here today. I'm sure Aunt Genevieve had something to do with it. To tell you the truth, Alicia kicked me out of the house this morning so I would assist Uncle Ned and Aunt Genevieve here like we do every year. Alicia didn't want to mess up our family tradition."

"Everyone would understand if you had stayed home this year," Edward said.

Rob was the first one in the family who had married and now had kids. Everyone loved the babies.

"I'm grabbing a quick bite to eat with Alicia," Rob said.

"Take your time and enjoy your lunch," Edward said. "We've got this."

The door opened. They glanced in that direction again before Rob joined his mate.

The tavern was filled with families coming in to share in the warmth and comradery with the other shifters who often came here: Arctic wolves, black bears, polar bears, you name it. Most got along with the rest and helped each other's businesses. They had a lot of human locals who were repeat customers, and a few passersby dropped in also.

A woman wearing a blue dickey over her face, her faux-fur hood still up, ushered two kindergarten-age boys into the tavern. At least he guessed that's about how old they were. They were buried in snowsuits, hoods, face masks and fur-lined, waterproof boots to keep them warm.

Ben didn't bother to say anything about the woman being a potential match for Edward, not when she had two kids in tow. Edward knew Ben would have otherwise. Though they didn't even know if she was a shifter or not.

She and the kids looked cold and worn out, hunched over, the kids huddling next to her, clasping her gloved hands with their mitten-covered ones. Edward headed for them, to make sure they got a table closer to the fireplace. All of the tables close to it were already taken, but he would ask someone to move for the woman and her children. At least he guessed they were her children.

"She's already taken," Ben said, carrying his tray of platters behind him, as if Edward didn't know that the woman had to have a mate already.

Edward was just being nice to the woman.

"There's always Joy," Ben said to Edward as he was headed back to one of his own tables to serve.

Edward ignored his cousin's suggestion. Joy wanted a dozen kids, and she was serious about it. Worse, she wanted a mate to stay home and babysit while she continued to work as a ski instructor at the nearby ski resort. She was eagerly searching for a mate, but most of the guys they knew were steering clear of her, except for having friendly chats with her.

Ben delivered the food to a table, then headed back to the counter for more platters.

When Edward reached the woman and her two kids, he greeted them. "You look cold. Come with me, and I'll find you a table by the fire so you can warm up."

He smelled her and the boys' scents and realized the woman was the same one who had left him some six years ago. *Robyn Conibear*. His heart rate sped up. The woman he had never stopped loving had his heart doing flip-flops again.

The boys were polar bear shifters too. He'd fallen so hard for her and she had seemed to feel the same for him, until he had to kill her brother in self-defense right in front of her eyes. She left and it was over between them. He understood why she'd left him, but the old interest roared to life. It didn't matter that she was mated now and had a couple of boys. The gnawing need to have her for his mate took hold and he had the greatest urge to pull her into his arms for a warm, bear hug.

He didn't blame someone else for falling in love with her either. He completely understood.

He'd never fallen out of love with her either. Even now his damn heart was tripping as she pulled down her dickey and lifted the fur-trimmed hood back off her face. She was older, like he was, but just as beautiful. Maybe more so now.

Robyn's and the boys' snow boots were covered in snow, their cheeks and noses red from the cold, their lips slightly blue.

"Are you okay?" He led them toward the fireplace where four tables were already occupied. The occupants watched him, as if wondering what he was up to when they'd already taken their seats at the tables. The three snow leopards hadn't been served yet, and he was certain when they saw how cold Robyn and her kids were, they wouldn't mind moving to another table.

"My truck broke down a couple of miles out of town," Robyn stuttered between shivers. She had the most beautiful red hair, and now it was hanging loosely about her shoulders.

"Hell. Alright. I'll call to have someone tow your pickup to the garage, if you would like." Edward paused. "It has been a long time."

"It...has. Thanks, Edward. I would appreciate that."

She seemed wary, maybe worried he would be mad that she'd left him and mated another bear. As much as he wished it had been him, he couldn't find fault in her leaving him.

"Are these your boys?" Edward looked them over, thinking if she'd stayed with him, like he thought she was going to, they would have been their sons. They looked like her to an extent. And like him too. Which made him wonder just how old they were.

He'd get them some coloring place mats and a package of crayons each to keep them occupied until he served up their food.

"Yes. I...I thought you might be busy with your tour business and not be here."

Had she hoped she wouldn't run into him here? Then why come here to eat, instead of at one of the other restaurants? "Rob and I always help Uncle Ned and Aunt Genevieve during the holidays. No tours at this time." Edward reached the snow leopards' table first. "Hey, guys. The lady and her sons' pickup broke down some miles out of town, and they're about frozen. Do you mind if I put them at your table by the fire, since you haven't been served yet?"

Jasper Wright winked at her. "Sure, come on, brothers. Let the lady and her sons have the table."

"Yeah," Simon said. "Anything for the young lady and her sons."

"I'll make sure you guys get a free dessert. Thanks," Edward said.

"We'll take you up on it, though we would have been good Samaritans without having to be bribed." William smiled.

"That's why I asked you and not anyone else," Edward said. And because they hadn't been served yet.

Robyn thanked them and the three men moved to another table farther away.

"Do you want me to take your coats?" Edward asked.

Robyn shook her head.

"Later, when you get warmed up, I can, if you would like. Menus are on the table there. What would you like to drink?"

"Hot chocolate," she said, "for the three of us."

"Alright, three hot chocolates coming up. I'll make that call about your vehicle. The tow-truck owner will drop in and get more information from you. It's...good to see you again, Robyn."

"Thanks, Edward. I'm glad to see you too. This is Garrett and Bryan."

"Nice to meet you, Garrett, Bryan." Edward shook their hands. "I'll bring something for you to color on." Edward thought she looked as worn out as the boys. He couldn't imagine trekking with two little boys in the cold for that long.

He hurried off, pulling his cell phone out of his pocket while he went to the hostess station, though they rarely seated anyone. Most of their patrons just found a table they wanted to sit at. He picked up the small packages of crayons and a couple of different coloring sheets—one of a Christmas tree with lots of lights and ornaments and another of a gingerbread house. All he could think of was he needed to stay away from her and have someone else serve her instead of himself, but he'd always been drawn to her. He swore it took him a good two years to get over her, thinking any woman who had the same color of hair was her, returning to tell him that she understood he'd had no choice about defending himself against her brother, that she'd made a mistake in leaving him, and she was ready to return and renew their relationship. Though the woman would turn around and he would realize it had been wishful thinking. He suspected Robyn was the reason he'd never found a woman to settle down with.

"Who's the woman and kids?" Uncle Ned asked, setting

another couple of plates on top of the counter for pickup, his hair and beard white.

They always told him he should be Santa Claus for Christmas and he always said he would be, once Rob's kids were older.

"Someone from out of town. She had car trouble. I'm calling Joe to pick up her vehicle and take care of it. And yes, they're some of our kind." Edward didn't know why he didn't just flat out say who she was. He guessed he was worried his family might be upset with her for leaving him, but they knew the reason too.

Uncle Ned smiled.

"She has got kids. Sheesh." Edward couldn't believe his uncle was even pushing to get him hitched. But when his aunt and uncle couldn't get their own three boys married off, they'd been eager to see Rob and Edward mated. Rob and Edward's parents had been killed in an avalanche and they'd adopted the boys to raise alongside their cousins. They had hoped Rob and Edward would provide them with grandchildren, well, great nieces or nephews, but they considered them their grandchildren. Now that Rob had twins, Edward thought they would be satisfied. But no, their aunt and uncle loved them so much, they wanted more.

"You chased off the Wright brothers to give them seats so you could still wait on the woman and her kids." Uncle Ned loaded a couple of more platters on the counter, while Edward tried to contact Joe on his cell.

"They had to walk some distance into town, and they were half frozen. They needed a seat next to the fire," Edward said. Then Joe answered the phone. "Hey, Joe, I've got a job for you." Edward told him what had happened.

"Okay, I'll be right over."

"Thanks, Joe." Edward entered the kitchen and made up

three steaming mugs of hot chocolate topped with twice the whipped cream they usually added.

Aunt Genevieve had returned to the kitchen while Alicia and Rob were finishing their meal, the babies in their carriers sound asleep. His aunt was studying Edward. "The hot chocolates are for someone special?" She arched a brow.

He explained what had happened again.

His aunt looked out from the kitchen to see what the woman looked like. His aunt's eyes widened, and she tsked. "Robyn Conibear? She has a mate?"

"That usually comes with the territory when you've got a couple of kids." Edward gave his aunt a kiss on the cheek and with the tray of hot chocolates, papers to color on, and crayons, he headed back to Robyn's table. He set the whipped cream-topped mugs on the table. "Here you go, boys." He gave them each the packages of crayons and the coloring pages. They eagerly took them. Their mom helped Garrett open his package, and Edward helped Bryan. "Did you decide what you want to eat?"

"We'll have the hot chicken soup, hamburgers, and french fries."

"Okay, got it. Joe, the tow truck operator, is coming over and will talk—" The door opened and Edward glanced to see who it was. *Joe.* He was always completely dependable. Edward waved to him, and he waved back and headed for their table. "That's Joe Cavender. He's an honest guy and he'll figure out what's wrong with the pickup, no problem."

"Thanks for everything."

"You bet. I'll just put this order in and get the hot soup out to you right away."

Joe joined them and began talking to Robyn. Edward returned to the kitchen to fill up bowls with chicken soup. His aunt just shook her head. "Do you know how many times you've come in the kitchen to help serve up anything to customers? Never."

"She and the boys are half frozen."

"Uh-huh. And she's a former girlfriend." Aunt Genevieve peered over the ledge to see what Robyn looked like. Then she smiled. "Well."

"What's *that* supposed to mean?" Edward lifted the tray of bowls of soup.

"She's still a looker and the boys are cute." Aunt Genevieve frowned. "They look a lot like you and your brother at around that age."

"She's still mated." Edward carried the tray to Robyn's table.

Joe inclined his head to Edward on the way out of the restaurant.

Ben and Rob were leaning against a post, arms folded across their chests as they watched Edward leave off the bowls of soup at Robyn's table and head back to the counter. He walked right past his brother and cousin to grab another tray, except this time to deliver to another table. He was trying to ignore Ben and his brother, but they followed him to the kitchen to pick up more meal orders.

"Who is she?" Ben asked.

"She's one of us. Robyn Conibear." Edward repeated what had happened.

Both Ben and Rob swung their heads around to get a better look at her. "Hell," Rob said.

"He made the Wright brothers move from their table," Ben said.

"He fixed them hot cocoa with mountains of whipped cream," Rob agreed.

"And bowls of hot chicken soup," Ben added.

"And she has two kids. Which means she has a mate. Either of you would have done the same for her, if you'd seen how cold she was when she first arrived," Edward reminded them. He glanced at the table where Alicia had been sitting, but realized she was leaving, and Aunt Genevieve was carrying out one of the sleeping babies, while Alicia had the other.

"So, Joe's going to tow her truck into town for her?" Rob asked, grabbing another platter.

"Yeah." Edward suspected that everyone was going to hear about his helping the woman and her kids out and it would be the talk of all of White Bear. Well, as far as the shifter population went. Especially since she'd been an old flame of his.

When he finally returned to her table with the hamburger and fries, the kids set aside their crayons and coloring pages.

"If you need anything else—" Edward said.

"Just a place to stay for the night."

Edward paused before he said anything. Rob had moved out of their home to one he shared now with Alicia and the babies. Edward was free to have house guests. But he chided himself for even giving it a thought. He could see having another black eye when her mate learned of it.

"Do you have a hotel in White Bear? I'm afraid my phone has gone out, and I couldn't check the internet," Robyn said.

"I can charge up your phone." Edward handed her his phone. "Here, use mine. We have three places to stay: a small hotel, and two bed and breakfasts. The hotel and one B & B is owned by our kind, and the other B & B is wolf run."

"Thanks so much, Edward," she said.

He was glad to see she'd finally warmed up enough to remove her hat, scarf, and coat. The kids had also.

Only shifters were sitting near her table, so he wasn't worried about talking about the shifters with her. Three tables of humans were seated on the other side of the tavern, and everyone was careful to watch what they said when they were around them. Not that anyone would believe they were shifters if they overheard some of the conversations. His aunt and uncle had thought about making the place a private club with membership only for shifters, though they would have to say it had a high-dollar membership to keep the humans out. And in truth, the shifters wouldn't have to pay the "club" fees.

But they decided they would rather have more business and not have the hassle of keeping track of who all entered the tavern. That meant they had to watch what they said around the humans though.

He took Robyn's phone back to the office where he could charge it up. He wondered where she was headed for Christmas without her mate. Unless she was joining him. And why she wouldn't be contacting her family. She'd made no mention of it, just that she wanted to stay someplace for the night.

If she was seeing her family, surely she would want to notify them as soon as she arrived at the tavern safely to tell them she'd had problems with her pickup. She was a total mystery, and he couldn't help being curious about her and her boys and wishing all over again that her brother hadn't attacked him with the intent to kill him that fateful day, causing Robyn to leave him so long ago.

3
———

When Robyn couldn't find a place to stay at the hotel or at the other establishments, she was exasperated and worried. At least Edward had helped her out with her pickup truck and the phone. But she needed to tell him about the boys too. Not here in the tavern though. In *private*. She was glad to see him, but anxious too.

Hopefully, Joe wouldn't find much of a problem with the pickup. What would she do if she couldn't find a place to stay? Surely, someone would put her up for the night. At least with her pickup in a garage, no one would see it, if anyone had realized she'd left Yellowknife and followed her in this direction. But she did have a problem. If anyone should follow her, they would be able to track her scent, indicating where she had walked with the boys and where she was going.

She should have picked up hunter concealer, but she hadn't thought she would need it. If she'd purchased some in Yellowknife and anyone had gotten wind of it, someone might have questioned why.

If she didn't do something though, and anyone stopped here, they would learn soon enough that she'd been at the tavern. She was torn between soliciting Edward's help, and not getting him or his people involved. If she did get stuck here for a day or more, and they did follow her here, she needed to let Edward know the trouble she could be in. Then again, she worried that he and the others of his own sleuth might not believe she had the right to take her children away from her mate's sleuth. But when she told him the truth? That the boys were his? She didn't think the damage between them could ever be undone. Yet, she knew in her heart, she needed to tell him as soon as she could.

She still didn't even know if he had a mate. Or if he was seriously dating another woman.

Still, she couldn't help but appreciate all of Edward's aid, especially when his brother and cousin were giving him such a hard time. She'd noticed them talking to him several times as he returned to get mugs of cocoa, bowls of soup, and then their hamburgers and french fries for them. And each time, they would glance in her direction, as if they knew she was going to cause the family real conflict. Which she could, if they took her in and didn't turn her over to her late mate's sleuth if they found her here. She suspected it also had to do with not wanting her to break Edward's heart all over again.

As much as she was afraid to tell him, she needed to warn him. He might be willing to cover for her, but it didn't mean the rest of his family would.

The food was really good, and they all were enjoying the warm fireplace, the hamburgers and french fries, and the kids were having a ball coloring the menus. Edward even brought them each slices of hot blueberry pie. She wondered if Edward still preferred chocolate, which was unusual for a bear shifter. And she remembered his brother teasing him that he would turn into a Kodiak bear if he ate too much chocolate.

She was glad they had reached the tavern alright, and that everyone had treated them well. Maybe Edward knew someone else who would put them up for the night. But she still needed to tell him about his boys.

EDWARD RETURNED to the counter to pick up more food trays, noticing Robyn kept looking in his direction. He kept thinking she would wave her hand at him, letting him know she needed something else, but when he caught her eye, she would look at her food and continue eating. Was she interested in him still? He scolded himself for even letting his thoughts drift in that direction.

Ben met up with him to grab another tray. "Has she warmed up a bit?"

"Yeah." Though Edward knew his cousin could see she and the kids had removed their coats already.

"I saw you exchanged phones with her."

Edward tilted his head to the side, trying not to look too exasperated. "Yeah, because hers died."

"Well, she's mated, cuz." Ben shook his head.

"I think that's rather obvious. I'm not interested in dating the lady. She has just had a bit of bad luck, and she needs a little help. She's past tense as far as I'm concerned." If he could have changed what had happened back then, he would have done anything to have made it happen.

"Right. A couple of women at table 12 look promising." Ben smiled.

Edward glanced in that direction, not that he was interested in striking up a conversation with any other woman right now, especially any that Ben suggested might work out.

Ben motioned with his head in their direction. "You can take their tray of food to them, if you would like."

"Thanks, but—"

"You would prefer to stick close to the woman and her kids who are in trouble."

Edward gave him a disgruntled look. "The last time you suggested I go out with someone, I ended up with a black eye. *That* woman was trouble. No, thanks."

"My mistake, but it could have worked out." Ben shrugged. "Alright. So Robyn had a broken-down truck and had to walk for a couple of miles in this frigid weather. She had no phone to call anyone. Is that why she's using your phone now?"

"She's looking for a place to stay for the night."

Ben frowned. "The places are all booked. I know, because I had a friend coming who wanted to stay with his girlfriend at one of them, but they couldn't. They're bunking with me. They had wanted to have their privacy, but..."

Edward glanced back at Robyn and her sons. She was making a call. Maybe she was calling family, though he suspected she would have asked him first if it was okay. He figured she was calling the local lodging.

"You've got plenty of room at your place now that Rob's moved out and it's close by," Ben said.

"Yeah, I do."

Ben shook his head. "I would ask my parents if they could put her up instead. I suspect she's in trouble, and that could mean problems for you."

That's what Edward was beginning to think. "I'll ask them if they think they could put her up for the night."

Ben slapped him on the back, then took the tray to the table where the two women were talking.

Edward delivered a tray to one of the tables, and Rob stopped to talk with him. "Joe called me and said he towed the lady's pickup to his garage. He tried her phone, but there's no answer."

"I'm charging it up for her."

Rob glanced at her.

"She's using my phone, trying to find lodging." Edward was tired of telling everyone what was going on, but he knew they were only worried about the situation. Concerned for her and the kids. Maybe anxious about Edward getting into a mess if he fell for her all over again because the last time he had nearly died. It was too late worrying about that now. He would never stop loving her.

Rob let out his breath. "Ben said he's putting his friends up because they don't have any room at the hotels."

"Yeah, he told me that. I'll talk to Uncle Ned and see if they can put her up."

"They can't. They've got friends coming in to stay with them tonight, and then they're heading to the mountain to ski. I would offer, but it's chaotic at home with the new babies," Rob said.

"Right. Okay, well, let me tell her what Joe said, and then I can learn if she has had any luck. Maybe there has been a cancellation."

"Good luck to her and the kids." Rob returned to get another order out.

Edward could just see offering for her to stay at his place could be one big mistake. Yet, if he were her mate and it meant she had nowhere else to go, how would he feel? Like he would want her to stay with anyone other than a single, male polar bear who had been her lover for several months.

When he reached the table, she shook her head before he could even ask her if she got a room for the night. "Everything's booked." She looked worried that no one would help her out.

"I was afraid of that. Okay, well, I was going to check with my aunt and uncle, but they have guests, and my cousin Ben does also. My brother has two new babies, so it wouldn't work out for them."

"Oh, congratulations on your brother and his family. We'll

figure out something." She sounded dejected and not at all like she figured they had any options left to them.

"You don't have any transportation. Joe picked up your truck and hauled it to the garage. He can't work on it tonight. He'll check it out tomorrow. I can put you up at my place, if you would like."

Her eyes widened a bit, and then she glanced at the boys. "I wouldn't want to put you out."

But she didn't say no. "It wouldn't be a problem. I've got three extra bedrooms. My brother moved out when Alicia and he mated. It's just me. And everyone will vouch for me."

She smiled a little bit at that, as if she knew he wouldn't be any trouble for her. Still, she bit her lip with indecision, then glanced around at his brother and cousin. Both were watching them. "They appear worried. For you? Or for me?"

He smiled. "Ben hooked me up with a woman who had a very, tightly-wound boyfriend. She'd failed to mention him, and they weren't done being together. Anyway, I got a black eye for it. I could have given him one back, but it was all a big mistake. The woman was to blame. She had no intention of leaving him. She just wanted a date while she was here."

"I, uhm, noticed, and I'm sorry."

Edward swore Robyn was fighting a smile, which couldn't help but amuse him. "Yeah, well, I'm not interested in making any more boyfriends or mates angry. If you need a safe place to stay, you're welcome to sleep over at my home."

The boys were watching their mom, looking tired, and hopeful, waiting for her to make a decision.

When she didn't decide quickly enough, Garrett said, "We can't walk all the way to your parents' home in the cold and the dark, Mom. And you said they might not even want us there."

Edward frowned. "You're on the outs with your family?"

"Yes, I am. But I still don't want to inconvenience you," she said to Edward again.

"It's no problem. Really. You can stay as long as you like. We'll get you a loner car if you need one to run errands in town until Joe repairs your truck." No way did he want Robyn to leave with the young boys if her family wouldn't offer her a safe place to stay.

"We can stay at your place though? Until we can get a room or the pickup is fixed?" she asked, sounding hopeful, but anxious.

He hoped it wasn't because she had a volatile mate. What if she'd run away from him? *Hell.*

"Sure, the place is yours. I'll be off here... Wait. Let me clear the table off, and I'll tell Uncle Ned I'm running you over to the house. It's just down the street and you can get settled in, watch television, play video games, whatever you want. I'll grab some more papers for the boys to color, if they would like."

The boys both nodded vigorously.

"Alright, thank you." She handed him his phone back.

"You're welcome."

"You didn't bring me the bill."

"It's my treat."

"Thank you."

"You're welcome." He pocketed his phone and then took their empty plates back to the kitchen and said to Uncle Ned, "I'm dropping Robyn and the boys off at my place to stay for the night. I guess I need to run over to Joe's garage so they can pick up a couple of suitcases, or whatever else they need."

"What's the mate situation?" Uncle Ned asked, acting like he was Edward's father, which was the way he'd been since Edward and Rob had lost their own dad.

"I don't know. But she and the kids can't get any lodging, and she's willing to stay at my place."

"Will we see you back this afternoon?"

"Yeah. I just need to get them settled."

"Alright. If you can't make it back, it's no problem. Just be careful. You know what happened the last time."

"Don't remind me. And thanks, Uncle Ned. I'll be back." Edward planned to learn about her mate when he could too. He grabbed her phone out of the office. It still needed to charge further, but she could finish charging it at his place. Then he dressed for the cold and saw that she was no longer sitting at the table with her sons. A family of four Arctic wolf shifters were there now. At first, he was afraid he'd scared her off, but then he saw her near the doorway leading outside, the three of them all bundled up for the cold weather.

He hurried to join her and handed her phone to her. "We can charge it the rest of the way at my home, but you can call someone, if you need to let anyone know you're not making it for the night or whenever you planned to arrive there."

"Thank you."

He walked her and the boys out to his van. The name of their excursion tour group—White Bear Wilderness Adventure Tours—was written on the side.

"Is that what you do still?" she asked, hesitating to get into the van. "I know you had just a little operation back when I dated you."

"Yeah. Rob and I, and a friend, run tour groups into the wilderness to show them the northern lights, wildlife, the glaciers, polar bears, all that we have to offer out here. We're a lot better organized than when you went with us that one time. We close down the operation during the holidays because this is the busiest time of year for our aunt and uncle, and we always help out at the tavern. Family helps family. You might recall that they have three sons. One is a state trooper, and one a pilot, and both are busy this time of year. Except they're always home for

Christmas, if they're not working emergency cases. You saw Ben at the tavern where he works."

"That's really nice." She climbed into the van with the kids.

He realized that if she was having issues with her family, maybe his mention of his family being there for each other would upset her. Talk about putting his foot in his mouth. Still, he felt that's the way they should be and that's how her family should be for her.

"Do you need me to drop by the garage so you can get your bags and have them for overnight?"

"Yes, I was going to ask if you would. Thanks so much for everything you've done for us. We really appreciate it."

"No problem. Any of us help others out whenever we can. Where were you headed before you broke down?"

"Here, and...and then...then to Anchorage."

"To your parents' place? But Garrett said you were having trouble with them." He thought she'd been living in Anchorage all along. Now he wondered where she'd been living. Then he worried that they'd been angry with *her* for getting her brother killed.

They all climbed into the van, and he drove them to the garage.

"I don't know."

"If you're unsure about being able to go home, stay here. With us." Edward wanted them to stay with him, which he'd hoped she would agree to, but he didn't want to push things too fast if she wasn't ready for it. Not to mention the little issue of her having a mate. He finally reached Joe's Auto Body Shop and parked.

"Boys, you stay here. I'll just grab our suitcases," Robyn said.

"I'll help." Edward and Robyn walked to the garage office where Joe was working on his computer. Edward opened the door to the office. "Hey, Joe, Robyn just needs to get some things out of her truck."

"Yeah, whatever you need."

Edward helped pull her large suitcase out of the passenger's seat, while she grabbed two smaller rolling bags out of the back seat and set them down on the garage floor. Then she pulled out the fire safe.

"Do you have any idea what's wrong with the truck?" Robyn asked Joe.

"No, I'll check it out tomorrow first thing, and then give you a call."

"Thanks."

"You're welcome. Good night, folks."

"Night," Edward said, and carried her fire safe and rolled her bag to the van, then put it in the back with the boys' bags.

When they drove to his house, she said, "I'm sorry you had to go out of your way to get the bags from Joe's shop."

"You'll probably need some things out of them. And really, it isn't any trouble. You'll have your own bathroom and bedrooms. If you get hungry, the fridge is well-stocked. Even though I live by myself, my cousins or my brother and his family drop by all the time, so I always like to have plenty to eat. Don't hesitate to ask for anything when I'm there or use whatever you want when I'm gone. And if you need anything that I don't have, I can run to the store to get it. Or you can borrow the van or the Wrangler Jeep I have and shop for yourself. We have plenty of transportation available to us."

"Thanks."

The boys pulled their suitcases into the house, but Edward rolled hers inside while she carried her fire safe. Everything was decorated in Christmas garlands and lights, the tree just for display because he always spent Christmas with his aunt and uncle and the rest of the family. But since his family was always dropping by, he liked having the house decorated for the holidays. He turned on the Christmas tree lights, then he showed them the bedrooms. The boys were going to take separate ones, but Robyn said, "Choose one. You can sleep together in the big bed."

"This one," Garrett said.

"I'll be in the room right next door," she said.

"Okay, well, like I said, you're free to watch television. I've got some board games and puzzles on the bookshelf over there. Just whatever you would like to do is fine with me. I'm heading back to the tavern for a couple of more hours, and I can fix dinner when I return. See you in a bit." He left them then, hoping they would feel relaxed and rest up a bit.

When they were at Joe's garage, Edward had noticed her license plate said Northwest Territories, and he wondered when she'd ended up there. That had been a hell of a long drive for her with the two boys. Was the guy she was mated to from there? And she hadn't resolved things with her family? He still didn't know where she had been living in the Northwest Territories. Or why she was traveling with two little boys in an old pickup across the Northwest Territories and the Yukon Territory into Alaska without her mate at Christmastime. Or why she would take a route that was way out of her way, adding more hours to an already long journey if she had been headed to Anchorage. He suspected she'd wanted to see him. But then he thought about the mate issue again.

When he arrived back at the tavern, he knew his brother and cousin were going to give him the third degree. He hadn't expected his cousin Craig, the pilot, and Andy, the trooper, to drop into the tavern for a meal today.

They greeted each other, but Andy did his usual thing with the police questioning. "Is she still mated?"

"She needed a place to stay. That's all."

"He avoided the question. Did you notice?" Craig grabbed a couple of bottles of blueberry mead from behind the counter.

"Hell, yeah. I don't want to be bringing her mate up on charges if he should beat you up, like I had to with that other guy," Andy said.

"I wasn't going to prefer charges on that guy." Not that Edward was always easygoing, but in that case, he could understand how the guy felt. In this case, Andy was right. Edward was just helping Robyn out, and if her mate got angry about it, it wasn't his fault. Not that the other had been either.

Craig shook his head. "You know Mom said those boys could be yours."

Edward had thought the same thing, but he hadn't wanted to believe the boys were his and Robyn hadn't told him all this time. Though if they were, he suspected she'd kept it secret to protect her and the boys from her own family, not so much that she was trying to keep the boys from him.

"They look like the spitting image of you and Rob at that age. Mom had taken pictures of the boys and Robyn while they were eating at the tavern and showed me those and pictures of us when we were that age, and she really thinks they could be yours. I agree with her. The timing is right too, for when you were dating Robyn and from the looks of how old the boys are."

"I know. I was thinking the same thing." Edward let his breath out. "I need to talk with her and learn the truth. If they are my sons...well, I want to help raise them. I don't want her leaving White Bear again."

Craig smiled a little evilly, then slapped him on the back. "Better you than me. At least your brother's raising his from the ground floor up. Little baby steps. Though you don't have to deal with messy diapers and they're the age where they can tell you what they want and can be a lot of fun. You know the whole lot of us will have your back, no matter what you decide to do. Even if they're yours or not. We all thought the world of Robyn. Not so much of her family."

"We just need to see if the spark is still there between us," Edward said, trying to sound upbeat about it. He might still be holding a candle for her, but it didn't mean she felt the same way about him. Or that what he felt for her had withstood the test of time. She had been mated and had kids and had lived with another sleuth in a world apart from them. She couldn't help but be a different person than he knew six years ago.

"You need to learn about the spousal situation as soon as you can. Where is she headed?" Andy asked.

"Here, but I suspect she was on her way to Anchorage."

Andy shook his head. "You know there's real conflict between our sleuths and that's never going away, if they have any say in it. Even if she has lost her mate, you don't want to get into that again."

"Yeah, I know." But he still felt compelled to be with her.

"Hell, Edward. Rob said you've been catering to her as if she were royalty. She has got you wrapped around her little finger all over again," Andy said.

Rob came up to the counter. "Give him some slack. He loved her once, and he obviously still feels something for her. You've never been in that situation before and you can't know how he feels."

"I could fly her there," Craig said. "To Anchorage, I mean. That way we could keep Edward from making a huge mistake with the lady. It's bad enough that she's here, but with two young 'uns? I can just see some angry dad coming to take him out."

"I'm sure she wants her truck fixed before she decides anything." Edward hoped he could convince her to just stay here, even if she didn't want to date him and the boys weren't his. She would be among friends no matter what, if her family was being hateful to her. He noticed the stack of lunch orders piling up and went to help out.

Andy grabbed a platter too.

"I thought you were here just to grab a bite." Edward thought his cousins were way too busy to be here to assist their parents.

"Dad called us and said you might be in a heap of trouble," Craig said.

Edward laughed. He loved his family. He only wished his parents were still alive to enjoy all the family gatherings.

Ben joined them then and grabbed a platter. "Good to see you all here. How's the woman and her kids?"

"Settling into the house. Joe won't know what's wrong with her truck until tomorrow."

Uncle Ned joined them. "If you want, we can swap house guests. That way no mate will think anything's going on between you and his wife."

Edward sighed. "I'll ask her, but I think they'll be fine."

"We're more worried about you," Andy said.

"Thanks, guys, but really, I should be fine. These meals are going to get cold. Talk to you all later." Edward headed for one of the tables and everyone else began delivering meals, but Andy and Craig finally sat at a table that Edward was serving, and he shook his head.

"You didn't think you were going to get by without us giving you more of the third degree, did you?" Andy asked. "Okay, while you were serving some tables, I checked with my sources in the Northwest Territories, and Robyn Conibear was married to a man named Callahan Gardner of Yellowknife. He drives a big rig for an oil company. Or I should say he did. He died in a hunting accident five months ago."

"Ah, hell." Edward hated to hear it, even though he had always envisioned *he* would have been her mate. But damn if her family hadn't taken issue with it. Now he was really thinking of ways to keep her here. Even if the boys weren't his, she could use some help raising them and they were cute kids. The whole sleuth would help. "Why would she be leaving Yellowknife? I mean, what about Callahan's family? Wouldn't they want to see the boys for Christmas? It seems an odd time for her to leave and not really have a destination in mind." If she had good relations with her sleuth and Callahan's family was her support system, he couldn't imagine her leaving there.

"Your guess is as good as mine. Maybe Callahan didn't have any family to speak of. I can check on that. Perhaps she came here to see you." Andy arched a brow. "Which makes me believe she has something to tell you that has been nagging at her for six years."

"Maybe." Edward served up their meals.

Or maybe she was no longer welcome in Yellowknife once her mate had died, and she'd needed to find refuge someplace where she was once welcome. Which gave Edward some hope that she might even consider staying here in White Bear. Permanently. With him.

4

F ive hours later, Edward finally finished his shift serving
meals at the tavern and headed back to the house,
eager to see Robyn and talk. He was having mixed feelings about her, sorry for her loss, hopeful that they might have a
chance together, but afraid he was going to lose her again. They
still needed to talk about what happened between her brother
and him six years ago. She'd left without a word, and he wanted
her to know the truth about what had happened, if she was in
any doubt at all.

When he arrived home, he smelled chili cooking on the
stove and he smiled. He was reminded of the time when Robyn
had made homemade chicken soup for him when he got so sick
and Rob and their partner, Casey MacIntosh, had to leave him
behind while they took the tour group out. Edward loved her
cooking.

Smelling the aroma of chili made him feel as though she was
living with him for good. He wished it was for real.

"Momma's fixing chili for us," Garrett said, running to greet
Edward at the door. Bryan rushed to greet him too, both kids

eager to see him and he felt good about that. Again, he was wondering if they were his own sons.

"She is." Edward smiled at the boys, not used to such a nice greeting when he came home.

"Yeah, and chocolate chip cookies," Bryan said.

That's what he'd smelled too. Though he wasn't sure at first. This was a real treat. He loved chocolate chip cookies, especially when they were homemade. He took off his parka and hung it up in the coat closet. "Chocolate chip cookies too? Great. I'm hungry. What about you?"

"Yeah," both the boys responded.

"But we gotta eat our chili first," Garrett said. "Momma said."

"Your momma's right."

They grabbed Edward's hands and hurried him into the kitchen, and he saw Robyn dishing up the chili, then she added shredded cheese on top. "Hey, are you ready to eat?"

"I sure am. Now *this* is a welcome meal."

She set the bowls of chili on the table. "I hope this is alright. I wanted to do something for you for being so nice to us."

"Yeah, it sure is." He poured glasses of water for each of them. "Are you seeing your family in Anchorage for Christmas?"

"I don't know," she said, taking a seat.

"Your license plate says you're from the Northwest Territories. Have you been there for a while?"

"With my husband's people. Yes."

"And your husband?"

She blinked away tears. "He died in a hunting accident and now his parents want custody of my boys."

Edward's jaw dropped. He couldn't believe it! Why hadn't she said something about it to him already? He was glad she finally told him about her mate so he didn't have to pretend not to know, but he couldn't believe her mate's family would try to take the kids from her. Wait, so she'd run away? Aww, hell. "I'm so sorry about your mate. Why would your in-laws want custody of the boys?" Edward just couldn't believe it.

"They've wanted them every day since my mate died."

"They're controlling, Momma said," Garrett explained.

"I can't even comprehend something like that. You're the boys' mother, and they obviously love you."

"Thank you. They do. My father-in-law was the mayor. Everyone thinks he can do no wrong. But I'm an outsider, and they tolerated me because I married one of his sons. But now that…my mate is gone…"

"We're not gonna live with Grandma and Grandpa," Garrett said adamantly.

Bryan shook his head vigorously, agreeing with his brother.

"Do you think they will come after you?" Edward asked Robyn, wishing she had told him this already.

"Yes. I imagine they will by Tuesday, if they haven't already started looking for us. I was supposed to drop the kids off with Callahan's parents that day. When I don't, they'll be calling. They've been saying they need to take care of them. They say I don't have time because of the business I'm conducting."

"Which is?" He added sour cream to his chili, trying to process what had to be done first with regard to her and the boys to keep them safe.

"Marketing. I've been trying to build my business so I can stay home with the kids and work as much as I can. But they get rambunctious when I'm trying to work, or I need to meet clients and videotape their business's products or services and so they couldn't go with me. Then they would stay with their grandparents. Before, if they'd offered to see the boys like that, I thought it was because they genuinely wanted to be with them and help me get on my feet with the business. Now, I know better."

Edward shook his head. Family meant everything to him.

She scoffed. "They never thought I was good enough for

their son. They only tolerated me because I'd birthed two beautiful baby boys. From the beginning, when Callahan had been off on jobs, they had wanted to take charge of the boys, as if I hadn't been caring for them suitably. Admittedly, I'd needed some help when they were newborns, and Callahan couldn't be there to assist me. But once he'd died, they'd even talked about me marrying one of their other sons."

"No way." He couldn't imagine Robyn doing that.

"Yeah. I knew that was only because it was a way to keep my sons in the sleuth permanently. Martha and Arnold have a lot of influence over one of their sons, and I suspect he might have caved, if I'd been agreeable. Not that I was. Since I'm from Anchorage and my mate was gone, I was quickly seen as an outsider again. I...I was headed back to Anchorage, hoping to reconnect with my family. Hoping they would side with me, though many had been angry that I'd left them to run off with Callahan and join the Yellowknife sleuth. Including a former boyfriend out of Anchorage. I have no intention of hooking up with Maverick again, not as volatile as he was. Which was some of the reason I'd taken off with Callahan in the first place."

"Hell, Robyn. You could have come to me."

"And risked an all-out war between your family and mine? No."

"But you *did* come here. You came to see *me*, hoping I'd help you."

She sighed and nodded.

"Aww, honey, we'll get it all sorted out." He needed to talk to her about his killing her brother, but he needed to deal with this other business right now. "Alright. I need to tell the rest of my family. And then we need to share this with the rest of the shifter community in the area. Everyone needs to know that a fight could be headed this way. Most likely, they'll help, but they have to understand the mess you could be in. Do you think your mate's sleuth will know which direction you went in?"

"I'm sure they would believe I headed to Anchorage because my family lives there. Hopefully, they'll think I took the most direct route there and hadn't gone out of my way to pass through White Bear."

She added sour cream to her chili too while the boys watched. Garrett tried some, but Bryan waited to see if he liked it first. Garrett ate a spoonful and smiled, then spooned up some more. Bryan added some to his bowl of chili also.

"Unless they believe I wouldn't go to Anchorage, so that I could throw them off our trail. Now I worry that if they happen to stop in White Bear, and if they eat at your tavern, they would smell our scent and know we've been there. I thought they could smell our scent from where the truck was abandoned, but now that it's secure in the garage, they won't stop along the way to try and track our scent that way."

"You need for us to say you continued on your way."

"I don't want you to have to lie for us, but—"

"I can't speak for the rest of the family, but I can say that I'll do all I can to keep your plans secret." Edward paused, then raised a spoonful of chili. "This is great chili, by the way. I know I haven't had anything better than this."

"Thank you. I've won the chili cook-offs several times."

"I'm not surprised." He looked at the boys who were listening in on the conversation and had stopped eating. They seemed worried and he wanted to alleviate the boys' concern. He realized then that not only had Robyn been fearful, but the boys had been too. "Hey, maybe we can make this a special movie night and have buttered popcorn."

Their expressions brightened.

"But you have to eat your chili first."

They started eating their dinner again.

She mouthed the words, "Thank you," to Edward.

He nodded. He would have finished his dinner in half the time he was taking so that he could start making calls, but he didn't want to show he was anxious about this business in front of the boys. He didn't want anyone telling any members of her sleuth about her staying with him or that her truck was at Joe's Garage.

He soon found a TV program for the kids to watch, made popcorn for them, and set out a plate of chocolate chip cookies, while she brought them glasses of milk. Then he grabbed his phone to make some calls.

"Aren't you gonna watch the movie too?" Bryan asked his mom and Edward.

"As soon as I make a few phone calls. We'll watch TV while I'm talking on the phone."

"Okay," the boys both said at once.

Wringing her hands, Robyn appeared anxious, but when Edward caught her doing it, she shoved her hands in her sweater pockets.

Edward knew Robyn was in a real bind, though he had never suspected it would be anything like this. They could have real issues with the polar bears of her children's sleuth and have a real fight on their hands. Everyone needed to be made aware of it right away.

He called Uncle Ned first because he was on the shifter council. The tavern would be open until eleven, but his uncle would know it was important and take the call right away.

"Uncle Ned, we have a situation. We could have some real trouble headed our way."

"The trouble has already found us. Four male polar bear shifters from the Northwest Territories are here right now. Since Robyn was driving a vehicle with a license plate from there, Joe said, and Andy told me her mate died five months ago, I figured something was wrong and she might even be on the run from her mate's sleuth."

"Hell." Edward glanced at Robyn, who was waiting to hear the news while the kids were engrossed in the movie.

"Yeah. They said she ran away with the kids and have put them in danger. They said they're the boys' uncles. So what the hell is going on?" Uncle Ned asked.

"You already know the boys' dad died, and she's the boys' mother and they want to be with her."

"That was obvious from the way they acted toward each other in the tavern. The men know she has been here. They're leaving now. They were talking about checking out the hotel and B & Bs to see if they stopped at any of them for the night under an assumed name. I called Joe to see if he could put a rush on fixing her truck, but he said he'd planned on checking it out first thing in the morning. In the meantime, he covered the truck in his garage with a tarp, something he never does, just in case these men had some idea her vehicle needed to be repaired. I doubt it though. I've called others on our list to spread the word that they haven't seen her anywhere else in town, which they wouldn't have, right?"

"Right. She was just at the tavern, and then at Joe's garage."

"What if they were seen leaving with you?"

"Hell."

"Yeah. Not that anyone's going to say anything, and the humans that had seen the two of you and the kids left way before these men showed up. Our people were suspicious of them when they came in, so thankfully, everyone's been wary of the situation. They came in four vehicles so they could go in separate directions if they needed to. Ben was acting as our spy, listening into their conversations while serving other tables close to theirs. They're looking for Robyn's pickup parked anywhere in White Bear for the night, making sure Robyn and the kids aren't here, unless they stayed for the night. By their calculations, Robyn and the boys should have been through the town and left already. I called Andy to have him check these men out. You might have to take Robyn and the kids to one of our cabins for safekeeping until her truck is repaired. We need to make sure that she can safely reach her destination, Anchorage, right? That she has a safe place to go once she reaches there?"

"I think that might be a negative."

"Hell, alright. Let us know as soon as you decide what to do."

"I will."

They ended the call, and Edward said to Robyn, "Four men are here looking for you. The word is going out that you must have continued on your way, but no one knows where you were headed. The men are searching for your pickup parked anywhere in the vicinity for the night."

"They shouldn't have started searching for me until I didn't show up to drop the kids off with my in-laws on Tuesday."

"Which means someone suspected you'd planned to run. You still got quite a head-start on them. You could have told me at the tavern when I first saw you. I would have done things differently." Like made sure her pickup was taken to someone else's garage and he could have brought her and the boys straight to his house and fed them there, just in case the men had showed up. They were lucky they hadn't turned up while she and the boys had been eating at the tavern. He could just imagine what a mess that would have been, dealing with her late mate's kinfolk, a bunch of growly polar bears.

"I couldn't know that you, or anyone else here, would want to help me. We...parted ways in a hurry and...I just didn't know. Also, I really didn't believe they would start looking for me this soon. I was certain I would make it to White Bear first and that they would believe I went to Anchorage instead."

"What *is* the situation with your own family?" No way was he letting her leave here on her own if she was on the outs with her family.

"I...I don't know. My parents disowned me when I left with my mate. They didn't want me leaving for the Northwest Territories to join another sleuth, and they didn't like Callahan. I haven't spoken to them since."

"Disowned you?" Edward snorted. "They didn't like me either. What about their grandkids? Don't they want to see them?" He couldn't imagine them not wanting to see their own grandsons.

"They *disowned* me," she repeated. "They don't know anything about the boys."

"Hell, Robyn. Then you can't go home." He said it in a way that told her he was glad that she wasn't going home. He would protect her with his life, if it came down to it. "You're safe with me here for now. If someone mentions you went with me in the van, and they connect that with where I live, we could have trouble. Otherwise, we should be fine." At least he hoped so.

5

While the boys were watching "A Christmas Story," Robyn spoke low for Edward's ears only. "I've got to tell you something about the boys." She took a deep breath and let it out. She was afraid he would hate her for not telling him the truth about their sons for all this time.

She opened her mouth to say it, but Edward pulled out his cell phone and showed her the picture Craig had shared with him of Rob and Edward when they were five years old. "They look just like Rob and me at that age. They're mine, aren't they?"

"Yes. I'm so sorry, Edward, that I didn't tell you before this. Garrett and Bryan *are* your sons. I didn't dare explain it to the boys when we lived in Yellowknife. They would have told my in-laws right away. In any event, I was going to bring them to see you before they turned five on the fifth of January, even if Callahan had still been alive. He had agreed that I should."

Even though Edward had seemed to suspect the boys were his sons, he still looked stunned. She didn't blame him. She'd been the same way that day once she learned she was pregnant. He glanced at the boys, their faces glued to the TV. He turned to look back at her, his eyes misty. "They're mine."

She couldn't stop the flow of tears then. Forever, she had thought about this moment when she would tell him, and she knew it wouldn't be easy, no matter how she broached the subject. "Yes, they're yours."

EDWARD STILL COULDN'T BELIEVE the boys were his own sons or that her brother had tried to kill him over some old gold claim that had been ancient history and screwed up everything between them. "Your brother told me to quit seeing you. And he said something odd, that I could never figure out. He said I would never be able to keep you because of what I'd done to you. Is that what he was referring to? That you were pregnant with the boys at the time?"

Tears filled her eyes again. She nodded.

He frowned at her. "Hell, Robyn. They were my boys too. So you took off and mated some other bear and pretended they were his."

"I was afraid my family would try to force me to give up my sons. Not to you, but to some other bear family not in our sleuth. They threatened to kill you. All of them did. We would have had a war between our sleuths, all because I had dated you and then was carrying our sons. The only way I could think to protect you was to go along with dating someone of their choice in Anchorage. But he was abusive to me because he didn't like that I was carrying your babies any more than my family did. Callahan was just passing through at a truck stop restaurant where I was a waitress, and I ran away with him. I was five months pregnant by then and he knew I needed protection and that I couldn't return to you because of the feud between our families. He was trying to protect me from my family, and ultimately, you from my family."

"*I* would have protected you from your family." Edward paced across the floor. He couldn't believe she'd left him six years ago, carrying his children, and had kept this from him all those years! "I want them to know who I am. I want to—" Hell, raise them as his own? He hadn't really thought about having had kids of his own. Especially when they believed another man had been their daddy. What a mess.

"You want to what?" she asked.

She was looking warily at him, knowing just the kind of reservations he had of becoming a daddy so all of a sudden. But he *was* a daddy already. They *were* his sons, and he wasn't going to shirk his responsibility. He knew he would love them as much as he had always loved Robyn, if she would give him half a chance.

"Raise them as my own, just as I should have done all along. That settles it. You and the boys stay with me. I have plenty of room at my place and you'll be safe with our sleuth. I want to tell my family though too."

"Of course. I'm so sorry I didn't tell you before."

ROBYN HAD to admit she'd been worried that he was married already and would want custody.

Callahan had never let on that the boys weren't his. She even wondered if her in-laws suspected that the boys were not their own flesh and blood and they worried she would take them home to their true father and cut them out of seeing them altogether. But why would they care then, if they weren't even blood relations?

To save face? At least, that's what she suspected. Robyn had never changed her name because of a sense of pride, which had annoyed her in-laws to great lengths. Her mother and grand-mother had kept their maiden names also. So it was a tradition in her family. Though she shouldn't have bothered to, once her family had disowned her. Still, that was another reason she *had* done it. They couldn't take her birth name from her. Callahan had been fine with it and that's all that had mattered.

"If my brothers learn I've gone back to you—" she said.

"They have no say in what we do." Edward looked so hopeful that she wanted to get back together with him.

She couldn't love Edward more than she already did, but that didn't change the problems she had brought with her. "And my deceased mate's people come after the boys—"

"They're not theirs by any stretch of the imagination." Edward didn't seem to want to let go of her or the boys, unless she really didn't want to be with him. The boys needed a father, however, and Edward seemed to want to spend time with them.

"I believe my in-laws fear losing face. They've bragged about the boys being their own grandsons since before they were born. They have no other grandchildren."

"Was your mate a good father to the boys?" Edward asked, sounding concerned.

"He was gone most of the time. Callahan's father tried to make up for it by taking the boys on fishing trips, but they preferred being with me. Arnold said they were going to be momma's boys and he didn't like it."

"When did you marry Callahan?"

"I married him shortly after I'd met him, just a quick justice of the peace affair. When I was waitressing at a restaurant in Anchorage, he came in to grab a bite to eat for lunch while he was on a job. I'd been crying and he asked what the trouble was. Of course, I wouldn't tell him, a stranger, but Maverick, the guy I was dating, was emotionally abusive to me because he hated that I was carrying your babies. Callahan asked me when I was getting off my shift and he ended up waiting for me when it ended two hours later. I unburdened my soul to him. I couldn't talk to my family. They felt the same way as Maverick did. I didn't know where to turn. A shifter with a couple of cubs on her own can mean real danger for all of them. Callahan offered me a marriage and a chance to leave Alaska. I was just desperate enough to take him up on it and prayed he was a decent man. Which he was. Right from the start, I told him that they were your sons and that my family hated yours.

"I...I told him you had killed my brother."

"God, Robyn, I'm so sorry for how that went down. You must have hated me for it."

"No, never. I knew Butch had tried to kill you. While Craig was flying in, we both saw you trying to get Butch to stop, backing off, indicating you were done and didn't want to fight any more. But he kept tearing into you and we knew then my brother fully intended to kill you. It wasn't your fault. I know you would have done anything to prevent what had happened. I saw how you kept trying to stop the fight, to back off from it like a bear who was willing to leave it be. Craig said the same thing. He said you were going to get yourself killed because my brother wouldn't stop trying to kill you. I was calling out to you to protect yourself with whatever it took. I was screaming at my brother to break off the fight. But neither of you could hear me. Even your cousin was so angry, he was yelling at you to fight back. Since Butch was there, I knew he'd started it and his actions proved he planned to kill you. My mother guessed I was pregnant, and she must have told him. I didn't tell them where we would be. I suspected someone had to have told them I was dating you. Someone who knows my family and came through White Bear and told them. I don't know how they would have known otherwise."

"I thought you'd finally told them we were seeing each other."

"No. I called my mom only to say I wasn't coming home over Christmas break. I'd hoped to spend it with you." Robyn brushed away tears again. That had been the worst day of her life, learning she was pregnant, nearly losing Edward, losing her oldest brother, and having to return home to a hostile family, when all she wanted was to be with the man she loved.

Edward took her into his arms and kissed her cheeks. "I didn't die. I'm here. With you now."

She loved the feel of his arms securely wrapped around her, not condemning her for leaving him, but loving her like he always had. "I...I didn't want my brother to die either, but I wanted you to live. I wanted you to...to win. I wanted the baby to get to know his father. I...I didn't even think you would make it. Craig didn't think so either, you had lost so much blood. He and I dragged you into the cabin and he started a field blood transfusion, then began bandaging your wounds. But I couldn't stay with you after that."

"You gave me your blood. Craig told me later that you had saved my life."

"I had to. I had to save your life. But I had to leave."

Edward held her tight. "You should have told me about the boys." He kissed her tear-streaked cheeks. "I was going to propose marriage to you that weekend. We should have been together."

"I was hoping you would. I was excited about it, but then I'd learned I was pregnant right before taking my last final exam and I was worried that you would be upset to learn we were going to have a baby. Two, as it turned out. I didn't expect my family to react like they did. After you killed Butch, my family promised me they would kill you, if I returned to you. We would have had a war between our sleuths. I couldn't have done that to you or your family. I was worried they might try to take my babies away from me after they were born too, and that was another deciding factor for me taking the chance and leaving with Callahan and never looking back. Not that I didn't think of you every day we were apart. The babies growing in my belly and after the boys were born reminded me of you and what we had lost—but I cherished that I still had a part of you to love."

"Aww, honey, we would have taken care of you. I should have helped you raise the boys. I take it they believe Callahan was their dad."

"Yes. But *you* are listed on their birth certificates. Callahan knew I put your name on them. He was satisfied with the boys having his name while he was alive. He knew I'd always loved you, and I loved him too, but not in the same way. He was good to all of us. The day he was killed, we were running as bears. The hunter shot and injured him badly. I was afraid the hunters would kill us too. I didn't have any choice but to run with the boys to Callahan. I carried him into the sea, the boys following us. The hunters didn't shoot at me, maybe because I had two young cubs to raise. When we were far enough out in the water, Callahan managed to tell me that I had to take the boys to see you and make things right between us. And then he died.

"I was heartbroken to lose him because I thought he had been such a good man. Though I learned he had a darker side to him that I hadn't known about. After the funeral, I'd planned to leave as soon as I could to see you and explain to you about the boys, but when I began to check on our finances, I discovered Callahan had put us into debt. He had convinced a female friend to sign my name on the second mortgage, using my ID to pretend she was me. He'd gambled our money away, yet he'd hidden his addiction from me all those years. I didn't have the means to leave there right away. I knew when I did, I wouldn't be returning. Once I had started my business, I was making enough money to put some away for when we left. I planned to see you and tell you about the boys. Then my in-laws began to make the move to take custody of the boys and I knew I had to leave right then and there. Our time had run out. Maybe Callahan knew something like that would happen if anything had ever happened to him. Callahan had never been close to either of his parents. He and his dad and mom were always butting heads. Maybe his parents thought they could start over and raise our boys as their own and get it right this time."

"They can't claim the bloodline. Not when the boys are yours and mine. They're not their real grandparents. And you can't go home. Not when your parents and brothers are so hostile to me. They already know the boys are mine, so how would they treat them? How would they treat you? Certainly not like my family and I will. And you can't subject the boys to mistreatment from your family."

"I don't want to drag you and your family into this." She was desperate to make Edward understand. She would rather be apart from him than see him killed because she stayed with him. But she could tell he'd never stopped loving her. She'd never stopped loving him either.

"You still use your maiden name. Was that after your mate died?"

"No. I wouldn't change it. Callahan was fine with it, his parents, not so much. You sent Butch's body home and I tried to make it work, but there were too many issues left unresolved. After I left with Callahan, my parents disowned me. I wouldn't give up my name."

"What about the boys?"

"They've been using Callahan's name," she repeated. "But he's not listed as their dad on their birth certificates."

Edward's brow rose. "If you've got the birth certificates saying the boys are mine, they can't claim them. If they try to contest the certificates, all we'd have to do is have DNA testing to prove it too. That would end any claim they make that the boys are their blood relations."

"I have their official birth certificates in the fire safe."

"Okay, we'll need to send copies to your former mate's family, so they know the truth."

She led him to the guest room where she'd placed the safe on the bed, the key in the lock, ready to reveal the truth to him. She opened the safe and stared at all the documents sitting on top. The kids' birth certificates had been on top, but now her truck title and her own birth certificate were. She had a bad feeling about this. She quickly pulled out all the documents, her heart hammering. "They've been...taken."

"Who would have done it? Who else's scents are in the inside of the safe?"

"Callahan's." She sniffled. "He's the only other one who had a key to the safe. Maybe...maybe he hadn't been happy that I had named you as their father after all. But you were, and I'd made that clear to him before we even were married."

"And he got rid of the birth certificates? Time can change people."

She blinked away tears. She didn't want to believe Callahan had destroyed them. What if he had shown them to his parents? And they had torn them up?

Edward rubbed her arm. "It'll take some time to get notarized copies of their birth certificates or DNA testing to prove they're mine. But we'll send away for them."

"We need to leave until the paperwork comes back. They won't believe the boys are yours unless we can prove it to them."

"We can go to the cabin. I just want to say I know a lot of years have passed since we were seeing each other, and we're different people than we were back then. But we've got to give us a chance, Robyn. To make this work between us. For each other. *And* for the boys."

"I'm willing to give us another chance. But I worry about the truck being at the garage and Callahan's brothers discovering it. Does anyone do paint jobs on vehicles?"

"Yeah. We can paint it. We can put a billet grille on it, new wheels, grill guard, new truck top. It'll make your vehicle look like it has never been yours."

"I can't afford—"

"I'll take care of it."

"But you don't even know us."

"Like hell I don't, Robyn. I..." Edward almost said he loved her, and he knew he still did, but he knew they would need time to work through any issues they might have between them. "Still, it doesn't matter. You're one of us, and you need our help."

More tears spilled down her cheeks and he knew she'd been managing on her own with hostile in-laws who didn't have her best interests at heart. Nor, from the sounds of it, did the rest of her mate's sleuth. And she didn't know if her own people would welcome her back home. And that was all because she'd been seeing him to begin with. Not that he'd known the trouble that could have caused.

She hugged him back and the boys suddenly peered into the room, their eyes wide, probably wondering where their mom had gone.

"Garrett, Bryan, I need to tell you that Edward is your real daddy." She reached out to them to give them a hug.

They hugged her, then looked up at him and smiled.

"I won't bite." Edward reached out his arms to give them a hug.

She hoped they would embrace their new daddy with all the love he deserved. And they did. They were so cute, and so was he.

Garrett said, "So you're our real dad? Dad told us he wasn't really."

Robyn couldn't believe it. She'd been so careful not to tell them the truth.

"Did you tell anyone? Your grandparents?" Robyn quickly asked.

"Grandma," Garrett said, "but that was Bryan's fault. She told him she would wash his mouth out with soap if he ever told anyone that."

Robyn was shocked to the core. "Ohmigod, Callahan's parents knew that already? Maybe that's why they wanted you so badly. When did Callahan tell you that you weren't his sons?"

Garrett shrugged. "Grandma made him mad, again, right before we went on our trip where the hunter shot him. And we were upset that Grandma was so angry with Daddy. When she left, he said she wasn't our *real* grandmother and that he wasn't our *real* dad. But he told us not to tell you that he'd told us. And we weren't to tell anyone else either. We asked him who our real daddy was and he said it was a secret. You were at the grocery store when he told us. Then we had to see Grandma, I don't know, a couple of days after that. Bryan got mad at her because she was being mean to us. He told her she wasn't our *real* grandmother. She got really angry."

Robyn couldn't believe it! Why hadn't Callahan warned her that he'd gotten angry with his mother and told the boys the truth?

"Grandma said she would wash my mouth out with soap if I ever said that again. She said Daddy lied to us. She said we were *too* her grandsons. And that Daddy was our daddy," Bryan said. "So he really wasn't our dad?"

Robyn hugged the boys again. "No. But he loved you like you were his own sons. Edward's your real daddy."

"You can call me Dad or...Daddy," Edward said.

"So, Grandma isn't really our grandmother like Daddy said?" Bryan asked.

Edward shook his head. "She isn't. But you'll have a great aunt and uncle who will be your loving grandparents who really are your blood-relations."

"Can we go back and watch the movie?" Garrett asked.

Edward and Robyn smiled at the boys. Dad issue aside, they were back to being little boys.

"Go and enjoy it." He gave the boys another hug and they hugged him back and then ran off for the living room. "Do you think that Callahan took the birth certificates with him to prove to his mother that the boys were not his own?"

"That could be. But then what? He didn't return them to the safe."

EDWARD WAS ANGRY WITH CALLAHAN. He had to be careful about what he said, but the fact that Robyn's mate had been deceitful about his gambling, refinancing the house, using a friend to sign Robyn's name, and hiding the fact that he'd told the boys they weren't his sons and made them promise they wouldn't tell their mom the truth was despicable. "Maybe Callahan's mother tore their birth certificates up and he didn't want to tell you what had happened. But he shouldn't have kept you in the dark about any of this." Then Edward had another concern. "You said that no one should have known you were here."

"Not unless they were suspicious."

"Would they have put a tracking device on your truck?"

"If...if they did, wouldn't they have gone straight to the garage, looking for the truck?"

"Maybe. Or maybe they knew White Bear is shifter run and wanted to learn something about us first." He pulled out his phone and called Joe. "Hey, sorry for the interruption, Joe, but could you check to see if Robyn's truck has a tracking device on it?"

"Hell. Yeah, I'll run over there and check it out. And if it does?"

"Craig can take it with him on his next flight out of here."

"Okay, I'll let you know. It'll take a few minutes."

"What if they're waiting for him to return to the garage?" Robyn asked.

Edward called Andy. "Hey, cousin, if you can, I need you to safeguard Joe. He's checking to see if there's a tracking device on Robyn's pickup truck. If the men who followed her here know her truck is in the garage, they may be waiting and watching to see if Joe returns to the garage and force him to tell them where she's staying."

"I'm on my way over there."

Edward wished he could go too, but he figured he could safeguard Robyn and her boys better here.

Suddenly, someone was knocking on the door, and he hesitated to answer it. "We've got company."

"Stay on the line with me," Andy said.

"Sure thing." Edward went to the door and waited until Robyn ushered the boys into one of the bedrooms.

Edward checked to see who it was, and saw it was Aunt Genevieve. He breathed a sigh of relief and let her in. "Hey, Andy, it's just your mom."

"Okay, I'll call back when I know something." Then Andy ended the call with him.

"Uncle Ned told you everything," Edward said, giving his aunt a hug. "The boys are mine. You guessed right."

Genevieve hugged him back, her eyes filling with tears. "Ohmigod, that is the best Christmas news ever."

Robyn and the boys joined them in the living room, looking relieved to see it was only Genevieve.

"You probably remember me. I'm Edward's aunt." She gave Robyn a warm embrace. Then she turned to the boys and crouched down. "You boys can call me Grandma." Genevieve gave them a hug too. Then she rose to her feet. "Our people will keep you safe. You won't be returning to the Northwest Territories unless you choose to."

Tears shimmered in Robyn's eyes. "They don't care anything about whether I return or not. Well, they probably would prefer that I don't. They just want to take the boys back."

"They won't have the chance."

Edward's phone rang and he saw that it was Joe. "Yeah, Joe, putting this on speaker."

"We found a damn tracker on the truck. Andy's here now with me. He saw a black pickup parked nearby, in view of the garage. We're going to pull a fast one on them. I've got a car in here that's been repaired. That's what I was working on tonight. Andy stuck the tracker on the car, and I'm going to drive it to the Howards' home. I already called them and told them I was going to. That way if these men were following the tracking device, hopefully they'll think it was moved off her truck and onto the other vehicle someplace between here and Yellowknife."

"Would they even think she would find it sometime between here and Yellowknife?" Edward asked.

"Yeah, I would," Robyn said. "If I'd been thinking right when I left the city. But then they'll question the Howard family, and they'll be caught up in the lies."

"They're grizzlies and they're tough. They don't put up with any guff from any other shifters. Not even polar bears," Joe said. "Andy talked to them, and they said they would be eager to help out. We just need to know where you transferred the bug over and then we can go from there with a story."

"In Chicken, Alaska, just across the border at a gas station. I stopped for gas there and I looked for a vehicle that had Alaska plates, but I didn't think the vehicle would end up in White Bear too," Robyn fabricated.

"Okay, we'll run with that story," Andy said. "I'll call them to let them know where they'd traveled and the rest of the route. Then I'll leave and watch to see if these guys follow the tracker to the Howards' house. I'll be close by and can intervene if the Howards tell me these guys are giving them grief."

"What if they believe the vehicle under the tarp at Joe's Garage is Robyn's?" Edward asked.

"We've already changed out the license plate, removed the truck top, and taken all of the stuff they had packed in there to my cubby hole," Joe said.

Which meant the hidden basement that had once been used as a speakeasy during Prohibition.

"It might look like her truck, but the tags will say it's someone else's, and with no truck top, it'll look different. Oh, and I had a new bumper grill that I added to make it look dissimilar."

"We thought of having it painted and the works, if you figure the truck is salvageable," Robyn said.

"It is. And we can sure do that. But I went ahead and checked the truck over after I finished repairing the other car and learned your truck needs a new transmission."

"Okay. Keep us informed," Edward said.

Andy said, "Out here."

Aunt Genevieve said, "We were wondering about splitting you up. The boys could go to different homes and then Robyn can too."

"No," Robyn said. "We stay together, no matter what."

"Alright. We thought of swapping out families. The family that's visiting with us would come here and stay with Edward and you could move to our place. Just in case any of these men learn that you came here with Edward. Or he can take you to the cabin we own. Craig could fly you out," Genevieve said. "Or he could take you to Anchorage. But if you're not sure that anyone would support you there, we would prefer you stay in this area with us."

"It's up to Robyn." Edward looked to her to make a decision. His cell rang, and he saw it was from Andy.

"Hey, Joe dropped off the car at the Howards' place and headed back to the garage. He's going to stay overnight there in case these yahoos think to break into his garage and check out the vehicle under the tarp. I'm running checks on their license plates so I have names if I need to charge them with breaking and entering."

"Okay, thanks, Andy," Edward said.

"I would say move the family to another location, but if your place is being watched, they'll know they were there and where they're headed," Andy said.

"Alright. We'll sit tight for now." Edward ended the call. "Okay, you heard my cousin. So we stay here until he thinks it's safe to move you."

"And the truck?" Robyn asked.

"Joe will have to order a new transmission for you. That'll take time. And it will stay in the shop until then. He can have it painted in the meantime."

"Do you need me to get you anything?" Genevieve asked.

"We'll be fine," Robyn said, hoping they would be. She was so thankful that everyone was helping her, but she couldn't believe her in-laws had been tracking her. How long had that been going on? Every time she'd taken the kids on an excursion? Poised to take after her if she went too far? She wondered if they'd been following her too, and she hadn't seen them. She'd been watching for any sign of them, but she'd never seen anyone trailing her. Then again, they would have caught up to her when her truck broke down if they'd been following her. So maybe whoever was supposed to be tracking her had dropped the ball in the beginning and then they had to rush to catch up to her.

"Let us know if you need anything," Genevieve said. "I'm heading back to the house."

"Night." Edward gave her a hug and a kiss on the cheek.

"Thank you," Robyn said.

"You're very welcome, dear." Genevieve gave her and the boys a hug too. She just smiled and sighed.

Robyn suspected she'd given Genevieve the greatest gift for Christmas, two more grandchildren to love on.

When Genevieve left, Edward and Robyn and the kids took seats on the couch to watch the show. She cuddled with the boys and kept feeling like she needed to run. Yet she knew she couldn't. That this was the best plan for now.

Edward got another call, this time from grizzly bear Mike Howard. "Putting you on speakerphone."

"We had a discussion with a man who asked me where I'd driven lately. I told him the story we all have to share about being in Chicken to fill up on gas. Had I seen a woman with a couple of young boys? Yeah. Andy gave me their description, so I was all set. He asked if she left before me or if she was still there when I left. I told him I had no idea. Why would I be looking to see if some woman and her kids left the place?"

"Did he buy it?"

"I don't know. But Joe said her truck is under a tarp at his shop, so I figure they'll be trying to break in to see if that's it or not. They might figure that shifters would stick together in a community. Especially to protect a woman and her kids."

"Thanks, Mike. Free meal on the house at the tavern."

"I'll take you up on it, but I would have done it anyway."

Someone pounded on the door, and Edward said, "Hey,

we've got company." He turned to Robyn, his voice hushed, and said, "Why don't you take the kids into the bedroom again."

Someone pounded on the door again.

Robyn's heart was skipping beats as she rushed the kids to the room where she was going to sleep for the night. She prayed Callahan's brothers weren't at the door, ready for a fight.

6

Pausing his conversation with the grizzly bear over the phone, Edward went to the door, peeked out the peephole, and saw a six-foot-four guy standing on his front doorstep, and three other men just as big, flanking him. "Hey, Mike, I think the four guys who were after Robyn and the boys are here."

"I'll call for backup."

"Thanks." Edward pocketed his phone and went to get a gun.

One of the men banged on the door again. "Edward MacMathan?" he called out.

Figuring the men weren't going to leave without Edward talking to them, he holstered the gun and opened the door. "Can I help you?"

"Yeah, we heard you gave our kin a ride, but we're not sure where to though. We figure her truck is in the garage. The damn thing is a piece of junk. Thanks for being a help to her. We'll take her and the kids home with us now," the darkest haired man of the bunch said, his blue eyes narrowed.

"You're mistaken." Edward moved onto the front porch and closed the door. He couldn't let them bully their way into the house or they would smell Robyn and the kids' scents inside. At least their scents wouldn't be on the front porch since he drove them into the garage, and they entered the house from there. "I've heard someone in town was looking for a woman and a couple of kids. If it's the same ones who had a meal at the tavern, I waited on them. I figured she and the kids went on their way after they finished their meals."

"You don't mind if we take a look in the house then," the one man said. He seemed to be in charge. Dark-haired, blue-eyed, tall, like the rest of the men. They all looked similar, as if they could be brothers.

"If you're police with the local law enforcement and you have a search warrant, I wouldn't mind at all." Edward glanced at the rear license plate of one of the cars parked next to his driveway. "I see you have Northwest Territories tags and so that eliminates that theory."

"Which means Robyn and the boys are here, just as we suspected."

Edward scoffed. "Just because I won't allow a bunch of strangers into my home? Who are you anyway?"

"Richard Gardner, and these are my brothers." He didn't bother to tell Edward his brothers' names, and Edward didn't care to learn them, except for the one who appeared to be the leader of the bunch.

Someone had to have told them that Robyn and her boys had left the tavern with him. "Why would you be chasing her down?"

"Why would you think that?"

"She would have told you where she was going and she would have waited for you to arrive at the tavern, if she'd expected you to meet up with her there."

Richard cast him a dark smile and then frowned. "The truth is she's an unfit mother and the boys' grandparents have custody of the kids. She ran off with them, ignoring the court order, and she's putting them in grave danger."

"You have paperwork to prove that a court order for the custody of the boys is in your possession, I gather." Edward was sure they didn't.

"We do." Richard didn't present any papers to say they did. Instead, he suddenly moved forward in an aggressive manner, as if he was going to break into the house and bodily remove Robyn and the kids from there.

Before Edward could reach for his gun, Richard balled his fist and swung at him. Edward blocked the blow with his arm, but Richard slugged him in the ribs. Edward grabbed his chest and Richard hit him in the eye. Hell! The man's glove helped to soften the blow, but the power behind the strike still slammed Edward back against his door. He knew the men intended to force their way into the house. Heart drumming, his eye throbbing, Edward drew his gun. "I won't hesitate to use this."

His eyes narrowed, Richard stepped back.

A patrol car pulled into the driveway, its lights flashing.

Edward sighed with relief to see that it was Andy. He suspected his cousin had been following one of the men all along and so he hadn't been far behind them when they ended up here, though he wished Andy had arrived sooner than this. Edward was certain he would have a fresh black eye and look like a racoon.

The men all moved aside to see the trooper coming up the driveway, but as soon as Andy saw Edward was armed, he pulled his own gun out. "What happened, Edward?"

"Assault and battery, and yeah, I'm pressing charges against this man." Edward motioned to Richard.

"Get on the ground. All four of you," Andy ordered.

"Hey, officer, this guy hit me first," Richard said, waving his hand at Edward. "I was only defending myself."

"Tell it to the judge. Get on the ground. All of you. Unless you want me to add resisting arrest to the charges." Andy called for backup, but he must have done so on the way over too.

"Hell," the one man said, as two more trooper vehicles pulled up and parked in the driveway.

The men finally complied, though it looked like it was killing them to do so, and they gave Edward a killing look before they were hauled off in the patrol cars.

Andy spoke with Edward then. "What happened?"

Edward told him everything.

Andy shook his head and took a picture of Edward's eye. "It's red and swelling already. You really need to leave the ladies alone for a while. You said he hit you in the ribs. We should get you checked out."

"I didn't hear them crack. They might be bruised but that won't show up for a while and we need to leave."

"Pull up your shirt."

Edward complied.

Andy took pictures of the red area where Richard had hit him. It was a good thing Edward was wearing a heavy wool sweater that had helped to protect him somewhat.

"As soon as I knew all four of these men were here, I called Joe and had him move Robyn's pickup to a new location, because, even though we changed out so many things on the truck already, and detailed it, Robyn and the boys' scents are still in the truck. It will be a few days before Joe gets the new transmission in. A few more days after that before the paint shop can paint the truck, and he can add all the accessories. Joe has another truck in the shop under the tarp, that he borrowed for the occasion. So if any of these guys break in, they won't find the right vehicle."

"Okay, good."

"Are you sure you don't want to have your ribs checked out?"

"No. I'm good. Robyn can take a picture of my eye tomorrow if it starts to look worse—and of any other bruising that might show up—and use it for the charges."

"We won't be able to hold them for long. You know they're going to be back here, trying to get into the place, smelling for Robyn and the boys' scents."

"Yeah. Someone must have told them we left together."

"I suspect so, before we knew the full story and the individual thought he or she was just helping out. I'll let you know when they're released, but you'll need to move them somewhere else. Not my parents' home. They don't need to deal with these men. And not your brother's place because of the babies."

"We need to go to the cabin. At least until we can get verification that I'm the boys' father to prove it to Callahan's family. It might be that his mother has already seen their birth certificates, but it needs to be shown to the others, in case she's trying to hide the fact."

"You can't go to our cabin. They might learn we own it and get a flight out there. The snow leopards said you could use theirs for as long as you like. They just stocked it with food for a visit, but they'll delay the visit, and you can use the place instead."

"That will be great."

"I'm going to take a swab of your DNA to send and process it on a rush order, and I'll order the birth certificates, same situation—police business."

"Thanks, Andy."

"Craig said he'll take you all to the cabin as soon as you're ready to leave. We need to do this before the men are released," Andy repeated, sounding worried.

"Alright. Let me tell Robyn. Do you want to come in?"

"No, I have to fill out paperwork at the office and get this other stuff going to prove you're the boys' father. I'll talk to you soon."

"Thanks, Andy, for everything."

Andy frowned at him and slapped him on the shoulder. "Don't let her get away this time. You have a hard enough time finding a woman you're interested in, and it's all because of Robyn." Then he chuckled under his breath and headed out to his car.

Edward locked the door and went down the hallway to the bedrooms. "Robyn, it's safe to come out now. If you didn't hear, Andy says my cousin Craig will take us to the snow leopards' cabin, where we can stay in relative safety."

Robyn opened the door to the bedroom, looking concerned. "Now?"

"Yeah. We don't want to wait for those men to be released from lockup. They might return here looking for you again."

"Alright. I heard Andy say he would take care of the verification concerning your relation to the boys."

"Yeah, he can expedite it through law enforcement channels."

"We have to leave again?" Garrett asked, sounding dismayed.

"You'll get to fly in a seaplane this time," Edward said.

The kids brightened at the suggestion. Edward called his aunt and uncle to let them know what they were doing, and then called Craig to tell him they would meet him at the dock where his cousin would take them up in his seaplane.

But they needed to go now before anyone else showed up to keep Robyn and the boys from going anywhere.

It was about an hour's flight to the snow leopards' cabin's location and the boys were really excited about flying. They'd never been on a plane before, let alone a seaplane. They finally landed on the frozen water, the seaplane wearing skis, and parked. With their enhanced polar bear night vision and a couple of flashlights, they could see the snow leopards' three-bedroom cabin situated in the trees, the roof covered with snow, the trees sheltering the cabin somewhat from the wind. Once they unloaded the seaplane, they trudged through the snow, carrying their bags, groceries—not wanting to eat all of the Wright brothers' food—and other supplies they might need, to the log cabin.

The whole time, Edward was thinking about Robyn and the boys and what he could do to protect them next. He was determined to learn what he could about her, her situation, and how he could rekindle her interest in him, so he could claim her for his own like he'd wanted to do six years ago. He'd tried to move on with his life and even dated several times, but his thoughts had always returned to her and wanting to be with her. Now that they had two sons together, there was even more of a reason for them being together.

Craig helped carry some of the groceries through the snow-drifts to the cabin, and then Edward walked him back out to his seaplane to say goodbye.

"Let me know if you need anything. We have some bad weather coming in, so it might be a while before I can return."

"Okay, will do." That was the thing about them being polar bears. The weather didn't affect them. This kind of weather was perfect for running in their fur coats. He said goodbye, watched his cousin leave, then turned to trudge back through the deep snow to the cabin.

Edward even wondered how he could get some alone time with Robyn, if she was so inclined, now that they had the twin boys chaperoning them.

He opened the door to the cabin, walked into the foyer,

closed the outer door, then opened the inner door, and stepped inside. The boys were in their bedroom, unpacking their bags, claiming drawers in an oak chest.

Robyn had removed her parka, gloves, hat, and scarf and was trying to start a fire. Edward came over to help her, crouching beside her, breathing in her she-bear scent that was all Robyn, like perfume to his senses.

"If you've got this, I'm going to put the boys to bed. After all we've been through today, and as late as it is, it's way past their bedtime," she said.

The boys came into the living room, rubbing their eyes and yawning and didn't even object.

"That's a good idea." Edward thought of offering to help her put them to bed, to take on a more fatherly-role—he really wanted to be part of the boys' life in every way—but he didn't want to intrude after they'd just learned he was their dad, and after everything else that had happened in their lives today. He was sure Robyn had her own way of doing things. He hoped one of these days he would have some routines of his own with the boys.

He hoped Robyn would return to the living room to visit with him before she retired for the night also. But after all the stress and exercise she and the boys had today while trying to reach White Bear on foot, and the situation with the men from Yellowknife trying to track her down, she might be so worn out that she would be ready for bed too.

He watched her retreat down the hall to the first of the bedrooms and enter the room while he continued to make the fire. Then he removed his cold weather gear and put it away.

"Time for bed boys," Robyn said.

This time they groaned, but they were opening drawers again. Boots dropped on the wooden floor, and he was sure they were removing their clothes and climbing into pj's after that.

The mattress squeaked and Robyn said, "I'll read you a story, and then it's time to go to sleep."

Edward smiled, thinking back to his and Rob's own childhood and how one story would never be enough. Unable to stay away, he headed down the hall to the bedrooms and peeked into the room where Robyn and the boys had gone, so that he could watch her read to them.

Robyn was sitting between the two boys on the bed, each of them looking at the book, until Edward poked his head into the room.

They all smiled at him. "Do you want to join us?" she asked.

"Yeah," the boys said, as if this was something new and different and they were excited about it.

Edward sat down on the bed with them, glad she had included him in the bedtime routine. He did wonder if Callahan had read to Garrett and Bryan too.

After she read "The Night Before Christmas" to the boys, they wanted her to read them another book. Only this time she gave Edward the honor.

He couldn't have been more thrilled. Once he had read them "Goodnight Pippin," they wanted them to read a third book to them. He knew the drill, keep asking for more stories until Mom, or Dad, said enough! What was it with kids wanting to put off the inevitable?

When the third request came to read another story, he smiled to himself. Was Robyn going for it, or would she stand her ground?

She smiled at the boys. "Nighty-night, boys. You can sleep in tomorrow, if you would like. We don't have anywhere to go for the moment. Don't leave the cabin at any time though, unless either Edward or I am with you. We don't want to lose you in the vast wilderness out here."

"Alright," both boys said.

Edward hoped they were better at listening to directions than he and his brother had been at that age. If Edward and Rob had woken early, and to avoid waking their parents, they would have gone outside and explored the wilderness. He was a really light sleeper though. He hoped if they did something like that, he would hear them and would go with them to make sure they were chaperoned.

Robyn and he left the bed and then closed the bedroom door and headed to the living room where he took a seat on the couch. She sat on a chair facing him, showing she didn't want to take up where they'd left off so long ago, snuggling together, loving each other. At least not right this moment.

Not wanting to leave it at that and hoping his encouragement would convince her to consider courting him again, Edward left the couch, took her hand, and pulled her into his arms. "God, you don't know how long I've wanted to see you."

She looked up at him with tears in her eyes. "I didn't care anything about the grudges my family was holding against yours. The feuding went back generations over a goldrush claim and territorial rights. It had nothing to do with us. When...when I met you—"

"You fell in love with me." She had to have. Edward had fallen head over heels in love with her. They had been inseparable. Until that fateful day that her brother had told him to quit seeing her and Edward wouldn't do as he commanded. Though Edward suspected, Butch would have tried to kill him anyway. As bad as it had been, at least only Butch had come to fight Edward, and none of the rest of her brothers had been there. If they had been, Edward would have been the dead man in that fight. Robyn and Edward's three-day weekend retreat had never happened, and instead, Robyn had left him behind—he had thought forever.

She pulled a tissue out of her pocket and wiped her tears away. "I...I didn't want to cause discord for you again."

"You came through White Bear for a reason. You could have taken a couple of different routes. Certainly, you went a long way out of your way by traveling to White Bear. After you arrived in town, you could have eaten somewhere else. Other restaurants were closer to where your truck broke down. You came to my aunt and uncle's tavern because you hoped to get in touch with me. You didn't want to just tell me about the boys. You wanted to know if we could make it together." He was hopeful that was the reason she had done so. He'd never stopped loving her and hoped she felt the same for him.

ROBYN WAS NO LONGER A SINGLE, carefree mother, but a widowed mother of two. But the boys were Edward's and she wanted to be with him in the worst way tonight. To see if they could make this work between them again like it did in the beginning. "Tell me we need to take this slowly between the two of us."

"Hell no, unless you need us to." Edward hesitated, waiting for her answer, but she only smiled, not wanting to wait, and he smiled back, then led her into one of the bedrooms and locked the door.

She hoped this wasn't a mistake, rushing into this, instead of taking it a little slower.

When he began kissing her, it was like no time had passed between them. The lust and love spilled into their lives all over again. He was kissing her like he loved her, and she was kissing him back with the same rampant, loving urgency. Only this time, they had two little boys in the other room, and she didn't want to disturb them for anything! Thankfully, Bryan and Garrett were heavy sleepers once they fell asleep.

Edward quickly began stripping her out of her clothes as if he was afraid that he was going to lose her or that she was going to change her mind about this. Unless they had a siege from her brothers-in-law at the cabin, or their sons made a sudden appearance at the bedroom door, she wasn't stopping where this was going.

She was trying to remove Edward's clothes just as fast, not because she thought *he* might change his mind. She knew that wasn't about to happen. And she loved him for it. She couldn't help worrying about the boys though. They understood about Mommy sleeping with Daddy when it came to Callahan. Hopefully, they would realize it was alright for Mommy to sleep with their biological daddy.

Edward stopped long enough to look over her naked body, her hips a little wider from childbirth, her body not as trim as it was before she had the children. His hands swept over her breasts with a gentle caress as he took his fill of her. "Beautiful," he murmured.

Likewise, she was looking him over, admiring the way his muscles were bigger, more ripped, really hot. "Sexy." She ran her hands over his hard abs. "Just for me."

"You better believe it." His voice deep and lustful, he pulled her in tight against him, sharing his heat with her, the contact between them making her body ache for him in all the right places.

And then he moved her against the blue and green, flannel-covered bed. But when she sank into the down-filled feather bed, he covered her with his body. She felt as though she was adrift in a blanket of warm clouds. And all his.

He began kissing her, rubbing his body against hers in a seductive way that had her body reacting with enthusiasm, her nipples tingling with the friction of his chest against hers, his cock making her wet between her thighs, needy, wanting his penetration in the worst way. His mouth latched onto hers with hungry desperation as if he'd been starved for this all along—this with her, not with any other woman. She had to admit she felt the same way about him. No one would ever measure up to him.

She kissed him back just as desperately, just as hungrily, wanting to taste and feel and smell him—to cherish the new memories, and the old, a reminder of how happy they had been before. But she was eager to make lots of new memories, *years* of new memories, though she told herself she needed to take it one day at a time. One moment at a time.

Their kisses slowed, their tongues touching and tasting, and enjoying each other. Their hearts were racing, and they were breathing hard.

He was still pressing his rigid cock against her when she lifted her leg around him and rubbed the back of his with the sole of her foot. He groaned and started kissing her again, ramping up her need to have him deep inside her. She felt cherished and desirable as much as she cherished and desired him. Then he moved his mouth across her jaw and his warm lips caressed her neck. She sighed with heady expectation, right before he latched onto a nipple and sucked. She about came undone. She groaned and he began to caress her other breast before he turned his attention to that nipple and took it in his mouth and tongued it with delicious strokes.

But when he moved his hand lower and began stroking the swollen, sensitive flesh between her legs, the tension inside her built, the need to find release escalating. "God, keep going," she breathed out, conscious of her sons in the room down the hall, tuckered out, thank goodness, and sleeping soundly, but she didn't want to push their luck either.

His eyes darkened with desire, Edward smiled and continued to stroke her as if he had no intention of giving up until he had her moaning with climax. Which was a damn good thing! His strokes continued until he dipped a finger into her, and she was so close to the pinnacle she could scream. But she couldn't, or she would terrify the boys. Edward swirled his finger around inside her, driving it as deep as he could. She felt the release coming and grabbed ahold of his hips and held on as the climax crashed through her. She groaned out loud.

"Are you ready?" Edward asked, his voice husky and strained.

Robyn was nodding. "Yeah, yeah, yeah...go ahead."

"Good, because I can't hold off any longer." And that was a promise.

"Good, because I don't want you too," Robyn breathed out.

EDWARD BEGAN KISSING HER AGAIN, rubbing his cock against her, before he slid into her wet sheath and began to thrust. And began to kiss her deeply. God, he'd had dreams of being with Robyn like this forever, wanting to wake up to her in his arms, to sleep the rest of the night through with her head resting against his chest, her leg crossed over his in a possessive way. He still couldn't believe she was with him like this, wanting to renew their relationship without reservation. He thanked his lucky stars he hadn't ever found anyone else, secretly hoping someday she would leave her family and come back to him.

It was as though they had never been apart. He knew her every torturous-pleasurable sigh, the look she had when she was about to come, the climax when it hit, the way she would openly receive him, and thrust against him to participate, to love him like he loved her. Despite being swept away with being with her like this again, a nagging thought tried to enter his brain, and he was trying hard not to think about it—how did she get pregnant the first time when she had been on birth control pills? Still, she'd never had any children with Callahan the six years she'd been with him and that gave Edward some peace of mind. He concentrated on the pleasure he felt with being embedded in her. He hadn't lied about being so close to coming, just by rubbing against her initially, and then making her come. It had been too long for him, and she did this to him. Turned the heat up and he was on fire. Every thrust brought him closer to the end. And yet, he couldn't help thinking of it being just the beginning for them. He just had to make sure that it was and that she didn't change her mind about being with him long-term.

He kissed her again, his eyes closed as he felt her muscles tightening around his cock, the scent of her sweet and tangy scent filling his senses right before he came. He groaned long and low and she wrapped her arms around his neck and kissed him again. She was beautiful and sexy, and he wanted to claim her for his own now and forever.

He slid off her and pulled her into his arms. He hoped she stayed with him tonight and didn't leave to go to the other bedroom, worried about what their sons would think if they got scared and went looking for her and didn't find her in her bed.

She didn't make a move to leave, and he cuddled with her, glad the punch that her brother-in-law had given him hadn't bruised his ribs like he thought it might. He kissed her on the top of her head, loving the feel of her in his arms. He thought back to the business of her getting pregnant and he wondered again how that had happened. He didn't want to spoil the moment, and instead tried to sleep, but lying here with Robyn in his arms like they'd done so many times so long ago, he couldn't stop thinking about how he had to convince her to stay with him for good this time.

THAT NIGHT, Edward had worried so much about Robyn's family, her in-laws, and convincing her to stay with him, that he had been awake for a long time. Not to mention Robyn had stirred and he'd made love to her again. Because of that, he slept in later than he usually did in the morning. But he swore he heard something that had woken him. He lay in bed for a few minutes, listening to see if he could hear it again, to determine what it was. Robyn was still sound asleep after all their love-making last night.

This time of year, it was dark still. He realized it was after nine in the morning, but *something* had disturbed his sleep. He slipped out from underneath Robyn and the quilt and blankets, trying not to disturb her, opened the door, and walked to the guest room where the boys were staying. Opening the door, he discovered they weren't in bed. A bit of panic crept in, and he hurried to check the room where Robyn had planned to sleep, just in case the boys had gotten scared and thought to join her in bed. They weren't in there either.

His heart beating wildly, he rushed out of the room and down the hall into the living room. He saw the boys' pajamas on the floor, the front door wide open, and he didn't have to guess what had happened. He ran outside, expecting to see them playing as polar bears nearby, but they weren't. They cried out and he swung his head in the direction of their cries, his heart thundering. In their polar bear forms, the boys were huddled together on an ice floe, crying out to him as they were being dragged out to sea. Hell! That must have been the sound he heard that woke him this morning.

He raced back into the house and to the bedroom where he and Robyn were staying. She was still sleeping. "The boys are on an ice floe!" he warned.

Still looking sleepy and like she wasn't sure what was going on, Robyn sat up in bed. "What?"

"Call my cousin Craig to fly out here. My phone's on the bedside table. He's on my contact list. I'm going to swim out to the boys. They're on an ice floe," he repeated. "They might not be able to swim that distance back here on their own. I'll stay with them until Craig can get here. You stay here. Wait for the boys' return. He'll bring them back in the seaplane."

"Ohmigod, Edward." She was out of the bed in a flash, grabbing clothes.

"I've got this." He kissed her, then raced off to the front door. He tugged off his boxer briefs, ran outside, and shifted. Then as a polar bear, he ran as fast as he could to the water, calling out to the boys in his polar bear roar that he was coming to get them. He prayed they didn't get off the ice floe and try to join him. As soon as Edward was in the water, he swam as fast as he could toward the darn floe that was moving out to sea just as fast.

ROBYN FELT PANICKED, and she nearly dropped Edward's phone as she hurriedly tried to call Craig. She was grateful to Edward for trying to rescue their sons. "Craig," she said, tears in her eyes, her voice unnatural. "We need you now! The boys are on an ice floe, and Edward's gone to be with them. But he needs you to pick them up. They're too far out."

"I'm coming. I'll be there in an hour."

An hour would be a lifetime.

7

Edward was swimming as fast as he could to reach the boys on the ice floe. They looked like they were getting ready to abandon their little, floating ice island, but he brayed at them, warning them to stay back, away from the edge. He was coming for them, to be with them, to protect them like their momma would have done.

Edward was a fast and able swimmer, but it was taking him too long to reach the boys. All he could think of for now was reaching the boys, joining them on the ice, and keeping them calm, warm, and safe until Craig arrived.

He was getting closer now and he was damn glad the floating ice island was big enough to accommodate him and the boys. He wanted to get to know them, but this wasn't exactly what he had in mind. Fishing trips, sure. Swimming, of course. But danger and peril? Not with the boys. He realized that he had a lot to learn when it came to raising a couple of kids too. He was getting his first real test on how to handle kids in a crisis situation.

Once he reached the ice, he slid up on top and the boys looked at him for a moment, not approaching, appearing scared, like papa bear was going to scold them for being so foolhardy and for disobeying him in the first place. They would have no idea how he would react, and truthfully, it was all new to him. It gave him new respect for his parents and all that they went through raising him and his brother before they died. To the boys, Edward was just a very big, menacing-looking, male, polar bear.

He lumbered toward them and then stopped, sat, and waited for them to join him. They both ran over to him and pressed themselves against him. He hugged them both, hoping no one saw the uncharacteristic scene of a male polar bear hugging two youngsters instead of momma bear being there for them and wanted to send scientists to document the unusual behavior.

He finally laid down on the ice, trying to relax so the boys wouldn't be so anxious. They could be here for a good long while. They probably figured he had a plan. Kids could be trusting that way. They snuggled up against him to stay warm.

About an hour later, Edward and the boys heard his cousin's seaplane flying nearby, searching the ice floes. He stood up tall, hoping Craig could spot him standing on the ice. Both boys joined him as if that would enable Craig to see them better. It was still dark out, but the sun was just beginning to come up. White bears in a sea of white ice floes could be difficult to spot. He hoped Craig could land safely in the water too. Edward could just imagine Craig crashing the plane, and having to strip and shift and join them as a polar bear also, and then what? No more rescues.

Then Craig was landing in the water some distance off, unable to reach them.

Craig called out, "I'll take the boys to shore and come back for you."

Edward had thought to swim back home, but he figured Craig was right. This was the best plan. He chuffed at the boys, telling them to join him in the water. Then he slipped into the water and one after the other followed him. He swam with the boys around other ice floes in their path and finally reached the seaplane.

Andy was in the seaplane also and helped to get the bear cubs inside, then Edward climbed onto the nearest ice floe to wait for his cousins' return. The cubs looked anxious about leaving Edward behind. He appreciated their concern.

"He'll be fine. We'll take you back to your momma and then come back for Edward," Craig said, then they flew off for the land mass.

Edward hadn't really planned their day as far as the activities they could do, but this certainly wasn't anything like how he thought of enjoying the day with the boys. Maybe helping them build a snow fort and having a snowball fight. Fishing. Exploring the area. Swimming as bears, but not hitching a ride out to sea on an ice floe and having to get a seaplane rescue.

ROBYN WAS SO upset with her boys and she was so proud of Edward for having the presence of mind to rescue them. She just hoped he wouldn't change his mind about having them around any longer, thinking they would disrupt his orderly, bachelor life too much.

She couldn't believe the boys had done such a thing. Then again, she remembered her own brothers doing something just as risky when they were little.

As soon as they were ashore, she thanked Edward's cousins and then she hurried the boys back to the house. "You go inside and shift, dress, and stay in your room until Edward returns."

The boys shifted and ran for the bedroom.

"He's going to be mad at us," Garrett said.

"Yeah, he is," Bryan said.

"*I'm* mad at you. *Go.* We'll deal with you when I return." She waited for them to enter their bedroom and then she went back outside to watch for Edward's return. It seemed like it took forever as she paced in the snow and watched for any sign of the seaplane. Then she heard the sound of the engine rumbling off in the distance and she prayed Edward was safe on the plane.

When they finally reached a safe place to park, Edward jumped into the water. So glad to see him, she took a relieved breath as she watched Edward swim to shore. He shook off the icy water and ran up to her and nuzzled her. She patted his wet, furry head and she thanked his cousins again. She couldn't appreciate them for all their help any more than she did.

"Sure thing," Craig said.

"Just call if you need anything else," Andy said.

"Hopefully, no more sea rescues," she said, still frowning.

Edward's cousins both smiled as if they knew the trouble Edward was in with hooking up with her again—except this time with two five-year-old, male twins—then they flew off.

As a bear, Edward walked beside her as they headed for the house.

"Thank you for risking your life to save the boys," she said.

He grunted, and she hoped that didn't mean he was really angry with them. She was still their protective mother, though she believed that Edward needed to be assertive in this case and she would let him decide the boys' punishment.

As soon as she and Edward went inside the house, the boys were peeking outside their bedroom door, not coming out, but just checking to see for themselves that Edward was there.

He grunted at them, then headed into his bedroom. A few minutes later, he was dressed and walking back down the hall.

"What did you want to do for punishment for the boys?" he asked her.

She pulled Edward into her arms and kissed him, tears trailing down her cheeks. "Thank you, Edward. I would never have reached them in time. Thank you. After you set the rules last night about not going out alone without one of us being with them, and because you risked your life to rescue them, you can decide their punishment."

He smiled and kissed her back. "I hadn't planned on that little adventure this morning first thing, but everyone's fine. We're all safe. We just need to set some ground rules. Again." He glanced back at the bedroom where the boys were still peeking out. "And when I say you don't go out to play without an adult being with you, I mean it."

They both nodded.

Then Edward said, "I'm starving. What about everyone else?"

The boys both looked at Robyn.

"I'll make us some eggs and ham." She glanced at Edward, thinking the boys should be confined to their room at the very least.

"We'll start building a snow fort while you're making break-fast. Just call us when it's ready. And thanks in advance for fixing breakfast. Come on, boys. Get your coats and gloves and hats on. We're going to have a snowball fight as soon as the fort is made."

She couldn't believe it! She could see the kids believing she was being the mean parent and Edward was the fun parent and not taking parenting seriously.

"Alright!" "Yes!" the boys said, but looked to make sure that she agreed, and she nodded.

They rushed back to their room to get their outside gear on.

She folded her arms and gave Edward a stern look. "That's your punishment for the boys? Don't tell me boys will be boys."

Edward pulled her arms apart and wrapped them around him and gave her a warm hug. "No, I wasn't going to say that.

The boys and I will have a little talk while we're snowball fighting outside."

She smiled then. Okay, so maybe he was right.

"That's how my father handled my brother and me when we did stupid and dangerous things."

She sighed. "Alright. Have fun then."

"You could join us and then we could fix food afterward," Edward offered.

"No. You need this time with the boys. I'll play with all of you later."

The boys raced out of the room and stood next to them, looking eager to play, hopeful she hadn't changed Edward's mind about his choice of punishment for them.

And then Edward headed outside with the boys.

Robyn still couldn't believe the boys and Edward could have died at sea, without Edward's quick thinking and actions. She was glad to see the boys were fine with Edward being their dad, though she wondered if they would have changed their mind if he had decided a harsher punishment for them.

She started making a breakfast casserole of shredded potatoes, eggs, ham, and cheese and set it in the oven to bake for an hour. She watched out the window to see the little boys and the big boy all having fun building a fort. She was so glad they were here with Edward, and for the first time in a long time, she felt she and the boys were safe from her late-mate's family, and her own family too. She loved watching Edward play with the boys. That's what they needed. A dad who was really there for them.

Glad she had told the boys the truth about Edward, confirming what her mate had told them about having not been their father, she felt relief.

She wanted to try to make it work between her and Edward and she was certain Edward did too. After last night and their making love, it was a perfect way to renew their feelings for each other.

She returned to the kitchen and set the oven timer. Since the food wouldn't be ready for another hour, she put her coat, hat, and gloves on, pulled on her snow boots, and headed outside to have some fun too.

As soon as everyone saw her, the boys yelled, "Mom! Be on our side!"

She laughed, not wanting to gang up on poor Edward, but he only smiled at her and gave her a hand to help her into the boys' fort. It had one partial snow wall up on a slight hill, but Edward said, "Okay, have your mom help you build your fort and I'm going to make my snowball pile."

And the battle was on. Robyn was trying to build their snow fort taller, and the boys were piling up the snowballs for ammunition. Edward started lobbing the snowballs over the fort's low wall and the kids took action—tossing their own snowballs. Robyn gave up on the wall and began throwing the snowballs at Edward too. Edward finally ran toward them with snowballs in both hands and the kids ducked behind the fort's wall. Robyn socked him with a couple of snowballs, but he didn't throw his. As soon as he reached the wall, he peered over and saw the boys smiling and hiding.

He dropped the snowballs on top of them, and everyone was laughing. They played for about an hour, and she remembered the casserole. "Who's ready to eat?"

"We are!" the kids shouted and scrambled out of their fort and into the house.

Edward drew Robyn into his arms and hugged her, then kissed her cold nose and lips. "Thanks for coming out and playing with us."

"I had to. You three couldn't have all the fun. Besides, it was going to take so long for the meal to be ready, it meant I had time to play too."

"You sided with the boys," he teased her.

"Yeah, well, I figured a big guy like you could take on the three of us and still win. Thanks for playing with the kids. They needed that more than a big scolding and being sent to bed for the rest of the day."

"They're good boys. They just need to know how dangerous the wilderness can be and learn to respect it. I think they learned their lesson as far as hitchhiking on an ice floe. They told me they thought it would be fun—just float around on it for a while. They didn't realize the currents could carry them out to sea. It doesn't mean they won't get into other mischief in the future though."

"And you know this because of you and your brother's shenanigans?"

"Uh, right, and because of what my cousins were up to. I mean, with five of us together, we could get ourselves in all kinds of difficult situations. Not intentional, just being kids. And not that our sons could inherit any of this from me." He walked her to the house.

"Right."

He smiled and wrapped his arm around her waist. "It's just in kids' nature to want to explore and be adventurous. Don't tell me you weren't like that too."

"Sure I was. But it's a lot different when you're the kid, than when you're the parent worrying about your kid."

"I agree with you there."

They headed inside the house and peeled out of their outerwear, hung it all up, and then Robyn and Edward served the meal while the boys set the table.

"I thought we would go on a polar bear run after we eat," Edward said.

"Yes!" the boys said.

"All of us, right, Robyn?" Edward asked her.

"Of course. I wouldn't be left behind." She loved to shift into her polar bear coat and go for runs with her cubs. It would be fun to do it with Edward too. She hadn't run with him in years.

"You really did hope you could run into me in town, didn't you?" Edward asked, all-knowing like.

"Yes. I didn't know how you or your family would feel if I showed up though. Or if you would even have a mate." And she wanted to tell him her kids were his too. But she really hadn't known how he would react. She should have known he would want to be part of their lives also.

"You made it impossible for me to ever find a mate. Everyone wants you back in my life, our lives. I know they were as upset as I was that you had left."

"Why did you go, Mommy?" Garrett asked.

"Yeah, why?" Bryan asked.

"Your uncles don't like Edward and his family. They threatened to hurt him. I didn't want them to hurt him, so I left. I was protecting him."

"I don't know those uncles, do I?" Garrett asked.

"No, you've never met them." If Robyn was going to be with Edward and his family again, she could never let her own family know of it. She didn't want to bring their wrath down on his family, not when they were still dealing with issues with her late mate's family. Someday, when the boys were older and could understand better, Edward could tell them what had happened between her brother and him, but that would be for another day.

8

After Edward and Robyn finished cleaning the dishes from breakfast, she sighed, examining his eyes. "The one black eye you had is gone, but the other is turning purple. I'm so sorry Richard hit you."

"All in the name of protecting you and the kids."

"Well, at least we heal faster than humans." She kissed his cheek and then they got ready to run, shifted, and dashed outside as bears.

The kids loped behind Edward and Robyn, staying with them and not running off. Edward wondered if the boys were still a little traumatized from their adventure this morning and were afraid to get into trouble again. Or maybe with both adults running with them, they figured they couldn't get away with too much. He was glad they were sticking close though, no matter what the reason was.

They saw moose roaming through the forested areas. They didn't see any humans on their trek, thankfully. Though the polar bears, the non-shifter kind, lived up north, the shifters went anywhere they wanted to go that they figured they wouldn't be seen by humans. Occasionally, a local Inuit would see them, and know they were not regular bears. The Inuit felt honored to see the bear shifters and only shared their sightings among their own people.

All the bears, black, grizzly, and polar bears had been seen around Anchorage though.

When Edward, Robyn, and the boys left the forest and were out on open snow, they saw a couple of bald eagles flying overhead. He enjoyed running as a bear in the pristine wilderness. He loved coming here with his tour groups and family and friends. He couldn't believe he was out here with Robyn again, and now with his own sons too.

He kept wishing that his brother or sister-in-law could have seen visions of Robyn and the boys showing up in White Bear and the difficulties they were facing. His brother had visions of the future, and Alicia had visions of the past, but oftentimes they couldn't see anything that related to close family members or otherwise they might have.

Once they'd finished having fun, he told Robyn and the boys to come with him and he would take them home again. For him, enjoying the wilderness was enough, fishing as a bear and cooking the fish at the cabin, taking wilderness hikes, enjoying the quiet, talking about things he and his family had done in the past, piecing together puzzles, playing cards, or board games. They didn't have TV out here and he hoped the boys would be fine with playing with other things. They could still go out and make a snowman or two. And they could work on more of their snow fort also and have another snowball fight. He wasn't used to being around kindergarten-age kids, so he wasn't sure what else they would like to do. So far, they seemed to be enjoying all the activities they'd taken part in here.

But he was thinking he needed to take her and the kids back to White Bear. They couldn't stay out here forever. He needed to tell his family that Robyn and the boys were staying with them.

They finally managed to arrive back at the cabin, and everyone was ready to shift and dress. The boys came out of the bedroom dressed and collapsed on the couch in the living room after their wild adventures.

Edward set out a puzzle for them to piece together and then joined Robyn in the kitchen where she was making grilled cheese sandwiches and chicken and rice soup for lunch.

Edward helped Robyn slice up cheese for grilled cheese sandwiches. The boys were piecing together the seal, puffin, and polar bear puzzle in the living room and talking away to each other.

She poured the soup into the saucepan to heat. "I've been thinking..." Then she glanced at Edward. "We need to get married."

Edward's jaw dropped slightly. He had hoped Robyn would want the same thing in time, but he thought he would have to do a lot more convincing before that happened.

He smiled and pulled her into a hug and kissed her. "Hell, yeah. I'm ready. Like six years ago ready." He'd been ready ever since he'd seen her at the tavern this time, hoping beyond hope her mate was no longer with her and that's why she was alone with the boys. Once he learned she'd lost her mate, he wanted in the worst way to make her his own mate. But he thought she might want to wait a bit and see how things worked out between them and see how he coped with the boys on a regular basis.

She smiled at him, looking just as happy about the prospect, not that she was only doing so because she was afraid, if they didn't, her late mate's family would still come after them. Or that she felt obligated in any way to marry Edward because it would provide more stability for the boys.

He couldn't believe how much it felt as though she'd never been away from him for any length of time.

"It's a little late to begin a courtship, I figure." She motioned to the boys in the living room.

"I have every intention of courting you, even after we're married." Edward kissed her again. "You don't know how happy that makes me."

"I have some idea." She smiled.

"I love you. I always have and I've never stopped."

"I love you too." She kissed him back. "Maybe if we're mated, my in-laws will give up on the notion that they have any rights to the boys. You don't know how much I was afraid you would reject me too."

"No way. Not when you were the only woman I've ever been interested in marrying. It feels like we've never been apart."

"Except that you've got a couple of boys in the deal—"

"Even better. I've always loved my family. And I couldn't be happier to make you and the boys part of it. My family already adores you. The only problem would have been if you had left again and taken them with you. My aunt and uncle will be ecstatic."

"Call them then." She rubbed Edward's arm. "Tell them we're returning to White Bear."

"We'll have difficulties."

"We'll deal with it, as long as your family is alright with it," Robyn said.

"You know they are. We always rally around our own kind, and others of the White Bear community, who are friends and like extended family, will too." Edward released her to grab his satellite phone and called Craig. Edward felt like he was doing a moonwalk, he was so thrilled Robyn wanted to be his mate. He pulled her into his arms again.

"Hey, have you had more issues again?" Craig asked right away.

"No. We want to return to White Bear and get married."

Craig whooped. "Halleluiah. You finally came to your senses. Is it okay to mention it to our family?"

"Yeah. Have your mom make arrangements for the marriage, and as soon as we arrive, we'll do this."

"Alright. As soon as I get off the phone with you, I'll tell her, and I'm headed out to pick you all up."

"Is there any sign of her husband's family in White Bear?"

"No. I think they've lost your tracks, but they're not in White Bear right now that we know of."

"Good." They really didn't need the conflict when they arrived back home.

"I'll be there in an hour." Craig ended the call.

Edward's aunt called right after that. He smiled when Aunt Genevieve said, "I'm so excited for all of you. This is just great news. Everyone will be so happy. Put Robyn on for me, will you? I'll talk to her about what she wants to do concerning the wedding."

"I'm sure she just wants something quick and official."

"Nonsense. That's a man talking for you. We had a lovely affair for Rob and Alicia. We'll do something a little faster this time for you and Robyn, but we're doing this."

Loving Genevieve for wanting to help with this, Edward smiled and pulled Robyn tighter in his arms. He hoped she wouldn't mind, because his aunt was going to do whatever it took to make this spur-of-the-moment wedding as grand as it could be, given the time constraints.

"Big wedding," Edward said, handing the phone to Robyn.

ROBYN COULDN'T IMAGINE THROWING A "BIG" wedding together in a hurry and it wore her out just thinking about it. But if his aunt was willing to get started on it while they were trying to return to White Bear, she would welcome it.

"I was just thinking of a simple wedding, a justice of the peace, or something. I think that as long as we have the paperwork, anyone can actually marry us off. Just as long as it's nice and official and we have plenty of witnesses, in case any of my late husband's brothers try to come and take the boys away from me."

"You deserve the best. If you don't mind, just let me know what you would like: color scheme, flowers, type of cake, food you would like to eat, and anything else you can think of. And I'll take it from there."

"I...I don't know. I didn't have a family wedding the first time. Just anything is fine."

"What about a dress?"

"There wouldn't be time."

"Alicia, Rob's wife, has a really good friend, Tamara White, and she has a new wedding gown. You look like you're about the same size. When she heard you and Edward were back together again, she said if you would like to use her wedding gown, she would be thrilled."

"Well, I don't know her, but if you really don't think she would mind. But tell her that I don't want her to feel in any way obligated if she doesn't want me to use it. I will totally understand."

"I'll ask her. She's eager to meet you. Beyond that, Ned and I can't wait to spoil the boys," Genevieve said. "Christmas is almost here."

Robyn smiled. This was such a change from the way her mate's parents had been. And her own family had been after she had met Edward.

"Edward has always loved you and no other girl could meet his expectations after you. I'm so glad you're back."

"We'll have issues with my late husband's pack," she warned her. Robyn didn't want her to forget that part.

"We have a judge who can handle this. Even if your late mate was listed as the father on the boys' birth certificates."

"He wasn't. Edward was. And Callahan knew they weren't his sons, but he was trying to protect them from my family. So was I. But then Callahan told the boys himself that he wasn't their father, though he told the kids not to tell anyone, including me. Anyway, my youngest twin, Bryan, told Martha."

"So they know the truth and they still want to take the boys away from you. Okay, dear. We'll get it all worked out. I can't tell you how excited we are that you're with us again."

"Thank you. Though I hate to bring this concern to you and your family, I'm glad to be here too. I just can't thank you and everyone else enough after...all that's happened."

"Nonsense. Craig's on his way to bring you here. He'll probably take his brother to help. I'll see you in a couple of hours and we can make final arrangements for your wedding, get the paperwork signed, and you'll be all set. You have nothing to worry about."

But Robyn knew how stubborn her late mate's family could be, and if they could stop this from happening, they would do it.

When they finished the call, Edward kissed her again. "I hope my aunt isn't making you feel that we have to go all out for this in such a rush. We could just get married on paper and then have a fancier wedding later."

"It's overwhelming, but no. I would much rather just do it the one time. I'm excited about it, really. And it was so good of your aunt to start coordinating everything until we can return, and I can help her."

"You and Alicia are like her daughters now. With all her sons and nephews to raise and all the shenanigans we pulled, she's thrilled to have you both. What about your own family? The Conibears still won't like that we're getting married."

"They gave up on me when I moved to the Northwestern Territories. I might not ever see them again, though all that matters is keeping you, our sons, and the rest of your family safe." She hugged him. "I bet you never envisioned your life to turn so upside down, just because you were working in your family's tavern before Christmas."

"Only in a good way. You're right about not expecting you to return and end up being with me like this again, certainly not with a couple of boys in tow. I'd always hoped you might return, but I had figured there would be no chance of that. I couldn't be more thrilled. It's like a Christmas miracle. In advance, I apologize if I don't meet your expectations as far as raising the boys go. I suspect it will be all trial and error to begin with, and our parenting ideas might be different."

"You've already shown just how good you can be with the boys. You rescued our sons. And I loved the way you dealt with them in such a positive way for their 'punishment'. You were so heroic, and I couldn't be prouder of you. I'm sure we'll have lots of ups and downs, as any couple raising a couple of bear cubs would. We'll have different ideas on how to raise them. And couple differences too. But we'll make it just fine as long as we continue to love and communicate with each other. I'll cherish every moment with you."

"The same with me. Have you ever wondered what it would have been like to be mated to me? I never stopped thinking of you in that way," he asked.

"Of course I did. And how dangerous it would have been if we had because of my family."

They heard a seaplane's engine and Edward said, "It's not Craig's seaplane." He immediately called Craig and put it on speakerphone. "A seaplane is landing on the water near the cabin. Simon and his brothers wouldn't be coming to their cabin, would they?"

"No. I won't be there for another forty-five minutes. But I've got Andy with me to help out."

"We're shifting and getting out of here and heading for our family cabin."

"I'm calling for reinforcements. We'll be there as soon as we can."

Robyn was already getting the boys to strip and then she hurried to remove her clothes.

"The brothers don't know this area, if it's them, which is the only advantage we have," Edward said.

"I'm radioing to learn which pilot took them out there," Craig said.

"Alright. We're shifting and taking off."

Robyn knew things couldn't be as perfect as they thought they would be. She and the boys shifted, and Edward said, "We stick together since you don't know the area well either."

She nodded. She knew all the bears would have to do was follow their scents and tracks and they could locate them quickly. She couldn't run that fast with a couple of cubs.

Edward opened the door and Robyn and their sons ran outside as bears. Edward shut the door and shifted. Then he led the way.

If all of the men had come, all four of them, she and Edward wouldn't be able to fight them off. She could see them killing Edward and her and taking the boys back to Yellowknife.

For a couple of miles, she and Edward and the boys had been running through the snow when she saw a grizzly bear off in the distance. As soon as he saw them, he stood up and grunted. Her heart was in her throat when Edward headed straight for the bear, and the grizzly tore off to meet up with them. That's all they needed was to have to fight off a grizzly bear first.

He growled at Edward, and Edward growled back. She and the boys stopped running to catch their breaths. But neither of the men were challenging the other's territorial rights. Edward motioned to Robyn and the cubs and then he growled at the grizzly. Then he motioned again with his head toward them.

The grizzly took in what Edward was trying to convey, and she thought he must be a shifter like them. Maybe he was even a friend.

What she couldn't believe was that the grizzly and Edward joined each other, stood on their hind legs and battled each other in friendly combat in greeting.

Edward called out to her, and she and the boys joined them and then Edward began to move again. She and the cubs followed. To her surprise, the grizzly came with them!

Polar bears were capable of traveling nearly twenty miles per day in search of food. She hoped that it wouldn't be that far from Simon's cabin to where Edward planned to take them because she felt as though they were just getting farther away from civilization. She was afraid that the cabin he mentioned he wanted to reach was so far away that they would never make it in time.

She wanted to trust in him, but she was certain he'd never traveled with a couple of young cubs before either. The boys had been good about staying with them, pushing themselves, not wandering off or complaining. But they were beginning to move slower and slower.

Then after walking and resting for about five miles, she saw a cabin off in the snow, but it wouldn't be any safer than the snow leopards' cabin had been, she didn't think. It would be awful to ruin someone else's cabin if they had a bear fight in it. But Edward was hell-bent on reaching it, nudging the boys on, trying to get them to move faster. When they saw the cabin, they began to pick up speed, as if the cabin meant they didn't have to run any more.

None of them had seen any sign of her mate's brothers, but the polar bears would all blend in with the snow, so it would be hard to see them. Likewise, they would have a difficult time seeing Robyn and the others. All except for the grizzly with them. Still, they would be following their scents.

She felt guarded relief when they reached the cabin and Edward shifted, opened the door, and ran inside. She and the boys did too, and she smelled Edward and more of his kin's scents in the cabin. This had to be the one he had been talking about with Craig.

The grizzly came inside with them, and Edward came out of one of the rooms dressed in boxer briefs and hurried to shut and lock the door. "Alicia's spare clothes are in the room on the right. Gary, you can grab some of my extra clothes. We'll have to fit the boys in some adult clothes. I've got two rifles here and a sat phone for emergencies. I'll let Craig know to come here first for us."

Gary went down the hall to the bedroom that was Edward's, and she and the boys went to Rob and Alicia's room. She hurried to dress. Then she tried to help the boys dress in adult clothes. Edward finished dressing also.

"These are a girl's clothes," Bryan complained.

"They're smaller than the men's clothes. We'll get your clothes soon."

Edward was already on the sat phone to his cousin. "Hey, Craig, we made it. No sign of the polar bears. Maybe it was just someone else who was landing the seaplane near there. Gary joined us."

"Good. I had learned he was in the vicinity and told him to try and meet up with you out there," Craig said.

"Great, he sure did. And we're much indebted to him."

"I think he still would like to make up for the fight he had with your brother."

"Well, he's sure going to be a great help now."

"Okay, I'm headed in your direction. I told the pilot, who left the four men off near Simon's cabin, that the men had it in mind to kidnap your young sons. He offered to help us, but he's human and we can't allow him to get into our bear business. I told him my brother will be here shortly, with handcuffs and arrest warrants."

"We know for sure it was them?"

"Yeah. We do now. Have you got your rifles ready?"

"Sure do. So far, we haven't seen any sign of them." Edward pulled the boys in for hugs in their oversized clothes. They looked like they were tired and scared. They hugged him back and then he motioned for them to sit on the couch. He embraced Robyn next and said to his cousin, "We'll keep you informed if we see them, Craig."

"Okay. Out here."

Gary joined them and loaded a rifle. "Do you want to tell me what's going on? Craig was trying to tell me the difficulties you were having, but I was in a real hurry to shift and get out the door so I could help you out if you got caught in the snow and had to face these men on your own."

"Thanks, Gary. You don't know how much this means to us."

"I think I do." Gary glanced in the direction of the boys and smiled at Robyn.

Edward explained everything to the grizzly who had fought his own brother over a case of mistaken identity when it came to a woman Gary had been seeing, but everything had been patched up between Rob and Gary. Edward was watching out the front windows while he was talking, and Gary was watching out the back windows.

Gary smiled at the boys. "They look just like you when you were that age."

"We hate dragging you into this," Edward said. "But I was really worried they would reach us before we could get the kids to safety."

"What are friends for? I know you would do the same for me if our roles had been reversed."

"I agree," Edward said.

Robyn sat down on the couch and hugged the boys. She prayed Craig and his brother would get here before the other bears did. She was glad they had Gary here to help out.

"What's your plan of action?" Gary asked.

"I'll shoot off a couple of warning shots to let them know we're armed and dangerous. Simon and his brothers didn't have any weapons at their cabin. I would rather we just let the bears know we're armed, and they no longer have the advantage. I would rather not have to kill them out here. But, of course, if it means they're going to keep coming after us and try to take the boys away, we'll have to do whatever it takes." Edward turned to Robyn. "Does that sound alright to you?"

"Yes. I'll do anything I have to, to keep them from taking the boys back to the Northwest Territories."

"Okay, good. We're getting married," Edward told Gary. "As soon as we're able to return to White Bear. You and your mate are invited."

Gary laughed. "That's a swift move. Looks like you got the cart before the horse."

"Absolutely, and we'll be glad to have you," Robyn said. "Though it's got to be a quick wedding."

"Those are the best kind. Plenty of food?" Gary asked.

Edward chuckled. "Yeah, you know my aunt and uncle. We will be well-fed." Edward moved closer to the window. "I saw movement."

She'd hoped the brothers had seen the tracks for another bear, smelled the grizzly's scent, and would worry Edward and she had more reinforcements they'd met at the cabin. But it appeared the bears weren't going to be persuaded to give up their mission. She wished there was some way to convince them that the boys weren't blood relations of anyone in their sleuth.

She got up from the couch and the boys immediately wanted to join her. "It's okay. Stay here." She grabbed some winter outerwear and began putting it on.

"What are you doing?" Edward asked, concerned.

"I'm going to tell them that the boys are yours. Maybe they'll realize what a mistake this is, and they'll back off."

"Do you think they'll even believe us?" Edward asked.

"I'm hoping so." But she really didn't know. "Callahan's brothers are only doing this based on what Martha and Arnold told them. If we could convince them what they believe is wrong, maybe we can stop this."

Edward hurried to put on some winter gear. Then he and she headed outside, his rifle at the ready.

The four bears stopped some distance from the cabin when they saw Edward and Robyn.

She called out, "The boys are Edward MacMathan's. This man standing beside me. *He* is their biological father. *Not* Callahan. Your brother mated me to protect the boys and Edward from my family, but he was not the father of the two boys," she repeated. "Your mother knows the truth. Callahan told the boys, and Bryan told your mother. I'm sure she told your father also. The birth certificates show Edward as the father. DNA will prove he is their father, and that your parents are not related in any way to the boys. Not only that, but Edward and I are married now. Martha and Arnold have no claim to the boys."

None of the polar bears made a move in their direction while pondering the news. Edward kept his rifle at the ready but was holding it in a non-threatening manner.

"Others are on their way here," Robyn warned the bears. "And we have three rifles between us and enough ammunition to stop you right now. We don't want this to end badly for any of us. The boys are already traumatized enough by your behavior. I understand why you thought the way you did, but I knew I couldn't have explained any of this back in Yellowknife, not with Martha and Arnold wanting to take custody of the boys so bad." She really didn't think the brothers would care that the boys were upset about all this. To them, the brothers thought they were taking care of an injustice.

One of the bears suddenly ran forward and Edward reacted just as quickly, firing a shot in the snow right in front of him. The bear veered off. The other bears were waiting, but they could see Edward was an excellent shot and could have taken out the bear easily, if he'd wanted to.

Gary joined them on the porch, wielding the other rifle. She was certain Edward wanted her inside with the boys, but she stood her ground, showing solidarity with the men. This was as much her fight as Edward's. She was just grateful Gary was helping them out too and that she hadn't been bluffing. Though she had been about the third rifle.

Maybe this wouldn't end in bloodshed. She didn't know what they thought they were going to do about the boys. Or how the men were even going to get a plane back to White Bear.

For the longest time, they just sat there, stubborn as usual, not liking the way things were going for them. Then she turned and headed into the cabin, wanting to be with her boys to offer them comfort while the bears made up their minds. The boys were scared, and she reassured them that everything was alright for the moment.

It seemed like forever that Edward and Gary were standing

on the porch. She watched the bears through the window. The sat phone rang, and she hurried to get it. "Callahan's brothers are here. We have a standoff. Edward had to fire a round at one of them when he charged us. I told them the boys are Edward's, Craig."

"We're landing in a few minutes. Andy is with me and well-armed."

Relieved, she let out her breath. "I'm so glad." She knew he couldn't arrest them, to go to trial and maybe earn a jail sentence for some time, not when they were bear shifters. Then they heard the seaplane coming in for a landing.

The bears all looked in that direction. She suspected then, they'd been waiting to see if she'd been bluffing about the seaplane carrying men coming to aid them.

"My cousins," Edward said. "One is a trooper, Andrew MacMathan. You met him already. I'm sure we can arrange for transportation for you to return to White Bear, get your vehicles, and head back to the Northwestern Territories."

The bears exchanged looks.

She hoped they would agree to it and leave without getting into a fight, but they must have left their clothes behind at Simon's cabin.

Another seaplane landed after that and Edward said, "Sounds like your ride home. Or to your vehicles in White Bear, at least. We don't want to have any more issues with you. If you ask Arnold and Martha about the boys' heritage, maybe they'll tell you the truth that they knew about it all along. I understand how you want to protect your own kin, but the boys are not part of your sleuth. And I understand how they feel about losing their son, and then realize that they have none of his offspring either to call their own. But that's the truth of the matter."

Robyn was glad Edward was so calm in a crisis.

Richard, the bear who seemed to be leading the pack, and

who had made the motion to attack them, inclined his head, acknowledging he would go along with their plan.

She didn't feel the bears had much of a choice at this point. Maybe they realized that their parents hadn't been perfectly honest with them. She suspected this wasn't the first time they'd lied about something to get their way either.

Callahan's brothers could have been taking the boys away from their true mother, father, and all the rest of Edward's family who were real blood relations.

It appeared the brothers decided to stay here and get a lift home. If they ran back the way they had come, they could get their clothes, but they would be stuck there, unless they could get someone else to fly them out. Maybe the pilot would fly them back to Simon's cabin and let them dress there.

Craig and Andy headed toward them, rifles in hand. Two more men followed them, the pilot of the second seaplane and another man, both armed with rifles, one carrying a backpack.

"Looks like you're flying these guys out," Edward said.

"Back to White Bear?" the other pilot asked.

"Yes, and then they're leaving for the Northwestern Territories," Edward said.

"Okay," Andy said. "One man at a time goes into the house, shifts, changes, gets manacled, and waits for the next man to do the same. We were already at Simon's place," he explained to Edward and Robyn, "and found their clothes, so we grabbed them before we headed out."

Good. Then they wouldn't need to take them back to Simon's house first.

The bear in charge headed for the house, Gary and Edward going in first to protect Robyn and the boys. She took the boys into a bedroom and shut the door. She didn't want one of the bears to attack them, if they were just pretending to go along with the plan.

9

———

Once Richard was dressed, Edward used wrist ties on him and made him sit on the couch. Then the next brother was ushered in. He shifted and dressed, and then was manacled.

Edward was glad Robyn had taken the boys into one of the rooms to keep them away from these men. He knew it had to have been terrifying for them, running for their lives from the sleuth three times already.

"We need the DNA analysis that proves the boys are yours," Richard said, stony-faced.

"We'll send you a copy of that and of the boys' birth certificates," Edward said.

After all four men were ready to be transported back to White Bear, Andy folded his arms across his chest, his expression stern. "Alright. Here's the deal. You leave, and if you come back, you'll be civil, or we'll deal with you in the way our kind sees fit. The kids aren't part of your sleuth. They're members of ours. And they won't be returning to your territory."

"Uncle Arnold and Aunt Martha have been raising the boys.

They should have some right to visitation," Richard said, but he'd lost his growl, more like he was hopeful they could get some concessions, if his parents still wanted some time with the boys.

Robyn came out of the bedroom and closed the door. "No. They wanted to take the boys away from me for good when they knew damn well they weren't Callahan's sons. And they haven't been 'raising' the boys. They've babysat them a few times is all. I'm sure you know how controlling they are."

The brothers glanced at each other, the telling expression saying they knew just what they were like, in charge and everything had to go their way, or else.

"If what you say is true, then you won't hear from us again," Richard said.

Edward sure hoped that this was the end of it. "You have my word you'll get the paperwork. I would prefer to send it to you, rather than to give it to them. We want to make sure that the information is disseminated to the rest of your sleuth."

"That's the way I want it done."

"Okay, then let's go," Andy said. "You can ride with me in the second seaplane."

Andy led the brothers out of the house, and they loaded up in the plane, the other man with them helping to watch over the brothers. He and the pilot were wolf shifters.

Craig said, "That went better than I expected."

"That's the same thought I had," Edward said.

"I'll take you to Simon's cabin and you can gather up all your belongings there. We'll have some men follow the brothers out of our territory to ensure they're headed home," Craig said.

Since the boys didn't have any shoes that would fit them, Edward grabbed up Bryan and carried him to the seaplane, while Craig carried Garrett out. Once they were airborne, the boys were having a ball pointing to the landscape below, the pristine snow, the choppy water, puffins diving, sea otters hugging each other, and even a couple of polar bears roaming across the snow, who looked up, stood, and waved at the plane. "Those are a couple of ours," Edward said. "Susan and Molly Winterberry. They just moved into the area, but they would recognize Craig's seaplane."

Edward had met them, just like his cousins and brother had, but like usual, he'd been so hung up on Robyn, no one else could hold a candle to her.

"Did the brothers ever have much to do with the boys?" Edward asked Robyn. It didn't appear the brothers cared about not seeing the boys further and if they'd been active in their lives, he would have expected them to say they wanted to see them anyway. It seemed as though the only reason they had made the effort to come after them was that they believed their parents had been wronged.

"No," Garrett said for his mother.

"Uh-uh," Bryan said.

"Truthfully? I think they were jealous of the attention their parents showed the boys. According to Callahan, their parents had been too busy to pay a lot of attention to their sons while they were growing up. So I think their sons were miffed," Robyn said. "Even so, sleuth ties are strong and I'm sure they didn't want me to get away with taking the boys from there where they couldn't easily see them."

"If the only ones who wanted to see the boys were Callahan's parents, it probably won't be as big of an issue." Though Edward did think of the presents they might have gotten the boys. Still, it didn't matter. Not when they had planned to take the boys away from Robyn for no good reason.

They flew to the area where Simon's cabin was located, and

Craig and Edward carried the boys to the cabin so they could put on their own clothes. While everyone was dressing themselves, Craig began hauling their groceries out to the plane.

Edward grabbed his bags and the clothes everyone had borrowed and the sheets off the bed so he could wash them and return them to the snow leopard brothers, stuffing them in a trash sack. Then he carried them out to the plane. Robyn finished packing her bag and the kids packed their own, then Craig and Edward returned for the bags.

The boys ran outside to the seaplane while Robyn hurried after them.

"You know," Craig said to Edward, following behind Robyn, "you and your brother are causing Mom and Dad to push my brothers and me to find mates. Here both of you already have kids even."

Edward smiled. "You'll find the right women one of these days. You're so busy flying that you don't take the time to look for the right girl. Ben's too busy matchmaking to work on his own match, and Andy is too busy trying to uphold the law."

"Not to mention finding a smart, beautiful bear who adores me can be an issue," Craig said.

Robyn climbed into the seaplane. "It'll happen when you're least expecting it."

At least that's what happened to Edward and his brother. Edward called his aunt on the sat phone to let her know they were on their way home, and he was glad that it truly was Robyn and the boys' home now too.

WHEN CRAIG and his passengers finally arrived back in White Bear, Rob came by with another of their tour vans and picked them up.

"Tamara is so glad you can use her wedding dress," Rob said, smiling at Robyn.

"Is she sure?"

"Yeah. I just sent a picture of it to Edward. We didn't have your email address."

Edward forwarded the picture to Robyn's phone, and she opened up the file to see the wedding gown. "Oh, wow, it's beautiful." She was so thrilled, even though at first, she was a little apprehensive. She would look like a fairytale princess for sure. "I would like to pay her for borrowing it."

"Don't think of it. She's so excited to have a new friend, that she was thrilled to do it."

"Thank you." Robyn brushed away tears.

Her sons looked at her, thinking she was upset about something. She smiled at them, to let them know she was fine.

"We scrounged up tuxes for the boys too. The tuxes the boys wore to Alicia and my wedding are too small for them now, so the wolves gifted them to the boys."

She couldn't believe the generosity of the local shifter community. "I just can't tell you how much all of this means to me."

"Everyone knows your circumstances and they're eager to help out. Once you and my brother found each other, we all knew that this was meant to be."

And here her family had been so awful about Edward and her being together. Edward had been so badly wounded after fighting with her brother and killing him, she knew then she would have to leave. Edward would never have provoked her brother, not when he wanted to marry her and make a lasting peace with her family. But her family would have wanted revenge. Edward could have easily covered up her brother's death and pretended his disappearance hadn't had anything to do with him. But he'd been honest about the whole situation.

"If it's alright with you, the rest of the guys are wearing black tuxedos, since we already have them," Rob said, breaking into her thoughts.

"That sounds wonderful to me. Can Alicia be my matron of honor and Tamara be my bridesmaid?" Robyn asked.

"They will be delighted. We're having a rehearsal dinner tonight and our aunt and uncle are hosting it at their tavern. Then tomorrow is the wedding. But we're formally marrying you off, paperwork-wise, when we get to the house, to ensure that Callahan's family realize you're not returning to the Northwest Territories. Uncle Ned is doing the honors. And then tomorrow afternoon, we'll have the formal ceremony with all the family and friends."

"Who will be there tonight at the house?" she asked.

"Uncle Ned, Aunt Genevieve, Alicia, me, and the babies. If we're lucky, the babies will be asleep during all the activities. Ben, Craig, and Andy are running the tavern while we're doing this. Then we'll head over to the tavern to the banquet room for the rehearsal dinner. We've reserved White Bear Hall for the wedding and reception and several people are setting up decorations for it tonight."

Robyn couldn't believe after she had left Edward like she did, that his family and their friends would rally together to marry them off, despite all the baggage she now carried with her.

"After the dinner tonight, we're going to move all your things from storage that we had unloaded from your truck so Joe could begin to work on your vehicle," Rob said.

"Oh, thanks so much," Robyn said. "We'll have to make room for all the stuff."

"Easily," Edward said. "When Rob moved out, he took all his belongings and half of the kitchen supplies, so we'll be good. And all the closets in the spare bedrooms are empty."

She was glad for that.

When Rob dropped them off at Edward's home, it was a whirlwind of activities. He helped carry the boys' bags into the house, and then said, "We'll see you in a little bit." Rob gave Robyn a big hug first before he left. "Welcome to the family." And then he hugged the boys too. "I'm your Uncle Rob," he said, smiling, then he left.

"Are you okay with all this?" Edward asked Robyn, carrying her bags into his bedroom. "I didn't realize they would pre-plan everything to such an extent and make it such a big affair."

"Oh, this will be the easiest wedding ceremony I've ever gone to." She saw the wedding gown laying on the bed, a princess ball-gown type, off-the-shoulder, tulle-lace long-sleeves, tulle lace covering the bodice, and a chapel train. "Oh, this is even more beautiful than the picture you sent me."

The boys were rolling their bags into their room, and she realized it really *was* her and the boys' home now too.

"You boys can pick a room for each of you," Edward said.

"Yes!" Garrett said and took the room they hadn't used already.

Edward smiled at her and rubbed her back. "You'll be beautiful. You *are* beautiful."

She smiled and hugged him. "I feel this is so right for us. I just wish we didn't have so many issues with the other families still."

"We'll be okay."

She wasn't so sure about that. "So what do we wear tonight?"

"Dress casual."

"I've got a wool skirt I can wear."

"That should work. I'll get changed. I suspect someone is going to take you away from me for the night so we're not together the evening before the wedding. But it will be someone who can protect you. I'll keep the boys here with me."

She smiled. "I think that would be nice for you and the boys to bond."

He laughed. "No wild bachelor party then."

She laughed. "That will be even better."

They had barely gotten dressed when Uncle Ned and Aunt Genevieve arrived, followed by Rob and Alicia and the babies.

"Andy called and said the Gardner brothers all drove out of White Bear. We had a number of shifters following them to make sure they were really leaving town," Ned said.

"Good," Robyn said, and Edward agreed.

They did a super quick marriage ceremony at Edward's home to ensure that if anything went wrong and they weren't able to have the fancy wedding tomorrow, they would still be a married couple tonight. Robyn told them she wanted to take the MacMathan name for her own, and the boys would also have the same Celtic name that meant son of the bear. Edward and his family couldn't have been more pleased.

Then Edward and Robyn kissed. Then they kissed and hugged the boys. Kissing and hugs with the rest of the family followed. Afterward, they headed over to the tavern for the groom's dinner. Ned and Genevieve seemed so thrilled to have her and the boys in the family. Robyn only wished her own family hadn't been so awful about everything. Though she could imagine how angry they might still be that her brother had died in a fight with Edward.

Robyn was afraid the boys would be upset with all the goings-on's, but they loved all the attention they were getting. And they were excited about being at the all boys' party tonight. The wedding would be at eleven the next day so that everyone could get some sleep in the morning. Edward's cousins were all going to be at the all-boys' party tonight. She thought that would be a fun way for the boys to get to know their uncles—as that's what all the cousins wanted the boys to call them—a little better too.

AT THE TAVERN, they all headed in to take their seats in the banquet room, many of the patrons congratulating them on the way past their tables. In the room, Edward's cousins gave Robyn and the boys hugs and kisses, welcoming them to the family. Tamara White was there too, and Robyn gave her a hug for loaning her the wedding gown.

Tamara smiled at Robyn. "If nobody's told you the story, I've never worn it."

Robyn's jaw dropped.

"Uh, yeah. It's one of those cases where the bride shows up for the wedding and the groom is a no-show. Best that we ended it before we actually got married."

"Does he live here?" Robyn asked, shocked.

"Lucky for him, no. He was from another sleuth further north and he ran back home with his stubby tail between his legs."

Robyn chuckled. "Well, he didn't deserve you. And thanks again." Robyn was delighted to have another friend among the bears.

"Seventy-five of our friends said they were coming to the wedding." Aunt Genevieve sounded delighted that so many had responded to the impromptu invitation and wanted to attend the ceremony to celebrate. "It's truly the miracle of having text and emails, or we would have had to go door-to-door. A lot of our friends are delighted to take part because of how much we've helped others out in a pinch."

"Not to mention the free food," Uncle Ned said.

Aunt Genevieve smiled. "Right, but they are also helping to

decorate for the wedding. It's just a fun opportunity for everyone who has been friends of ours for all these years."

"No alcohol, right?" Robyn said. "Tonight, at the groom's dinner is fine, but I would rather not have it at the wedding reception because of the kids. I've been to enough of them to see a bunch of drunken bears ruin it for everyone else."

"Uh, yeah, no alcohol," Edward said. "I agree."

"No problem at all," Uncle Ned said. "We put that on the invites because we felt the same way."

"I can't believe you went and got married and I didn't have a chance to match the two of you up in the very beginning even," Ben said.

Edward laughed. "We were already an item before you saw her."

"Yeah, but when I saw she had two sons this time, I knew she was already mated. Shows what I know. Next time, I won't assume," Ben said.

"So now you're going to work on your brothers?" Edward asked.

"I've got to. You and your brother are mated now. Though I'm sure my brothers will be tougher to pin down." Ben ordered a glass of wine. "So what are we going to do for your 'bachelor' party?"

"Movies, appropriate for five-year-old's, ice cream, popcorn, games we can come up with that the boys would enjoy."

Ben smiled. "Man, I never thought you would be having a bachelor party for kids."

Edward laughed. He hadn't either. His aunt and uncle had offered to watch them tonight, but he was glad to have some quality time with his sons. "It'll be a fun way for them to get to know all of you too."

"True. Except for helping out some with your brother's little ones, and they're so little that has meant changing diapers or rocking them to sleep, I haven't had much experience with kids."

"Garrett and Bryan are easier to take care of," Edward said. "At least they can tell you want they want or don't want."

"But they get into more trouble too."

"Uh, yeah. The ice-floe incident was a real reminder of what little boys could get into."

"Like us." Ben smiled. "Sounds like something we could have pulled when we were that age."

"My thoughts exactly."

"I don't envy you. Yet, I kind of do."

Robyn smiled at Ben. "Someday, you'll be just as happy as we are."

"Oh, I'm sure of it. I'm really glad for the four of you. We've all had to do some last-minute Christmas shopping too. We always just share lists, so if there's something you would like, just let us know, Robyn."

"Thank you. I need to get lists from all of you too," Robyn said.

Edward hadn't even thought of Christmas because every-thing else had been so up in the air. He knew she was strapped for money, and he didn't want her to feel she had to go out and buy a bunch of gifts for the family. Though, if she felt the need, his money was hers too.

"It's covered. Everything is from the two of us," Edward said.

Robyn squeezed his hand, but he wasn't sure what she was thinking. He suspected she wanted to do something for the rest of the family to show how much she appreciated everyone. "I want to get my marketing business up and running here." She smiled. "Everything else has been a higher priority, but now that we're settling down here, I want to get my business going."

He suspected it wasn't just that she wanted to work, but that she felt the need to help add to the family income, though she didn't have to.

"Rob, Casey, and I will be your first customers. We could use a great video showing the fun we have on our tours. If you help us with setting up a better website and anything else you can think of to help showcase our business, we would be grateful. Which means you and the boys will have to come with us on some of the tours to take the videos and pictures and show how much fun the trips can be with kids."

She smiled so brightly, he knew he'd made her whole day. It would be fun for the kids, not having to stay at home with someone, but to see what their father and their mother did. And even their Uncle Rob and their friend did for a living. "Alright. And I can do that for free to use it to showcase the kind of product and services marketing I can provide for businesses."

"Our business," Edward said, because she and Alicia were every bit as much important in their business as the guys were.

Rob shook his head. "We'll pitch in money to help pay for the marketing."

"No way am I going to charge your company when I'm mated to Edward now."

Alicia shook her head at her. "It's only right. The guys would have to pay someone else to do their marketing otherwise. If they can pay you, it still stays in your family's finances, so it's a win-win for all of us."

"Oh, and we want you to do a marketing campaign for our tavern. Believe me, with all the special holidays and different kinds of festivities we have here throughout the year, we could really use the help to spread the word. We'll need so many marketing videos, we'll keep you well-paid. You'll have examples of your marketing talent that you can showcase to encourage new business," Uncle Ned said.

Edward thought Robyn didn't want to charge her own

family, but he knew they wouldn't have her do all that work for nothing. And they were eager to help her become profitable on her own. He wanted that for her too, if that was something that she felt she really needed to do.

"Okay, thanks," she said.

"You can do promo for my seaplane excursions. I take people on sightseeing trips and deliver people and supplies to different locations across the state. I do a lot of rescues too, and you could do a feature on that," Craig said.

"I'm a video photographer also," Alicia said. "Though I usually do pieces for magazines and the like. But if you can use some of the pictures or videos that I've taken to help you get started on some of these projects, you're welcome to them."

"Thanks so much, Alicia. And thanks to Tamara for loaning me her beautiful gown."

"You're so welcome. I'm so glad you could use it," Tamara said.

"It's just beautiful. I never had a real wedding, so I'm looking forward to it."

"As far as your marketing business goes, it looks like you've got your work cut out for you," Edward said. "And you don't ever have to worry about the boys. They'll be well-taken care of."

She looked thrilled with the prospect. He was glad for it. Then he wondered if she'd ever had a chance to finish her marketing degree after she'd left White Bear so suddenly.

"We've converted a back room for our grandkids as they get older," Uncle Ned said. "It has a kid-sized house, table, and chairs, puzzles, building blocks, stuffed animals, cars and trucks, a TV, Play Station, you name it. We set it up for Rob's kids for when their babies are older and for when our sons have kids of their own. But your sons are the perfect age for it now. So anytime you need a break, they can be in there and Ben and

Genevieve and I will check on them periodically," Uncle Ned said.

"Oh, how wonderful," Robyn said.

"Yeah," Ben said. "We keep asking why Mom and Dad didn't set up something like that for us when we were that little."

Everyone laughed.

"Can we see it?" Garrett asked all ears.

"After dinner." Robyn pointed to their chicken and broccoli and french fries.

They began eating their meal faster.

"What about a honeymoon?" Genevieve asked. "We'll take care of the kids while you take a trip somewhere. You really need to have the time alone, just like before."

"We haven't even discussed it. I hate burdening anyone with the boys this soon after we just arrived," Robyn said, "or making them anxious about me leaving them."

Edward assumed she was worried about the boys staying with other families this early in their marriage.

"The boys will have a ball. Between their uncles and us and if you would like, we would love for them to think of us as their grandparents, we'll keep them busy," Genevieve said. Even so, she glanced at the boys to see what they thought about it.

Garrett had finished his meal. "It's okay with me, Mom."

Bryan finished his meal too. "Me too. Can we see the playroom?"

Robyn laughed.

"I'll take them," Ben said, and he and the boys left the banquet room to go to another room.

"We have video cameras in there," Uncle Ned said. "I'll send you the app. You can check on your sons at any time."

Robyn uploaded the app and saw Ben turning on the Play-Station for the boys. That was it. They took seats on beanbag chairs and began playing a game.

"Wow, that's fantastic. They could play that way for hours," she said.

"What do you think, Robyn? Do you want to get away for a little bit?" Edward asked.

"Yeah. Just for three or four days maybe. Somewhere not too far away in case the boys get homesick."

"We can do that." Edward was eager to have a real honeymoon.

R obyn was thrilled that Edward was really eager to have a honeymoon alone with her. She didn't blame him. She wanted one too. It would be the perfect way to get to know him again like she knew him before. She really wanted to be with him tonight, but she knew that they needed to do the traditional thing and be apart the night before the wedding because of the boys.

"We have a school for shifters here," Genevieve said. "I didn't know if you homeschooled or not. This is a special, private school for all ages and your sons can attend it, if you would like for them to. It's a mix of shifters and no child is allowed to shift at school. If a child does, he is sent home. Since we have Arctic foxes, polar bears, snow leopards, grizzly bears, Arctic wolves, and gray wolves, we have to have strict rules about it."

"Oh, that sounds wonderful. We can certainly try it out." Robyn thought it could be a great experience for the boys to learn how to get along with other shifters and to make friends with them too. She never thought she would become friends with a grizzly shifter herself even. Not that she was averse to it, she'd just never met a grizzly that was a shifter.

The dinner ended and they went to the hall where they would practice the wedding ceremony. The boys wanted to stay at the restaurant playroom. Robyn could see it was the perfect place for them when they had to stay with their new grandparents. They might even want to go there when she didn't need them to. As long as they weren't underfoot, she could agree to it.

"Where did you want to go for our honeymoon?" Edward asked Robyn, after they had practiced the ceremony.

She was searching her phone for a location. "McKinley's Riverside Chalet Resort? It's only two miles from the entrance to Denali National Park. It's not rugged, which would be fine with me either way. I'm good with not having to shift as polar bears. But they have two restaurants, an espresso bar, fire pits, live entertainment at a saloon, hot tubs, and a view of the mountains. The park has six million acres with only one road in. Bears, moose, wolves, Dall sheep, and caribou live there. We might even be able to move well off the road as polar bears, but we don't have to. Or we could even just stay home, if your parents or cousins take care of the boys."

"Denali it is. Sounds like a good plan."

"Or we could take a drive where you go on your tours. I could start working on the marketing video."

Edward smiled and pulled her into his arms. "No work. All play."

She wrapped her arms around him. "Good answer."

THAT NIGHT ROBYN stayed with Alicia and the babies. It might have seemed unfair that she was staying the night with a nursing mother while the guys had more fun things planned, but Robyn didn't mind. Her boys hadn't been this little in a long time and she loved cuddling the babies. And she was their aunt now.

The grizzly bear, Gary, was there to provide them security for the night, just in case they needed it, but he stayed in the living room, while Alicia and Robyn and the babies were in the den. "From everything Edward's already told me about you, I feel like I already know you," Alicia said.

"I was really surprised to hear Rob had mated. He and his cousins had always been confirmed bachelors."

"I agree. We really connected because of our psychic abilities. If Edward didn't tell you about it, Rob can see glimpses of the future, and I can see glimpses of the past. It's something we haven't shared with everyone, though I've done some police work with my gift."

"Oh, that's great. And it's amazing." The baby Robyn was rocking was sound asleep in her arms and she wondered if the babies would have one of their parents' abilities.

"We don't see things that are going to affect close family members. Not normally. Or else I'm sure Rob would have seen you return to White Bear."

"Right. Because of all the danger I brought here."

"We see other things. Not just about danger or disasters."

"That's good. I can imagine how distressing that could be otherwise."

Alicia put the babies in their crib. "True. I don't know if anyone has told you yet, but I was bitten and turned. Edward might have told you. I would have either frozen to death as a human or Rob had to turn me, and I would become a polar bear so that the fur would quickly warm me, and because of your advanced healing abilities. So he turned me, and though it has been an adjustment, it has been incredibly wonderful too. I haven't shifted since the babies were born yet, waiting for the babies to get a little bigger. Everyone keeps telling me I need to.

That it's the most natural thing in the world, but I'm afraid to hurt them. And I finally have gotten the shifting under control, for which I'm grateful."

"I've been in your shoes as far as shifting with the babies, but it was easy. If you would like, when the babies wake, we can shift and you can see just how easy it is."

"Ohmigod, you wouldn't mind?"

"Not at all." Robyn was glad she could do something for Alicia after she had welcomed her like she was already family. Robyn hadn't realized how much she'd missed that once her family had disowned her.

AN HOUR LATER, the babies woke in their crib, and Robyn began to strip. "You can do this. Take off your clothes and I'll put the babies on the mat there. I'll remove their clothes and diapers, and you shift. We can take them out in the snow for a couple of minutes, teach them to relieve themselves and they can come back inside with us."

Robyn was already undressing one baby and Alicia had removed her own clothes and began to take off the other baby's clothes and diaper.

Then Alicia shifted and the babies turned into small bear cubs. Instead of taking them outside first, she let them find their way to her teats and fed them.

Robyn smiled to see the special bonding that Alicia had with her cubs in their bear form, recalling how it had been for her when she finally chanced doing it. She had already shifted and when the cubs were finished eating, she and Alicia each carried one cub outside. Alicia might be fairly newly turned, but she was a natural at this, the maternal instinct for caring for her cubs coming to the forefront.

Gary soon joined them to watch out for them. Robyn really didn't believe anyone would try to cause problems for her right now. But she was glad Gary was willing to help out, just in case.

The cubs were so small, they stayed with their mom, while Robyn watched for any sign of danger. And then Alicia finally took them inside. Gary returned to the living room. Robyn and she shifted in the house, and the babies shifted. They both dressed, and then put on new diapers for the babies and clothed them.

After that, they cuddled them.

Alicia was all smiles. "Rob will be so thrilled I did it. I didn't want to do it with him for the first time. He doesn't know any more than I do about raising infant bear cubs."

"You are a natural, Alicia. You and the babies did great."

"I know you'll be off on your honeymoon after the wedding, but when you return, can we do it again?"

"Tonight even. And yes. Anytime you would like."

"That's great. I get strong urges to shift still, and I fight it because I wanted to wait. I think everyone worried the babies might not learn what they need to as cubs if I didn't shift right away."

"Well, you've done it. And if you need proof, I can videotape it the next time."

"I'm so glad you and Edward are together again. I'm thrilled to have a sister-in-law that I can call a sister."

"After having so many brothers, I feel the same way about you. And I adore your little ones." Robyn got a call from Edward, and she worried there was some problem with the boys.

"Hey, just checking in on you. How is everything going?"

"Alicia and I took the babies outside as cubs."

"You're kidding. That's great. I'll let Rob know. He'll be thrilled."

"How are the boys doing?"

"They're having a blast. We're watching *A Christmas Story* and both of the boys want bb guns."

"No way."

"I told them they get to learn how to fish with their bear teeth. They said you never did that with them and neither did Callahan."

"That sounds like a great job for papa bear."

"All the guys want to get involved in it. Including Ned. They were eager to do so with Rob's kids when they get older, but they'll have had all the practice with ours."

She smiled. "That sounds good. What do you think of sending the boys to the special shifter school?"

"That works for me. I think the kids will love it."

"Okay. At the end of summer, they can go to school. And I can work on marketing promotions while they're in school. They didn't have a special school like that in Yellowknife. I had to homeschool them."

"Well, now we have a choice. Garrett wants to talk to you."

"Momma?" Garrett said.

She was afraid he was going to tell her he wanted to leave. "Yeah, Garrett?"

"Daddy said he and our uncles and Grandad would take us fishing as bears, but he said you had to say okay. Can you say okay?"

She smiled. Her boys were going to grow up too fast, but she could see how the other males could be a good influence on them. "Absolutely."

"Will you come too?"

She knew they would want her to. "Sometimes. Sure. Sometimes I think you guys all need to do fun things together. At the end of summer break, I'm going to put you and Bryan in a special shifter school. There's no shifting allowed though."

"Are there other polar bears in kindergarten?"

"I don't know. We'll see when we enroll you."

"Okay."

She had been afraid that Garrett and his brother would fuss about going to a regular school. Hopefully, it would all work out.

"I'm going back to playing with everyone," Garrett said.

She was glad they were having so much fun. "Okay." Coming here and joining Edward's family had been the right move to make, all away around. She couldn't wait to get started on her marketing either. She loved doing it. She talked to Bryan too and he was so excited about being there.

They finally ended the call so he could get back to the fun, and she walked one of the babies when Alicia got a call. Alicia smiled. "Yes. Robyn was really sweet to help me out with the babies." She chuckled. "I know you offered a million times but it's different with Robyn. She has been a new mother too and it hasn't been all that long ago. We're doing great and having fun. You want to go fishing with the boys? Sure. Sounds great. You'll be all set when ours are that age. Love you, hon. Talk later."

When she got off the phone, Alicia said, "Probably nobody's mentioned it with everything else that's going on, but we're having Christmas dinner at Uncle Ned and Aunt Genevieve's place. We open presents at our own homes in the morning. But when my kids are older, we'll probably open some of the kids presents at their home, so the 'grandparents' can enjoy it too."

"So we'll probably need to do that," Robyn said, thinking how much Callahan's parents would be furious over all of this.

"If it's something you want to do. I think they would be thrilled, and I'm sure the boys will love having two Christmases too."

"What about Christmas Eve dinner?"

"We've been reciprocating. Last Christmas, prior to having babies, Rob and Edward hosted it, and this year, Ben and Craig are."

"Okay, sounds good. We'll be home in time for it."

"You'll have fun at the resort. Rob and I stayed there before the kids came, our last hoorah." Alicia laughed.

THE NEXT MORNING, the wedding was a grand affair, and everyone who had come was dressed up for the ceremony. Even Edward's black eye had faded so it was imperceptible for pictures, thankfully. And he was glad their tour-guide partner, Casey, had made it back from Fairbanks where he'd been visiting other relatives for the holidays. He was glad for Edward and Robyn and gave him all kinds of grief too about getting the girl.

Edward thought Robyn truly looked like a fairy princess, and the boys were dashing in their tuxes, though Bryan kept pulling at his bowtie and making it askew. No objections were made during the ceremony, though he kept thinking of Robyn's family. If they only knew what was going on, he was sure *they* would violently object.

But everything went smoothly and when the wedding was over, they all feasted and danced.

"Are you sure you boys will be okay with your grandparents and your uncles?" Robyn asked her son Garrett as she danced with him. Bryan always went along with whatever Garrett wanted to do.

"*These* grandparents and uncles? Yeah! We're going to have lots of fun. But you'll be home for Christmas, won't you?" Garrett asked.

"Absolutely."

"Okay."

Robyn smiled, then danced with Bryan. She asked the same question of him.

"What did Garrett say?" Bryan asked.

"He said you would have lots of fun." Robyn was glad that her sons were okay with them leaving for a while.

The song ended and she released Bryan. "Go, have something to eat with your brother." And then Edward pulled her into his arms for another dance, keeping her close while Bryan hurried to join Garrett. "You look just like a princess."

"I feel like one. This has been wonderful. The turnout was great. I wasn't sure everyone would show up, but it looks like everyone has, number-wise. I guess the free food drew them here."

"And to show loyalty to us and our family. Especially when they learned what was going on with you and the boys. Besides, any chance at having some fun is a real draw. The boys said they understand we're leaving after this so we can reach the resort to check in on time."

They ended their final dance, and everyone cheered them. It was time to leave, and Robyn and Edward hugged the kids, but the boys were excited to go with their uncles to play more games and Robyn was so thrilled they were fine.

"Looks like the boys are going to be just great with the family all loving on them," Edward said as he quickly got the Jeep door for her.

"I agree. I'm so glad too." Robyn got into the Jeep, and he climbed into the driver's seat and drove them back to their house.

Their bags were already packed in the Jeep, but they needed to change clothes for the trip.

"Alicia said your shoe size is the same as hers. She loaned you her skis and boots and snowshoes."

"Good. I left mine at home, not wanting it to look like we were moving out and they weren't essentials I needed to take."

"If there's anything you need replacing, I'll get it for you and the boys."

She sighed. "I wish we'd been together all along."

"We will be, here on out."

She was so glad for that. She'd only hoped everything would work out between them, but she'd worried he had a mate already! Or a girlfriend. How would that have been if the bear had lived here, and Robyn had stolen him away? All kinds of new trouble for all of them. Though, she could have said she had him first, leaving out the part about abandoning him.

When they got home, Edward helped her out of the wedding gown in the bedroom, so she could put on warm clothes for the trip, and he could remove his tux and do the same thing. But once he carefully helped her out of the borrowed gown and set it aside on a chair, she had other notions in mind. Even though she'd needed help with the gown, he didn't need help with his clothes, yet, she removed his bowtie, then his tux. It didn't take her long to remove his cufflinks and then start to work on his shirt. He was kissing her neck, running his hands over her shoulders, his heartbeat ramping up.

So was hers.

She knew very well where this was headed. Dressing warmly wasn't the next step. "We probably should get on the road and do this once we're at the chalet," she said, her voice breathy, thinking that they could drive to the chalet and then make love as a brand-new married couple in their hotel room.

He smiled down at her as if he was checking to see if she was serious, his hands caressing her bare shoulders.

"Or not." She hadn't envisioned being married to Edward so soon and making love to him at his place, and no kids here either so they could be as wildly passionate as they wanted to be.

He leaned down and kissed the swell of her breasts with his

warm mouth, and she knew then he really didn't want to drive to the resort before they made love. She didn't either. Not really.

He removed his shoes and socks, but before he could take off her heels, she pulled his shirt off the rest of the way and pressed kisses against his neck and throat. He began to unfasten her strapless bra. And then he tossed her bra aside, exposing her. She felt deliciously sexy in her white stockings, garters, high heels, panties and nothing else. He molded his hands to her breasts, then began kissing her mouth again. He started massaging her breasts, and then his thumbs brushed over her nipples, and they tingled with his touch.

Their hearts were thumping with need, and she could already feel his cock swelling in his pants as he pressed his body against hers. Which meant they needed to remove more clothes!

She slid her hand over his cock, and it moved beneath his tuxedo pants. "Your pants have to go," she whispered against his mouth, licked it, and kissed him again.

He smiled against her mouth. "Easily remedied," he said huskily. And then he moved his hands from her breasts and began to unfasten his pants, but she pulled his trousers down, kissing his hard abs on the way.

He groaned, stepped out of his pants, and ran his hands over her upswept hair. When she stood, he pulled the pins from her hair, letting the strands fall to her shoulders. Then he was combing through them. "Soft, silky, beautiful."

She licked and kissed his nipple. "Hard, mine, exquisite."

He smiled and lifted her onto the bed and pulled off her heels. He kissed her mouth, his hands working on her breasts again. Wanting his cock thrusting inside her now, she reached down to remove her garters, but he quickly shifted his attention to them. He clearly wanted to undress her all the way and she loved how he kissed each leg, his breath warm and whisper-soft against her flesh as he removed her stockings. Wet with need, she was past ready to remove her panties.

He slipped his hand beneath her panties and cupped her ass.

She reciprocated, sliding her hands beneath the waistband of his boxer briefs. "Hmm, I love your firm butt. I wish mine was that hard."

He chuckled and squeezed her buttocks with appreciation. "Nice and soft and feminine." Then he pulled off her panties and she slipped off his boxer briefs.

She climbed into bed, and he joined her. She couldn't help regretting that it had taken them this long to get back together, but she was just thankful they were and that they'd finally tied the knot like they had originally planned so long ago.

He spread her legs and kissed her belly, then started to minister to her needs first. But just kissing her and removing her clothes and his, had already made her eager and desperate for climax. He sweetly tortured her feminine nub, making her arch for more of his strokes. When he pushed his finger into her as deep as he could go, she hadn't thought she would be ready. But the intimate contact made her blood surge, and her body caught the peak of the wave, the high before she plummeted.

"I love you," she breathed out as the arousal swamped her body.

"I love you too with all my heart, honey." And then Edward pressed his rigid cock between her thighs and began to thrust, holding himself still, afraid he would come too quickly. He thrust again when he felt he was in control.

Sliding into her wet heat, deeper, pushing for the top, he felt her hands caressing his skin in a loving way. Her foot was rubbing the back of his leg in a sexy caress. He slid his arms around her legs and wrapped them around him so he could penetrate her deeper. Kisses were exchanged, tongues danced, and he felt the climax coming no matter how hard he fought finishing too quickly. He had no control when it came to being with her.

He stopped thrusting and kissed her mouth again, and then he drove in until the end and released a long, low, satisfied groan. He wanted to just stay like this the rest of the day and night, sharing the space as one, but they needed to hit the road and they could continue this for a few days before they had to return home. Yet even so, he couldn't make himself leave her and the bed for several more minutes. They just snuggled together on the mattress.

"If we stay here too long, we're going to fall asleep. And then we're going to wake and want to do this all over again," she said, very seriously.

He smiled at her. Hell yeah. "And miss our reservation." He sighed and got out of the bed and began to dress, smiling at how beautiful she was, lying naked on the bed, her nipples dusky rose and taut, her skin creamy, her silky hair splayed across the pillow.

She frowned and got out of bed. "When we get there, I want a repeat of this, only afterwards, we're not going anywhere."

He chuckled. "My thoughts exactly."

AFTER THEY DRESSED in warm clothes, they climbed into the Jeep and headed out to the resort. It would take them four hours to get there, and they talked about all that had happened in the last six years on the drive in the dark, snow covering the ground on the side of the roads, but the pavement was clear. The full moon was out, shining on the snow, stars twinkling across the night sky.

Once they arrived at the resort, Edward parked in the lot,

then they grabbed their bags and headed inside the chalet. Now this was nice. In the lobby, chandeliers were sparkling overhead with brilliant white lights. A Christmas tree was decorated in multi-colored lights, red and green balls, and gold bows, wreaths hanging on walls, and red bows and garlands and poinsettias also decorating banisters and counters. Water from a fountain poured from a fish's mouth and the fish's tail sported a red bow. It was perfectly festive for a quick honeymoon getaway right before Christmas. After such a mess with her former in-laws, she couldn't believe that things were working out so nicely with Edward and his family and the boys were happy with their new circumstances. She just hoped Edward and she didn't have any new troubles follow them there.

———————

Once Edward had the keys to their room, he and Robyn headed upstairs. "Dinner in the room?" Edward asked, opening the door and they stepped inside, and shut the door, then set their skis, boots, and bags out of the way.

"I thought you would never ask."

He pulled her into his arms and kissed her and she kissed him back, but before they got too amorous, he needed to tell her the schedule he'd worked out. "I thought we would have dinner, then go down to soak in the hot tub before it's closed." He was still holding her in his arms, loving that she had returned to him, and she was truly his mate now.

He had even more of a reason for going down to the hot tub to share some intimacy at that time though. They couldn't make love in the hot tub because it was exposed to the view of the chalet, but he'd arranged for a honeymoon hot tub extravaganza as soon as he'd made reservations for the room. He wanted it to be a surprise, and he hoped his mention of the hot tub closing at a certain time would convince her that was the only reason he wanted to take her down there after dinner, instead of making love to her right away.

That was until she began pulling off his sweater and unfastening his trousers, wanting to take this in a different direction. So much for schedules when his mate wanted to play.

He smiled down at her and quickly removed her clothes and the rest of his. There was nothing in the book on the art of seduction that said they couldn't have a quickie before dinner, then a longer lovefest after the hot tub romance, which he *had* planned for.

He jerked the covers aside and she tackled him to the bed. He hadn't quite expected her move, but he was game. She straddled him, leaning down, pressing her body against his to kiss him. He smiled and speared his fingers through her hair, their mouths fused together in a melding of heat and skin and need. Now that they didn't have to worry about the kids being about, it was as though they'd transported to the time six years ago when they were carefree and could make love at a moment's notice as soon as she'd finished with classes, and he was home from managing a group tour and taking a breather.

He even stopped thinking about their schedule for now and concentrated on the way her body slid against his, making the fire burning in his veins grow even hotter. Their hearts were pounding hard as he rolled her onto her back and began to kiss her again, but this time he was eager to stroke her and kiss her beautiful breasts. And so he did, circling his finger around the feminine nub between her thighs as she moved them farther apart for him. Then he began sweeping his tongue over her nipples, loving how they responded to his warm, wet touch. He sped up his strokes, slowed them down, watched the way she was arching under his ministrations.

"Hurry, oh, yeah, ohmigod, yes!"

He smiled as her belly tightened, and then he eased into her and began to thrust. If anyone had told him he would be making love to Robyn on their honeymoon right before Christmas, he would have thought they were crazy. He couldn't even believe himself that he was making love to the only woman he'd ever truly loved. Placing his hands on her hips, he maneuvered to his back so she would be on top and then she rode him, her hands stroking his chest. She was arching back, and he was stroking her thighs. She was beautiful, her breasts full and bouncing, her eyes wide open, her lips parted, her hair hanging over her shoulders, caressing her soft, creamy skin. He moved his hands from her thighs to her hips and set the pace. He could feel the end coming, everything about her—the delightful smell of her spring-scented soap and jasmine shampoo and her unique bear scent, the smell of her arousal, the feel of her tight around his cock, hot and wet, the sound of her soft sighs and low moans, and the taste of her kisses and taut nipples, and the appearance of her now in rapture—all pushed him to the edge.

He groaned out loud with the orgasm, and she continued to rock him until he was completely spent, and then she settled against him and hugged on him until he remembered to order their dinner so they could head down to the hot tub afterwards before it was too late.

She rolled off him and he pulled the menu off the bedside table. They read it over and decided what they wanted. "Does champagne or wine appeal more?" he asked.

"Champagne would be perfect."

He called room service and ordered alder wood grilled salmon, charred cauliflower, and mashed potatoes for himself and for Robyn, king crab fettuccine, cherry tomatoes, and corn.

Then they got dressed before the food arrived and they returned to bed to snuggle. "I meant to ask you, did you ever finish your marketing degree?"

"No. Between moving back to Anchorage, then leaving there

with Callahan, and then having the babies, there wasn't any time. And besides, I was doing really well with starting up my business and didn't need the degree after that."

"You're sure you don't want to go back to school and finish it?"

"Nah. If I really needed it for work, then sure. But I really don't need it and I would rather spend the time on my business and being with you and the kids."

"Okay, but if you ever change your mind, you can go back to school."

"Thanks, Edward."

"Do you have a house in Yellowknife?" he asked.

"Yeah. I've talked with a realtor already, and she's getting it ready to put on the market."

"Good. What about your furniture?"

"I'm selling it along with the house, or separately. She said she would set up an auction for it and try to get me the best deal for everything. I didn't leave anything behind that I would miss. *You* are what I needed in my life more than anything. The kids. Your family. That's all that's important."

"Are you sure? We could always go there and rent a truck to move your things." He couldn't imagine Robyn had taken everything she'd wanted with her in the bed of the pickup truck.

"No. Truly, I don't want to return."

He suspected that was because she and the boys had been traumatized by having to escape her in-laws and still felt that she and Edward wouldn't be safe if she returned with him. "Alright. Do you think your in-laws will try to sabotage the sale of the house?"

"It won't matter. I didn't realize Callahan had taken a second mortgage out on the house. I won't get much out of it and if I have to let it go, then I will. You and your kin can't do anything about it. If you went there to protect the sale of the house, the whole sleuth could be up in arms."

"Okay, but I'm still helping in any way that I can if you need it."

They watched a cop show set in Hawaii on TV after that and then someone knocked on the door and called out, "Room service."

"Good, I'm starving," Robyn said while Edward got the door.

The man brought the cart into their room and set the food on the little table for two. Edward tipped him, and the waiter thanked him, then left with the cart.

They enjoyed their meals and talked about the future that he thought would never have included a life with Robyn and certainly not with a couple of his own sons. Once they were finished, he said, "Are you ready to soak in the hot tub?"

"Sure. Or we could just watch a movie and enjoy whatever else happens after that."

"We could just make a really quick trip down there, take a dip in the hot tub, and return to the room to watch a movie and enjoy whatever else happens next." He quirked a brow and smiled.

She laughed. "Alright. You seem to have your heart set on a trip to the hot tub. I'm just being lazy."

They grabbed a field pack carrying their swimsuits and then headed down to the changing room before they went outside and slipped into the hot tub. He couldn't wait to see her reaction or to even see for himself how the staff had set everything up.

They finished stripping out of their clothes and hung them up in lockers, then put on a couple of terrycloth robes. He took her hand and kissed her mouth before he led her outside. Hanging up on the glass door was a heart sign with two polar bears nuzzling and his and her names written underneath it.

"Ohmigod, did you do this?" she asked.

"Yeah. They usually just do a heart and flowers, but I sent them a photo of us as polar bears that Rob had taken that one time when we all went out to have some fun at the cabin years ago, and they added it to the card."

"I remember. This is just beautiful." She took the sign off the door and hurried back to their lockers. "I'm tucking it away as a keepsake so we don't forget it."

He smiled at her and was glad that was a hit. While she slipped the sign into her locker, he glanced out the door and saw a trail of red rose petals leading to the hot tub, twinkling lights surrounding it, and candles lit and set around the whole tub, except for a space left free where they would enter it.

Really nice. He hadn't expected to see the trail of rose petals leading to the hot tub. He turned as Robyn joined him and he reached out and opened the door.

"Oh, oh, this is too cute." She quickly ran back to the locker, and he wondered what she was up to now. She pulled her cell phone out and hurried back to the door and took several shots of the rose petals and the candles lighting the hot tub. "I've got to show everyone what a sweetheart you are. This is so romantic." Then she brought the phone with her as they crossed the deck to the hot tub.

Romantic instrumental music was playing around the tub, giving it just the right ambience.

The deck was heated, and the wood slats were wet, not iced over. He held her hand to keep her from slipping on the wet deck. The chilled air surrounded them as they hurried to the tub. There were three other hot tubs close by, but no one else was outside in this weather. He imagined in the summer it would be harder to get a spot in a tub, so he was glad they were here now, enjoying the tub and the deck all to themselves.

He would have liked to have seen the sun set as an added

romantic touch, but it set too early in the winter. Instead, he hoped they would get lucky and see some northern lights.

She peered into the tub and saw the red candles floating in the water and smiled, then snapped some more shots. He helped her into the tub and then joined her, but she was smiling, her eyes bright with excitement as she snapped pictures of the candles floating on the water and the bottle of peppermint aromatic sitting on a shelf. She set her phone on the shelf away from the water, though her phone was waterproof like his was.

"I could have requested green sage, as it's supposed to be an aphrodisiac too, but peppermint suited the season. It's a product made for hot tubs too." He slipped into the tub and joined her as he pulled her into his arms and kissed her.

"I so agree. It's just perfect," she said, grabbing her phone again and snapping pictures of him putting a couple of drops of the peppermint liquid in the water. "You are such a romantic."

"I wanted to do something special."

She set her phone back on the shelf. "You've done it. I never expected this. No wonder you were anxious to finish supper and head down to the hot tub. I just figured we couldn't make love in it, so I wanted to do so before we came down here. And then after we had dinner, I was getting sleepy. But here you had this all set up for us."

He chuckled and kissed her cheek. "I didn't want to give up the surprise, but once we started undressing each other, I figured we would just go with the flow."

"I kind of wondered. I mean, I know you're always on a schedule with your tour group. You have to be, but you were never that way with me when we had free time together."

He laughed. "You were making it awfully difficult for me to keep the secret."

She smiled up at him and then kissed his chest. "This was such a beautiful surprise."

While they were seated in the tub, the hot water over their shoulders, they were facing away from the chalet, their backs to it so that they had a view of the snow-covered trees and the dark, star-sprinkled sky. Even though they had eaten, the staff would bring them food that was meant to be aphrodisiacs—oysters, avocados, cherries, strawberries, and hot chocolate topped with whipped cream. Which is why he hadn't started the massaging ritual yet. He wanted to wait until their food was delivered. They would enjoy what they could, and then he would begin the massage.

They heard the door open to the chalet and she sighed. "I figured it would be too much to ask for, that we would have the whole deck out here by ourselves and no one would intrude on our intimate fun."

He glanced over his shoulder to see who was coming, but it was just a waiter carrying a tray of their treats and mugs of hot chocolate. "No problem. It's just the next phase of the seduction."

She glanced back and laughed. "*Ohmigod,* Edward. I am so keeping you. *Forever.*"

"Good. Because I feel the same way about you."

"Congratulations are in order," the waiter said, smiling, as he placed the dishes of food and the mugs of hot chocolate on the shelf. "Is there anything else I can get you?"

"We're good. Thank you." Robyn squeezed Edward's hand and he knew from her expression, he had made her day.

The waiter bid them a good night, then left.

It might not be as special tomorrow night when they came out to the hot tub because she might think it was old hat by then, but he'd paid for another two nights of sensual, hot tub seduction. While they were here, he wanted to do it up right.

They had fun feeding each other oysters and avocados. "Boy, these are so good," she said, kissing his lips in between. "We might not last long out here, you know, eating all this sexy food."

He chuckled, feeling the need to return to their room too.

But they had to stay out here for a while, because he wasn't about to leave until he'd massaged the peppermint scent all over every part of her silky body that needed massaging.

Then they began to eat the fruit, feeding each other cherries and strawberries, licking the strawberry juice off her chin, and she tongued his mouth when he finished.

"Hmm"—she slid her hand up his bare thigh—"are you getting ready to go back up to the room?"

"We've got a couple of more things to do." Come on, northern lights, he said silently to himself as he handed her one of the mugs of hot chocolate.

"You know, your bathtub is a whirlpool tub and I bet we could schedule dates like this when the boys are with family or at school." She smiled up at him and nuzzled his whiskery chin.

He smiled back. "You've got a deal."

She sighed and moved onto his lap. "You sure know how to spice up a honeymoon."

"There's more. If you could reach the bottle of peppermint liquid and hand it to me"—since she'd pinned him down when she'd sat on his lap—"I'll..."

She reached for the bottle and handed it to him.

"Work on this." He poured a little peppermint liquid on his hands and began to massage the tension out of her shoulders, though the way her buttocks were butted up against his erection, and the way she was moaning with ecstasy, he was having a hard time controlling *his* need to take her straight to the room and have wild and crazy sex with her!

Then he began to work the tension from her neck, and she melted against him. But the miracle of the northern lights began after that, the sky hosting swirling arrays of green, teal, and purple at the edges, providing them with the most natural light show on earth. It couldn't have made the ambience any better than this as the lights reflected off the hot tub water, the music played on, and he massaged his mate. He knew, after all the pictures she'd already taken, she would want to take some of the lights stretching in brilliant, colorful bands across the sky and reflecting off the water in the hot tub. "Go ahead," he said.

"I hate to move, or lose the touch of your skillful hands, but—"

"You've got to do it. You can show off the beauty of the experience with everyone that way."

"Okay, thanks for understanding." She scooted off his lap, grabbed her phone, and nestled back against him so she could take pictures while she sat on his lap. But he wasn't stopping his mission and continued to lightly massage her so he wouldn't disturb her picture taking.

"Okay, I'm putting my phone up." She sounded like she wanted to enjoy his touch more than she needed to take pictures now.

The northern lights could last ten minutes to all night long, and since they were continuing to ripple across the sky, he concentrated on really massaging her body. He moved his hands from her shoulders to her breasts, her nipples peaking. And then he slid his hands down her arms, over her hands, and finally moving them to her thighs.

When he finished massaging the rest of her, he said, "I've got to take care of your feet now."

Overhead, the beautiful colorful lights continued to swirl.

She quickly turned around and offered her feet to him, but she also poured some peppermint liquid on her hands and began to massage *his* feet. Before long, she was working her way up his body, his legs, stopping to skim her way up his board shorts and his erection. "Hmm," she said, and kept going up, massaging his abs, hands, and arms, making him feel relaxed, all except his cock, and that was ready for further action. She finally reached his shoulders. But she was on her knees by then, straddling him, and he was kissing her mouth and caressing her breasts as the colorful lights from the heavens above washed over them.

"Ready to take this somewhere more private?" he asked, pulling her into his arms.

"Am I ever!"

He got out of the hot tub and picked up her robe for her, and helped her into it, before he put his own on. Then he grabbed her hand, and they hurried across the wet deck to the changing room before they returned to the room for a wild night of sex. They certainly had done everything beforehand to prepare for it!

12

After taking a shower together the next morning, Edward and Robyn dressed, then went down to one of the restaurants. They were seated at a table with a view of the snow-covered trees and mountains and there was a light scattering of snow. They ordered a hearty breakfast of mushroom, swiss cheese, and avocado omelets, home fries, and buttery biscuits. Since it was their honeymoon, they decided to have mimosas, in addition to mugs of coffee.

"Skis or snowshoes on our hike this morning?" Edward asked Robyn.

"Well, we could see more of the park on skis. But we couldn't cuddle. And that's what I want to do."

Edward smiled. "We just could return to the room after breakfast." She'd been so amorous all night long, he figured she was trying to make up for lost time. Not that he wasn't eager to fulfill her needs just as much as he needed to satisfy his own. He suspected that she was a little worried they couldn't be as free to make love when they were at home with the boys. But they would find a way.

By the time they were finished with breakfast, the sun had started to rise, a golden blush sweeping across the pristine white snow. This far north, the sun hung low in the sky for as long as it was up, making for a soft light, rather than harsh sunlight on bright snow further south. Photographers on their tours always mentioned how much they loved the natural lighting as if the golden hour of photography existed for the whole four and a half hours that the sun was in the sky.

Wearing snowsuits and carrying backpacks with bottled water, snacks, and snowshoes, they headed out to the shuttle that would take them from the resort to Denali National Park. The road was closed further into the park due to the snow conditions, but at least the shuttle could take them to the entrance of the park. No one else came out to use the shuttle and the driver finally left to drop Robyn and Edward off at the park.

Once they had exited the shuttle, they put on their snow-shoes and began to walk along a trail, the upper crust of snow crunching under their footfalls. They noticed a couple of moose were eating branches and twigs of willow trees nearby.

Edward and Robyn kept out of their path to avoid confronta-tion, keeping trees between them and the hungry and unpre-dictable moose. Edward's arm was around Robyn's waist, and they'd walked about a mile when he whispered to her, "Kind of nice coming here in winter. It's so quiet because hardly any humans are visiting the park."

"It's just so peaceful and beautiful."

They were quiet then, watching for signs of any other animals when they saw a couple of white ermine chasing mice through the snow.

They observed the hunt and then the mice and ermine disappeared from sight.

Way ahead on the trail, they saw two men walking and

Edward swore they were a couple of the grizzly shifters who lived in White Bear. Hearing Edward and Robyn, the men turned to look to see who was following them, so reminiscent of shifters who could hear better than humans. They smiled and Edward waved as the men waited up for them. Edward was happy to introduce them to his wife. "Robyn, this is Josh and Jeremy Black, and guys, this is my wife, Robyn."

"Robyn Conibear, right," Josh said, frowning. "Well, congratulations, you finally got the girl, Edward."

Jeremy nodded. "Yeah, that was quick."

Edward didn't think six years was quick, but he knew what Jeremy meant. "It was past time." He didn't think the grizzlies knew Robyn from sight but had most likely heard what had happened. Any interesting news traveled quickly through a sleuth. Maybe his aunt had even invited them to the wedding, but they hadn't been able to attend on such short notice.

"She was worth waiting for," Josh said. "Care to join us on the walk?"

"They're honeymooners, can't you tell?" Jeremy asked his twin brother.

"We would love to," Robyn said, before Edward made sure it was alright with her. "So you're from White Bear? I don't remember seeing you before."

"Yeah, we're from there. We own the White Bear Gift Shop. We sell a lot of merchandise to gift stores in Alaska, and also online to shops all over the world. We even personalize some of the gifts we carry," Josh said, then he changed the subject. "We heard what happened when you left White Bear the first time, Robyn, because of how bad a shape Edward had been in after fighting your brother."

"Yes, well, I hadn't wanted to leave, but I had to, or the rest of my kin would have wanted Edward's blood."

"That's what we told Edward," Jeremy said.

"What are you doing here?" Edward asked, surprised to see the grizzlies here at this time of year.

"Delivering orders in the surrounding towns. We dropped off some gifts at the chalet gift shop and took some more orders even. Whenever we come out this way, we always drop by the park for a hike, no matter the time of year. But we're also looking for a cousin of ours, Lisa Black, and we'd heard she was staying at the resort. We wanted to make sure she spent Christmas with us, if we could convince her to come home with us. If we hadn't had appointments with stores in this area already though, we would have gone to your wedding to show our support. Genevieve had sent us the invite, but we had to decline the invitation. But we'll be sending a gift as soon as we have time."

"Do you have any of your products with you that you haven't already sold?" Robyn asked.

Josh and Jeremy smiled.

"I need to do some Christmas shopping."

"Oh," Josh said. "Sure. We were thinking you might want to pick out a wedding gift, but we'll do something special for that."

Edward really didn't want Robyn to feel that she had to buy anything for anyone, not even to try and make friends with business owners she didn't know. But then he realized she probably hoped to help her *own* business along, and he was glad she wanted to be part of the business community. Even though he and his brother and Casey did well in their business, he knew it meant a lot to her to help contribute to the family funds. And she seemed to love to do it too.

"You probably know some of the merchandise Edward's family have purchased and so I won't be buying any duplicates of anything."

"We can sure look up the items on our computer when we return to the resort." Josh appeared eager to make some more sales.

Jeremy was smiling too, and Edward knew she'd instantly won the brothers over. She was a good business woman, but he knew she still felt she needed to give gifts to the family for all they'd done for her.

"We...understand you and Edward have a couple of sons," Josh said as they continued to walk along the trail.

"Yes. Bryan and Garrett. They're nearly five-years-old," Robyn said.

"That's a great age," Josh said. "Are you up for it, Daddy?"

Edward smiled at him. "Yeah, I sure am."

"We've heard that you've already had some difficulties. Seems it follows Edward and his brother around wherever they go." Jeremy sighed. "But, Edward, at least you both ended up with lovely mates, so it's all turned out well in the end. Gary told us what had happened, by the way."

Edward had wondered. But then the bears all kept each other apprised of news that might affect them.

Josh agreed as they continued to stroll through the woods. "If only we were so lucky. We're really sorry that we missed the wedding."

"That's totally understandable," Robyn said. "I was surprised so many showed up, despite having such short notice."

Jeremy pulled a snow-covered branch aside. "We all try to show each other our support in the community."

"Do you have a picture of Lisa? If we see her, we could let her know you're looking for her," Robyn said.

Edward already knew what she looked like. He'd forgotten Robyn didn't.

"Yeah, sure, thanks." Josh pulled out his phone and showed the picture of a redhead with blue eyes and a pretty smile. "If you see her, tell her we'll be in the area for a couple of more days and then we'll have to head back to White Bear for Christmas. We'd hoped we could take her with us."

"Do you know for sure that she's here?" Edward asked.

"She told our mom she was going to be. She writes articles for different sources. She was doing a story in the area. She's all alone now and we know she's feeling blue about it. It's the first year for her without her parents at Christmastime. She needs to return to White Bear and be with the rest of her family."

"We'll tell her if we see her. If you leave before us, we'll try and convince her to return home with us," Edward said.

"You're honeymooners. We couldn't ask you to do that," Josh said.

"We'll be headed back home. It'll be no difficulty at all," Robyn said. "Are you going to run as bears while you're here? Though if anyone sees you, they'll wonder why you aren't hibernating."

The brothers laughed.

"We haven't smelled Lisa's scent out here, or we would have done so to see if we could locate her as bears. What about you? Are you going to run as polar bears?" Josh asked.

"Maybe tomorrow," Robyn said. "There are so few visitors in the winter at the park, we could probably get away with it without being spotted. But if we were seen, talk about a shock to visitors. Of course, if they reported it and they didn't capture a picture of us, no one would ever believe it. Or if they did, I can just see droves of people invading the winter wonderland to search for the two polar bears that had somehow found their way down here. So maybe we won't take a run on the wild side."

"We heard that you make marketing videos. We'll have to check them out when you get started on your business in White Bear," Jeremy said.

Robyn smiled and pulled a card from her pocket. "Marketer. I always have business cards on me. The phone number and email address are good."

Josh pulled out their shop card. "Shop owners. We always have a business card on us."

Jeremy chuckled. "Not me this time, brother. Good thing you have one to cover for us. I gave all of mine out. Well, I guess we'll head on back and visit a few more stores. Good to meet you and we'll be returning to the chalet for dinner, if you would like to see what we have to sell."

"That would be great, thanks," Robyn said.

Before they parted ways, Josh asked her, "What about your family? Have they come to terms with you being mated to Edward?"

"No. They don't know."

"Good to know." Josh gave her a hug.

Then Jeremy did. "We'll be seeing you tonight around six?"

"That would be good," Edward said.

"And we'll have to get back with you about what you offer in the way of marketing also." Jeremy shook Edward's hand, and then Josh did.

She smiled. "Sounds great, thanks. And good luck finding your cousin."

"Thanks," both the brothers said at the same time, then headed back to the chalet.

Robyn and Edward didn't say anything for a while, then Edward sighed, letting his breath out in a frosty fog. "Lisa's parents were killed in a plane crash. She was the only one who escaped, and she felt it was her fault they all died, when she lived."

"But it wasn't," Robyn said. "Though I understand how she feels. When the hunter killed Callahan, I felt it was my fault that I hadn't done enough to keep him alive. I know I couldn't have done anything more, but still, it gnaws at me sometimes. It didn't help that I knew his parents would have wished that he had returned home with the boys and that I hadn't made it out of that situation alive. If that had happened, I believe Callahan would have brought the boys to see you and told you the truth about you being their father."

Edward wasn't so sure about that, not that any of it mattered now. Robyn had returned to him, bringing the boys with her, and that's all that was important.

She snuggled next to him. "I don't have anything for you for Christmas."

"You and the boys. That's the best Christmas present I could ever receive. It's the gift that keeps giving. Are you ready to go back to the resort and get warmed up?"

"Yeah, if the way you mean to warm me up amounts to more time in bed with you. It'll be different when we're home with the boys."

That's what he was afraid she'd been worried about. "When they go to school, if I'm not on tours with Rob and our partner, Casey, and you're not busy with your marketing, we'll have to be sure to get in some loving. After the boys go to bed, it's our time. Even my brothers and my aunt and uncle will give us the time we need for dates."

"Good. I'm so glad you waited for me, Edward."

"I didn't have a choice. I wasn't marrying just anyone. Once you stole my heart, there was no getting it back. Not until you were mine."

"Thanks for not coming after me. That would have been a sure way to get yourself killed."

"Believe me, I wanted to. I was too injured to fight anyone for a while. And my family convinced me that you needed to be the one to come back to me or I would get myself killed and they would have retaliated. No telling how many would have been hurt or even killed over it. I truly believed you hated me for killing your brother."

"I hated that he'd died for no good reason, but I didn't blame you. For a couple of months, I called your aunt and asked how you were and kept getting updates on your injuries and progress."

He scoffed. "She never told me. I thought you hated me. I would have done anything I could to make things work out between us."

"It wouldn't have worked. Not back then. Even now, we could still have real problems. But I couldn't keep the boys from you any longer. I did send Callahan's parents gifts. They should arrive tomorrow. I didn't want them to get them too soon, but I did want to send them something."

Edward admired her for it. He wouldn't have given them the time of day, had he been faced with what she had been.

"In the spirit of Christmas," she added.

"You're a more forgiving person than I am."

She shook her head. "Not forgiving. It's more of a peace offering. I doubt they would want to make the trip here to see the kids. If they did travel to White Bear, I would let them see them, but only with all of us watching the situation. And truly, it would be up to the boys if they wanted to see them. I wouldn't force it on them. I purchased my in-law's presents a couple of weeks back when I knew I was going to have to take the boys and run."

"You should have let me know your plans."

She wrapped her arm around Edward tighter. "What could you have done about it? If you had turned up in Yellowknife to help move us, they would have made you disappear for good."

"I could have flown in with Andy and Craig and rescued you."

She smiled up at Edward, and he loved that she wasn't annoyed with him that he'd wanted to be her prince and swoop down and take her away from all of the trouble she'd been in.

"Besides, I didn't even know if you were mated or were courting someone." She took a breath. "I want to get you something for Christmas. And a wedding present too."

He smiled. "After-Christmas sales are the best."

She laughed. "Alright. But I had an idea. What if I make a marketing video of your family at the tavern for the lunch meal on Christmas Eve? I know they'll be closed for Christmas Eve dinner so we can have our family dinner. But that way I can give it to them for Christmas."

He laughed. "Sure, honey, if you would like to, we can do that."

She breathed a sigh of relief.

"Though you know you don't have to do anything for the family. They're just so glad you are part of our sleuth and a member of the family now."

A snowshoe hare wearing its white winter coat jumped across their trail, startling them. They laughed.

Edward kissed her cheek and they saw the shuttle arrive with a couple of more people to drop off to hike in the park. "Just in time." He waited for her to board, then followed her into the toasty warm shuttle. "Jingle Bells" was playing overhead.

"Oh, this feels good," she said, snuggling with Edward on one of the seats as the shuttle driver drove them back to the resort. "We'll have to return here with the boys next summer. They would love to visit the park and see if they can spy any of the animals that live there. Then again in the summer, you're probably booked up on tours at the height of the season."

"We can always arrange for a getaway. There are enough of us who don't mind lending a hand. When Rob's babies were due, he took off a whole month, not wanting to be out in some remote area when Alicia had the babies. Aunt Genevieve was over there constantly helping out too, after Rob returned to help with the tours."

"Okay, good. That would be fun when the kids are out of school. And if you have room on the tour, we'll come along."

"Absolutely. Maybe the boys will want to be tour guides when they're older. And you wanted to take some tour videos too. What better way than to show the boys having fun, along with whoever else is on the excursion."

"Okay, super idea. In fact, I need to do one for every season to showcase what your tours look like any time during the year. When I look up photos for resorts, they often show only the summer scenes. It makes it appear they're not open for winter."

"Hell, good point. So you want to show folks who are looking to take a later tour or spring tour what it's like. I think we're guilty of showing off only the summer pictures too."

"Easily remedied once I get to work on it." Robyn got a text, and she pulled out her phone. "Oh. Great. My in-laws. They said I haven't heard the end of this."

Edward wrapped his arms around her shoulders and hugged her. He didn't want her to believe she'd made a mistake in being with him. The one good thing about Yellowknife was that it was a *long* way from White Bear. "Don't let them get to you."

"They were so popular in Yellowknife among our kind, mostly because he'd been the mayor, and she was such a social butterfly, that they could do no wrong. I'm sure they've riled up everyone there over this."

"They still don't have a leg to stand on. Hopefully, Andy will send Richard all the paperwork proving the boys are ours as soon as he can. Which is probably why your in-laws are angry with you. They thought they could take custody of the boys before you had any say in it. And they might have believed Callahan was named on the birth certificate, though DNA would prove I'm the boys' father."

"I still wonder if Callahan showed them the boys' birth certificates already."

"He very well could have after Bryan told them they weren't their grandparents and Callahan had to prove it to Martha."

The shuttle parked, and they thanked the driver and got out, hurrying inside the chalet to the warmth of the lobby.

"We still have time until dinner. Why don't we find something entertaining to do in our room before then." Edward wondered if she could even afford the gifts she intended to buy. He suspected she wouldn't want him to pay for them, though he would if he could. If he could surreptitiously contact the brothers and tell them to discount the items and he would pay for the rest of the cost later before they met for dinner, he would.

After they unloaded their gear in the room, Robyn called the boys and put it on speaker so they could both talk to them before they did anything else.

"Your dad and I arrived at the resort and wanted to see how you are doing," Robyn said.

"We're having a ball," Garrett said. "You're not coming home already, are you?"

Edward laughed. "No. What are you doing?"

"We're playing videogames with our uncles," Bryan said.

"And we get to stay up late too, they told us," Garrett said.

"We're glad you're having fun. Love you both," Robyn said.

"Love you." Edward still couldn't get over that he had a couple of sons, but he was glad he did and gladder still that his brother and cousins seemed to be having fun with the boys too.

"We'll call you again tomorrow," Robyn said. "But not too early, in case you're sleeping."

"Okay, love you," Garrett and Bryan said at the same time, then they ended the call.

Robyn put her phone down on the bedside table and she and Edward began removing their boots and snowsuits.

The notion of trying to contact Josh and Jeremy secretly to

have them reduce the prices for Robyn when she picked out merchandise for gifts from their catalog was now the furthest thing from Edward's mind. All he could do was undress his mate as fast as she was attempting to undress him.

13

After making love, Robyn and Edward were lying in bed, snuggling, having a nice rest, when she suddenly realized they were going to be late for dinner with Josh and Jeremy if they didn't hurry. She yanked off their covers, jumped out of bed, and began pulling on clothes.

Edward laughed. "They won't be upset if we're a couple of minutes late." He got out of bed and began dressing.

"Maybe, but I hate to be late for dates." She went into the bathroom to freshen up her makeup. She was in kind of a quandary though. She wanted to get nice gifts for the family members, even though she was going to do the video also for Ned and Genevieve. She didn't want to just get them something to be getting them something. It had to mean something special. Oh, and she wanted to get a gift for Tamara also for loaning her the wedding gown. She needed to have it dry cleaned too. She couldn't believe she'd forgotten to do that right after the wedding and before they came out here.

Edward finished dressing and hugged and kissed her. "The brothers know we're on our honeymoon and will understand." Then he took her hand, and they left the room.

When they arrived at the restaurant, both men smiled and waved at them from a table near the window.

They joined them at the table and the server brought them menus. They all ordered beef tenderloin, stone oven roasted, seasoned and roasted fingerling potatoes, asparagus and baby carrots, with Bearnaise sauce.

"So has business been pretty good?" Robyn asked as they waited on their meals.

"Oh, business has been up and down. Some months are better than others. Some years, the same way," Josh said.

"I know how that goes," Edward said. "In the winter months, our tours are way down."

"We'll have to work on that, unless you want more time off with me," Robyn teased him.

"If you put it like that... But you have the right of it. We don't do a lot of promo on our website for winter tours. After you mentioned it, I was looking it over and it does appear we're closed for the winter season. No winter pictures at all. Not any for spring or fall either. All of them are summer shots," Edward said.

"See, our slow time for sales is spring. In the summer, tourism is big, and we move a lot of merchandise. Christmas, same thing, mostly because of our personalized products, giving gifts a special touch and selling worldwide. But after Christmas, things die down. I mean, polar bears are our motto. And in spring, everyone's thinking of flowers and bunnies," Jeremy said.

Their meals arrived, and they began eating.

"Okay, so we'll see what you can do to market more spring things with polar bears," she said.

"Everyone thinks of spring as flowers, baby chicks, lambs, and bunnies, not polar bears." Josh carved into his steak.

"But some places, other than Alaska, still have snow in the spring. It makes your gifts unique. White polar bear, white snowshoe hares, Easter eggs. For displays, you could have a few purple crocuses poking up through the snow, like they do."

"Okay, I think you're right." Jeremy leaned back in his seat and turned to his brother. "I told you she could help us."

"I could shoot some footage of a snowshoe hare sitting in the snow amidst Easter eggs, crocuses, and one of our bears. Now, nobody will have that kind of remarkable photography to use for merchandise. If no one has a real snowshoe hare, we can maybe find a couple of Belgian hares. They're not really hares but rabbits. Still, they can look like hares, and they do come in white, and they're bred as pets."

Josh took a sip of his water. "You seem to know a lot about them."

"Yeah, well, I used them in a different Easter promotion for a local business in Yellowknife, no polar bears though. And no crocuses, strictly the hares and Easter eggs in the snow. It turned out really cute and was totally successful. I had dressed up the boys for the venture, they were four at the time, and they might have helped to sell the idea even more."

"Can we borrow the boys?" Jeremy asked.

She chuckled. "If we can figure out an angle where it won't get us into any...uhm, hmm, maybe they can be cubs with the Easter bunnies. What about that? Everyone loves babies."

Josh snapped his fingers. "That's it. What about Rob's babies? They would even be smaller."

"By next spring, sure, if Rob and Alicia are agreeable. We could do a couple of takes to see which works the best. My kids will sit still for photos now; the babies might not at that age."

"You got a deal." Josh started cutting up his steak again.

"I think you just got another job," Edward said, smiling. "You may end up being too busy to do *our* marketing."

"No. I can handle it." She wished she could do business in Anchorage, a bigger market than White Bear, but for now, she was sure that word of mouth would spread, and other businesses would hear about the marketing she did for them and how it had helped to improve their sales. She was excited to prove her worth, she supposed. A lot had to do with the way her in-laws had believed she would never make a real go of her business. She had all kinds of ideas. She'd just needed someone to help with the boys who didn't want to take them from her.

Once they finished dinner, she and Edward and the brothers took seats by the fireplace in the lobby, the flames flickering and the wood crackling. Josh opened up his laptop and showed her some of the merchandise he suggested she might buy for the various members of the family. She loved this because he knew the family well enough to know what they would like. She had enough savings to swing it now that she was married to Edward, as long as he didn't mind that he supported her for a while. She still had to pay the mortgage and taxes on her home until she could sell it.

Edward was on his phone, texting someone as she began looking through the merchandise and Jeremy got a text, then responded. He glanced over her shoulder and told her, "Everything is fifty-percent off. We have a big, before Christmas sale going on right now."

Josh looked up at Jeremy and he smiled. She thought Josh appeared to be surprised to hear it. She glanced at Edward to see what he thought, but he was still texting someone.

"Okay, great. I'll take the White Bear Tavern sign, Est. 1865, with the polar bear on it. Will it be ready in time?" she asked the brothers.

"We'll drop it off at your house on Christmas Eve," Josh said.

"Okay, and I want to get the New Year's polar bear apron for Genevieve, and Grandma and Granddad mugs for Ned and Genevieve. What should I get for Rob and the cousins?"

"They all barbecue but not one of them has a special set of tools. We can personalize those too," Josh said.

"Alright, sold. What about Tamara? She loaned me her wedding gown. And Alicia? Wait, maybe we can run to a couple of shops in Anchorage." Not that Robyn wanted to really go there and chance running into any of her family, but with a population of nearly three-hundred thousand, how likely would it be that they would run into anyone there that she knew?

"Are you sure?" Edward sounded concerned.

"What if you tell us what you would like to pick up and we'll get it for you?" Jeremy asked. "We have a couple of stores we need to deliver to in the city tomorrow."

"I won't know until I see the merchandise."

"I can take some pictures of the items in the stores that you want us to check out and send them to you. Then you pick out what you would like."

"Are you sure you don't mind?" Robyn couldn't believe they would help out like this.

"Yeah, it's no problem. Really."

"Okay, deal."

Edward rubbed her shoulder, and she knew he didn't want her to go into the city. She just hoped she could find what she wanted, doing it this way. She gave them the name of a couple of boutiques and then they said goodnight and the brothers headed to their room.

"What do you want to do first?" Edward asked Robyn as the guys left.

"Hot tub time? After all the exercise we got, I thought it would really be nice to take a short soak and then we can retire for the night."

"That sounds idea to me." He was eager to show her another night of hot tub romance.

After they returned to the changing room and put on their bathing suits, they found a new sign for the two bears and Robyn immediately secured it in her locker. Pink roses were leading out to the hot tub and the petals and new candles were floating on its surface. The lights twinkled in the dark around the hot tub, while candles had been set all about the rim again. The northern lights were already on full display, as if they were ready for them to finally make it down to the show to watch them.

The waiter served them chai tea, artichokes, pine nuts, figs, and pomegranates, all purported to be great aphrodisiacs too. This time, the aromatic scent was vanilla crystals and Edward put them into the water and then he began to massage her again. "I was afraid that this wouldn't be as special for you the second time around."

"Are you kidding? I could do this every night and just love it. And of course all of what comes after."

FOLLOWING another night of mated bliss, Robyn and Edward went down for breakfast. They met up with the brothers again, though Josh's ears turned a little red and he looked embarrassed that they kept intruding on the honeymooners. Robyn didn't mind as she and Edward sat down with them and ordered alder wood grilled caribou patty, cheesy grits, reindeer sausage, gravy, and fried egg. The guys had waffles smothered in blueberries and honey, typical bears.

Then the brothers told them to have a great time while they took off to do their shopping for Robyn and to visit a couple of the stores they had appointments with.

"What do you want to do now?" Edward asked Robyn.

"Our usual walk in Denali, only this time I want to ski out

and then we can see more of the park, get further away from civilization, and we can shift."

"I was thinking the same thing."

"Yeah, I really wanted to see some caribou or wolves, and Dall sheep, if we can," she said.

"Sounds good to me."

Eager to make the most of the short amount of daylight they had, they returned to the room and grabbed their skis, and their snowshoes, just in case. Then they headed out. But then she worried. What if the Black brothers were shopping for her and she was busy with skiing and then running as a polar bear and missed their texts?

She sighed. "I guess I need to scratch the plan of having the brothers look for gifts for me. If we're going to be busy with activities that mean I can't stay in touch with them, it wouldn't be fair to them."

"Maybe they can drop by the shops and then take pictures of a few items. You can check your texts every once in a while on the trail. They know we're going to be on the trail all day until it's nearly dark."

"Okay." Still, she texted them as they headed outside to the shuttle while Edward carried both their skis. Like before, the shuttle was empty for their trip.

Josh texted back.

"Okay, they said they figured that. They're dropping by the stores they have to do business with first. I can check in with them in a couple of hours."

"Perfect. Before we shift, you can get with them."

Once the shuttle dropped them off at the park entrance, they saw a couple of more moose nibbling on willow twigs, and Robyn and Edward put on their skis. They began to ski along Denali Park Road since it was the easiest for cross-country skiing and took them to where they ultimately wanted to go. For a while, they followed dog-sled trails and then moved off the trail to one of the remoter ones. They continued to ski as much as they could. Snowfall had been heavy in the last couple of weeks, which worked well for them. Sometimes the snowfall wasn't this good until February. She loved that Congress had made much of the national park off-limits to vehicles, which helped to preserve the pristine wilderness area.

"Some visitors might be camping in the park," she said.

Edward said, "What I wouldn't give to pay them a visit as a bear, but I know the concern that could cause too."

She chuckled. "Yeah, me too."

They kept going, having more of a time navigating since the snow wasn't plowed or groomed.

"Are you up for going to Hines Creek and the backcountry?" Edward asked.

"Yeah. The boys and I did a fair amount of cross-country skiing so we could get away from civilization and then shift. So I'm used to it."

They finally reached the creek and saw no sign of anyone in the area while smelling for scents and listening for voices that would carry across the snowy terrain. "Let me check really quick with the guys to see if they're at one of the stores."

Edward pulled out bottles of water for them while she checked. "Perfect. They're at the store." She chuckled as Josh sent her a picture of Jeremy holding a cashmere sweater against his chest, looking heavenward. She texted them to tell them to get each of the ladies one of the cashmere sweaters that were fifty-percent off since it was so close to Christmas, one in pale blue for Alicia and one in ivory for Tamara. She'd noticed that Alicia wore a lot of blue. Tamara was more of a neutral girl. She told the brothers thanks, though she showed Edward the picture of Jeremy and the sweater.

Edward laughed.

Then she pocketed the phone. "That's it."

"Okay, let's do this," Edward said, taking her into his arms and kissing her before they shifted.

The shift would warm them up as they transitioned from human to bear in a jiffy.

They unpacked an emergency blanket to stand on while they stripped, then she shifted, and he hurried to pack everything away and shifted.

Then they raced across the snow, through the icy river, and back up the other side. They headed for the mountains but took a bit of a detour when they saw a red tent near the bottom of one of the slopes. They didn't see any campers. They could have been hiking or climbing or skiing even.

They continued to move, stopping to drink water from the river and then looked for animals they wanted to see, finally spying some Dall sheep on one of the hills. No wolves, grizzlies should be hibernating, unless a shifter was running around like them in their fur coats, but then they saw a group of caribou, pawing at the snow, looking for something to eat.

It would take Robyn and Edward a considerable amount of time to head back to the chalet before it was dark. If they were staying out here, that would be one thing. Of course, they had good night vision also, but they would just prefer to be closer to the resort when it grew dark.

They ran into the river and crossed it, then saw three men on skies heading in their direction. The men couldn't cross the river like the bears could, but she noticed they kept stopping and one of the men was taking pictures with a long, zoom lens.

Great. Not that anyone would find any polar bears here when she and Edward were going to soon turn into humans again, but she really wished no one had seen them, much less recorded their presence. She could imagine pictures going up on the Denali National Park website. Not only were there grizzly bears, moose, caribou, wolves, and Dall sheep, but a new large animal could be seen—the polar bear. Two in fact. A male and a female. And they could speculate what would happen in the spring. Bear cubs.

She could just imagine scientists and bear enthusiasts descending on the area, searching for the very elusive polar bears and for the cubs that would be born in the spring.

When Edward and Robyn finally reached their clothes, he shifted and spread out the emergency blanket. She shifted and both of them hurried to dress. Then they packed up their gear, pulled their backpacks on, and wearing their snowshoes, they carried their skis and headed back to the road.

Edward chuckled. "They will be coming in here in droves looking for us, don't you think?"

"Yeah. I just hope the guy taking the pictures was doing a lousy job of it. Maybe, if we're lucky, we were just moving white specks in the white snow."

"He had a telephoto lens."

"But it doesn't always mean it's someone who knows what he's doing. He might have had the wrong setting on the camera and shot overexposed photos. Then everything will be white on white and no definition. At least, we can hope."

"At least no one will ever find the bears. They will have done the best disappearing act ever."

"Oh, crap. What if the pictures were decent and he airs them? Or video, if he took that. What if my family sees the media and knows we were at Denali?"

"Okay, what if we just do what we've been doing. Just have fun and in the meantime, we'll monitor the news to watch for anything about a couple of polar bears that were spotted at Denali. Even if they're lousy photos, or video and your family can't identify who the bears are, they might want to come here to check it out. And if they do, they'll smell our scents."

"So we leave early."

"*If* the news is posted. Otherwise, we'll go about our business. I mean, what if the guys don't even leave their camp for a couple of more days, so they don't download the information until they return. They could be looking for the bears to get more shots of them and just wait to prove their case after they leave their camp."

"True. It's not like they're staying at the chalet. They're camping out."

"Right."

Robyn breathed in a sigh of relief. "Okay, I'll stop panicking."

"Well, it's a good thing to be thinking ahead, just in case."

"If we see any hint of news about us running in our bear coats, we head home." That meant they had to really keep monitoring the situation too.

"Yep, that's what we'll do," he said.

They finally reached the road and removed their snowshoes and put on their ski boots and skis. Then they skied toward the entrance of the park.

"Those men would have a time crossing that river," Robyn said.

Edward chuckled. "You're worried."

"Sure I am. I don't want to have to leave before we want to."

"Hopefully, we'll be long gone before anyone does anything with the pictures or video. Do you want to have room service when we get back in?"

"I would say yes, but I need to pay the brothers for the sweaters and get them from them. So I figure we'll have dinner and then maybe room service in the morning?"

"Okay."

When they returned to the gate, there was no shuttle. "Should we just walk back, or wait and call the shuttle?" Edward asked her.

"Let's work off the rest of our meal we had this morning so we can be ready for the next big meal."

They removed their ski boots and skis and put on their boots, then began the walk back.

Once they returned to the chalet, they glanced at the local news on a big screen. No mention of polar bears sighted in Denali National Park. They went up to their room and removed their snow gear, then checked the TV again. While the TV was playing the news, they also checked their phones, just in case anyone put something up on YouTube or some other social media site.

"Nothing that I can locate," Edward said, sounding relieved.

"Good. I don't see anything either." She knew they wouldn't try shifting again if the news went out about them being in the area. Even if it didn't, the men who had spied them could be on the lookout for them.

Their room phone rang, and they both stared at it for a minute, as if they knew the caller was someone in Robyn's family. Edward grabbed up the receiver. "Hello?"

"Hey, it's Josh."

"Josh," Edward told Robyn. "We're coming down for dinner. If you have the sweaters, just bring them with you. We'll give you a check for them. Okay, see you in a few." Edward hung up the phone. "Are you ready to go downstairs and join them?"

"Should we tell them what happened to us?" She figured they should, but she wondered if Edward would rather keep it a secret. She'd been doing things for herself for so long, and making all her own decisions, it was going to take some getting used to having a mate to confer with.

"Yeah, just in case the brothers are monitoring the news and see something about it first."

When they finally reached the restaurant, Jeremy and Josh

had already gotten a table and waved to them. The bag from the boutique she'd sent them to was sitting on the floor next to Josh.

They joined them and she wrote a check for the sweaters. "Thanks so much." She pulled each sweater out of its tissue paper and admired the soft cashmere and then put them back in the bag. "Beautiful. Thanks."

"You're so welcome. No problem at all," Jeremy said.

"We have to let you know about something that happened at the park while we were out there," Edward said.

"Don't tell me. A couple of polar bears were out for a run." Josh smiled. "We knew you couldn't resist, not when you're on your honeymoon."

"Someone might have caught us on camera," Robyn said, frowning.

"Oh." Josh leaned back in his seat. He didn't seem worried about the news, probably because they were sitting here, safe and sound, and about to have dinner with them.

"If my family sees it, they'll be able to recognize it's us," Robyn added.

"Oh," Josh said again, but this time he was sitting straighter and frowning.

"But the men were camping out there. They might search for our paw prints in the snow for some time and not even be leaving the area for another few days. It could be well after we've left. So we'll just keep monitoring social networks and the news until we're ready to leave." At least Robyn was really hopeful that the men wouldn't post anything about them until much later.

"We'll do the same," Jeremy said, then chuckled. "Robyn probably doesn't know about the time we did that. Everyone was sure that a couple of male grizzlies woke up from a short winter's nap and were roaming the area. We were way out too and hadn't expected to see any humans out there in the wintertime. But at least we 'belong' in the park, unlike you guys."

"Right, and sometimes a grizzly will come out of hibernation for a short while in the dead of winter if they're disturbed, picked a bad location for a den, were hungry or sick, or sometimes are old and maybe get confused. But two male grizzlies running together?" Robyn smiled. "So what happened?"

The server brought them menus, and they all ordered hamburgers and fries.

When the server left, Josh said, "It was all over the news. We were here for a few days, but only the one time as grizzlies. We did get a kick out of all the media looking for them. Crazy bunch of people. If pure grizzlies had been roaming around out there, it could have gone badly for all the thrill seekers."

"Did anyone in White Bear see any media about it?" Robyn asked, suspecting someone would have, especially since they were some of their own and would recognize them in their bear coats. In fact, any mention of bears being in the news would make other bear shifters take notice, checking to see if the bear was one of their own.

"Hell, yeah," Edward said, answering for the brothers. "Everyone in White Bear of the shifter community, and those who weren't, were talking about it."

That's something Robyn wasn't used to either—that there were other kinds of shifters in the area. In Yellowknife, she knew only of the polar bears.

"Yeah. All it takes is for one person to see it on the news and all these scientists are on talk shows explaining why these two male grizzlies were running together in the dead of winter. Of course, we didn't chance getting caught in our fur coats running again that winter in Denali, though it had been awfully tempting," Josh said.

"Josh kept wanting to sit in the hot tub as a grizzly late one night after everyone was in bed though."

"You didn't, did you?" Robyn thought the smile Josh was wearing meant he had.

"For about twenty minutes. Maybe less time. We really prefer being in cold water when we're wearing our fur coats," Jeremy said.

"You both did it together?" Robyn laughed. She thought the guys were fun, though it could have ended badly for them. "Too bad we all couldn't do that together one night. Two grizzlies and two polar bears having a nice soak in the tub. If anyone captured videos of it, it would go viral for sure. Wait, even if everyone was asleep, what about security footage? I would think they would have security cameras that would monitor the hot tubs. Video could have caught you in the tub."

"If they had any footage of it, no one ever said anything. Maybe they were afraid people would be upset to learn grizzlies had used the hot tub, left fur behind, and who knows what else." Josh smiled.

Robyn laughed.

The server delivered their hamburgers and fries. "Does anyone need anything else?" she asked.

"No, we're good, thanks," Edward said.

Everyone thanked her for their food, and she went to the next table.

"You two are crazy," Robyn said to the brothers.

"You don't know the half of it." Edward salted his fries and steak.

They just laughed, but she was curious about what else they'd been up to.

"We'll be in the area, but we won't be returning here to the chalet after dinner," Jeremy said.

"We'll let you know when we leave the area though," Josh said. "And if we run into Lisa and take her home with us."

"We'll keep an eye out for her here," Robyn promised.

After dinner, the brothers gave Robyn a hug and shook Edward's hand.

"Congratulations again, to the both of you," Jeremy said.

"Have a great time, and we'll see you back in White Bear at some point," Josh said, "but we will be calling you before we leave, just to let you know we're no longer in the area."

Then the brothers left the chalet and Robyn and Edward returned to their room.

"Hot tub—" Edward started to say.

"If our hot-tub time is anything like what it has been for the last two nights, I'm ready. Do we have time for me to call the boys first?"

"Oh, absolutely, honey."

She was sure it would take Edward time to think about the kids, but it might just be her momma's instincts. She called Rob's cell phone number, figuring Alicia would be busy with the babies. "We weren't sure who the kids were staying with." She put the phone on speaker.

"They're here now. They were talking to the babies, making faces at them and making them smile. But everyone's kept the boys so busy, they were worn out and went to bed already."

"Oh, okay. We'll check on them in the morning then."

"Alright. Everything's been fine. They've been too busy to worry about you not being here," Rob said.

"Good. I'm glad for it," Robyn said.

"Thanks to everyone for taking care of them," Edward said.

"It's made for good memories all around," Rob said. "I've got to run. Alicia needs me to change diapers."

Edward laughed. "I never imagined you being a father and being stuck with diaper duty."

Rob chuckled. "Me either, but the babies are well worth it. Talk tomorrow."

14

This time when Edward and Robyn went down to the hot tub, a trail of bright pink rose petals led to the tub and Robyn seemed just as pleased to see the new setup. She was still taking pictures of the different settings. "I'm going to be so spoiled; I'll want this every night when we return home."

Edward was thrilled he'd made the trip so special for her because she meant the world to him. "If it makes you happy, we can, though it will be in the warmth and privacy of our house and we won't have to trudge through the cold, back to the changing room, dress, take the stairs to our room, strip out of our clothes, and get to the business of making love."

"I agree, and we can be naked in the tub from the start. So we won't have to go anywhere."

"Even better." He smiled, removing her robe, and helping her into the tub before he disrobed and settled into the hot tub with her. He was glad no one else was there to impose on their romantic interlude, all but their faithful waiter who came out to serve them a tray of crackers topped with salmon, pan-fried honey bananas, watermelon, dark chocolate-covered almonds, and hot mulled wine.

Once he left, Edward and Robyn enjoyed their appetizers, but before they could start the massages, they saw two Arctic wolves headed their way.

"Well, I'll be. That's Noah and Isabella."

"I remember them, though I wouldn't have recognized them as wolves. They came to our wedding."

"Yep, that's them." Edward waved at them in greeting.

Robyn did too then.

The wolves ran up to the hot tub and woofed in greeting.

"We didn't expect you to be here," Edward said.

Smiling, the wolves bowed their heads.

They heard someone come out of the chalet door and Edward was afraid whoever it was thought to shoot at the wolves to protect Robyn and him, but a couple of men had come out to take pictures of the "tame wolves."

The wolves woofed at Robyn and Edward, then turned and ran off.

"They must not be staying at the resort," she said.

"Maybe camping. Or staying someplace else, or I'm sure we would have seen them some time or another."

They listened to the music and didn't see the northern lights tonight but enjoyed the sensual massages and afterward, went inside to enjoy the rest of their night.

EARLY THE NEXT MORNING, Robyn called Rob and put the cell on speakerphone before they went down to breakfast so that she and Edward could learn how the boys were doing. She could hear the boys playing in the background and she hoped they weren't disturbing the babies.

"Hey, we had some worrisome news, and I was just getting ready to call *you*," Rob said, before he put the boys on the phone.

"What?" Robyn asked, thinking they needed to return home, even if it meant leaving now.

"Is that Mommy?" Garrett asked.

"Yeah, just a minute, bud. I have to tell her and your daddy something first. We saw the news of you and Edward running through Denali National Park as bears."

Edward had his phone out right away and was looking up the news.

"Yeah, we never thought we would get caught at it, when we took a run on the wild side," Robyn said. "Though we were hopeful the guys who saw us wouldn't post anything for a couple of days until we had left the area. I guess we're out of luck." They weren't running again as bears, but if her family saw the news, they might check out the chalet to see if they were staying there.

"I see it." Edward showed the video to Robyn of the two of them running through the snow, and then swimming across the river. "It was just posted a few minutes ago. We'll be leaving then. We'll get breakfast and head out." They learned everyone in White Bear had heard about the polar bears' sighting.

"This is as exciting as last year when two grizzlies woke from their winter's nap and stirred everything up. Apparently, the rooms of the chalet are booked now as a bunch of people are out looking for the polar bears," Rob said.

"They ought to pay us for all their business," Robyn said.

"I agree. Let us know if you have any problems. The kids are eager to talk to you," Rob said.

"Mommy, you got caught!" Garrett said, as if he was anxious. Probably because Rob sounded worried.

"And Daddy too," Bryan said. "I can't believe that was you and Daddy in your bear fur."

"Yeah. We didn't mean to. But you have to be so careful about getting caught where the other polar bears don't live." She'd tried to explain that to the boys, that there were polar bears that weren't shifters and they only lived further north and then the polar bear shifters lived where they could get work.

"We'll be returning home today," Edward said, "as soon as we eat breakfast, but it will take a few hours for us to drive home."

"Okay," Garrett said. "Uncle Ben is gonna take us to the movies today. Is that okay?"

"Yeah, we'll be in after that. You enjoy your movie," Edward said.

"We're gonna eat breakfast now," Bryan said. "We helped make dinosaur pancakes with chocolate chips."

"Oh, yum, that sounds good." She needed to get some fun molds for the kids.

"Bye, Mom," Bryan said.

"Love you," Robyn said and Edward echoed her sentiment.

"Love you," both boys said.

Then they ended the call and Edward and Robyn headed down for breakfast. "Maybe we should just get on the road and get breakfast somewhere else," Edward said.

"No, we'll eat here. And then get on our way." She wasn't going to be chased off.

Then she got a call from Josh. "Hey, since you gave me your card, I called you, but we wanted to know if you've seen any sign of our cousin before we leave."

"No, not at all. We're leaving right after breakfast because of the news concerning us being seen in the park."

"Oh, great, do you need our help?"

"If we do, we'll give you a call. In the meantime, if we see Lisa, we'll try to convince her to come with us."

"Okay, thanks."

They finished the call and Robyn and Edward took seats in the restaurant and quickly ordered breakfast so they could pack up, check out, and leave before they ran into any trouble from her family.

Once the food arrived, Robyn and Edward ate their scrambled eggs, ham, and toast they'd ordered from the menu. They noticed the restaurant, that had been practically empty all along, was filled with people now, probably like Rob had said—they had come to look for the polar bears, but a couple of men had seen another strange phenomenon. Arctic wolves visiting the hot tub. She overheard someone at a table next to them talking about the wolves and she recognized them then—the two men who came out to take pictures of them.

The two women who were sitting with them just shook their heads. "They could have attacked you!" one of them said.

Then the men saw Robyn and Edward and the one asked them, "Hey, you were in the hot tub last night, talking to the wolves. Do you think they were half tame?"

"I'm sure they smelled the salmon we'd eaten and came to investigate," Edward said.

"Did they growl or anything? They were wagging their tails and seemed really friendly," the other man said.

"They woofed. But they're still wild wolves," Edward said.

"Well, that was damned cool," the one man said. "Hey, Roger, what if we take our wives to the hot tub tonight and have salmon. We can take our waterproof cameras and maybe capture some shots of the wolves up close."

"Are you kidding?" one of the women said. "It's freezing out there."

"I'm game, but only if you add the flower petals, candles, and all the fun food and drinks they were having," the other woman said smiling.

Robyn realized that if the men had taken pictures of them

and the wolves, that was bad news. Then she remembered they had their backs turned to the men. She glanced at the buffet line and her heart gave a little start when she saw a woman who looked like the photo of Josh and Jeremy's cousin. "Is that Josh and Jeremy's cousin, Lisa?"

"It sure is." Edward jumped up from his seat and strode toward her.

So glad to see Lisa before they left the resort, Robyn waited at the table, not wanting to overwhelm Lisa if she were to head over there too. Edward talked to Lisa, then motioned to Robyn and Lisa turned to look. The lady and Robyn exchanged smiles, then Lisa finished filling her plate, and she and Edward joined Robyn at the table.

"Your cousins hoped to catch up with you here," Robyn said, though she knew Edward would have already told her that.

"Yeah, Edward told me. And that you and he are married and have two sons. That was quick."

"Not quick enough," Edward said.

Robyn smiled at Edward and took ahold of his hand and squeezed it. "Will you come with us so you can spend Christmas with your cousins, Lisa?"

Lisa nodded. "Sure. Thanks for the offer of a ride. I was working on a news article in the area, but I just finished it up, so came to the chalet to spend Christmas. I had an offer of a ride to White Bear after the weekend. I lost my phone on this trip, so I didn't have any way of getting a call from Josh and Jeremy, but they knew I was in this area. They just didn't know who I was doing the interview with or I'm sure they would have sent me word that way."

"Well, we're leaving after breakfast, if that works for you," Robyn said.

"Yes, that will be fine. I had a friend drop me off and he was going to pick me up after I was here for a couple of days and take me back to White Bear. I'll call him when I pack up my things in my room and let him know I'll be going home for Christmas. He'll be glad to hear it. I'll cancel my reservations at the chalet also."

Robyn wondered if the guy was a boyfriend, but then he would have been here with her for Christmas, she figured. They talked about the boys and the concern they'd had with Robyn's in-laws. She didn't mention the problems with her family with Lisa, thinking she might already know about it anyway. And she felt Lisa would think everyone in the world had a grudge against Robyn if she mentioned them too.

They had a nice visit in any case, and Lisa seemed pleased she hadn't been alone for the meal.

Once they finished breakfast, Lisa said, "I'll bring my bag down to the lobby. I'm going to the front desk to cancel my reservations."

"Okay, see you in a few," Edward said.

He and Robyn headed for the stairs.

"I'm so glad we saw her in the restaurant, and she wanted to come home with us," Robyn said.

"I think she was really pleased. We can have a nice visit on the way back to White Bear. I didn't mention anything about the situation with your family. I'm sure she knows something about it."

"I was afraid to bring it up after mentioning about my in-laws. She might think I made enemies of everyone."

Edward smiled down at Robyn, his expression totally warm and loving. "Only with those who don't count. Everyone in White Bear loves you."

That's what she loved about Edward. He knew how to turn the darkness into light.

In their room, they grabbed their skis, snowshoes, and their bags and left. After taking the elevator, they walked through the lobby and headed outside and loaded their gear into the Jeep, then went back into the lobby to wait for Lisa.

As soon as they saw her pulling her bag behind her, they joined her, and they all headed outside to the Jeep. So far, so good. No sign of any of Robyn's family.

"Thanks so much for taking me with you. I've got to let my cousins know I'm going home with you, and my friend know I don't need him to pick me up. Can I borrow someone's phone?" Lisa asked. "It's amazing how much we're hooked on them and how useful they can be when you have them and how lost we can be when we lose them."

"I so agree." Robyn gave her phone to her, and Lisa began texting someone.

They piled into the Jeep and drove off toward White Bear, hoping they wouldn't run into Robyn's family on the way out of here.

15

On the way to White Bear, they'd been on the road for about half an hour when something felt wrong with the Jeep, Robyn noticed, as Edward tightened his grip on the steering wheel. "What's going on?" She immediately glanced in the direction of the trees. They were swaying, but not from the wind. "An earthquake!"

"Okay, the rule is to slow down when you're driving a vehicle during an earthquake"—which Edward had already done—"pull off the side of the road, park, and stay in the car. But there's no shoulder here."

"Keep going until you find one," Robyn said, her heart drumming, and Lisa agreed.

Tension was high in the Jeep as the road was swaying and the vehicle was rolling back and forth. Then the road began to break up, the noise of cracking pavement filling the air. That was the thing with their bear senses, their hearing was much better than human's. Robyn prayed they wouldn't get stuck out here, or worse, injured or killed. All she could think of was her boys losing their mom and dad. The road buckled and Edward slammed on his brakes. The trees continued to sway, the pavement breaking like an asphalt puzzle being ripped apart in a spiky, nonsensical way, with chunks of the road caving into the earth, other sections solid and level as if the rest of the road hadn't just been torn asunder.

Robyn began taking pictures.

Some of the pavement was twisted downward into an area of about ten-feet long and ten-feet deep. Edward continued to drive down one section of road that had collapsed, scraping underneath the Jeep, then turning onto another section far to the left. He stopped the Jeep. "I've got to get out and see how far down the pavement is. I can't tell if we would make it down the ragged incline." He opened the door, got out, and peered down at the pavement below.

"Can we make it?" Robyn asked, joining him and looking down at the pavement way below. She didn't want him risking damage to the Jeep. They could be stuck here for who knew how long.

"Yeah. I think so. I'm willing to risk it, but how about you, ladies? Are you willing to chance it?"

Lisa joined them and looked down at the collapsed road. "It's your Jeep. I'm sure you know how it performs in bad situations better than we do. It's up to you."

"Alright, let's do it."

"Are you sure, Edward?" Robyn asked.

"Yeah, let's go before more aftershocks unsettle it further."

They got back into the Jeep, and then Edward eased the vehicle down as slowly as he could, scraping the undercarriage. She hoped that didn't mean the jagged asphalt had done damage to the vehicle.

She felt like they were on a roller coaster, doing a nosedive in slow motion, but then finally making it to the base of the road. The whole while, she was taking a video of their ordeal.

Edward took a relieved breath and continued to drive across

the broken segments of road. This time he had to make a sharp right, climbing up a section of road tilting up. He was really good at this. She wouldn't have had the nerve to try it. Though, with her pickup, she definitely couldn't have made it, she didn't think.

Then he maneuvered to the left again, navigating a section of serrated pavement, until he could make it to a patch of snowy earth. He finally drove back up onto the road, again scraping underneath the Jeep with a loud, grinding noise, making her skin crawl.

"Do you think everything is okay?" Robyn asked.

"I hate to say it, but we need to make an emergency run into Anchorage to the nearest garage so we can have the vehicle checked out. I don't want us getting stuck somewhere in the middle of nowhere on the way back to White Bear if the Jeep has been damaged." Edward finally made it past the torn-up part of the road. As far as they could see, the rest of the road was in great shape.

"We have to do it." Despite regretting that they would have to go into Anchorage, she knew they couldn't chance continuing on their way until they ensured the vehicle was safe.

"I know someone who can fix it, as long as he hasn't closed his garage and gone home for the Christmas holidays, and he didn't have any earthquake damage to his place of business. He's a grizzly and he owes me a favor. I did a great write-up on him last year after he took care of some people's vehicles who were stranded when their cars were damaged in another earthquake," Lisa said. "He received all kinds of great publicity from it and lots of new business. As long as he's available, I'm sure he'll get right on it."

Robyn hoped he would because she didn't want to run into her family in Anchorage while Edward was with her. She wasn't even sure how they would treat her if he wasn't here. She handed Lisa her phone again so she could call her friend or text him.

"I sure hate not having a phone. That's something I need to do right away when I get home. Buy a new phone." Lisa called him. "Hey, Billy, I'm with some friends who are taking me home for Christmas in their Jeep, but we ran into fallout from the earthquake." She paused. "Earthquake damage to the road we were on, and we hit the road a couple of times hard on the undercarriage. Are you open for business?" She sighed with relief. "Okay, good. Your place is okay? Alright, thanks. See you as soon as we can get there." Lisa ended the call. "He said his shop is fine, he's open for business, and to bring the Jeep right in." Lisa gave Edward the directions to Billy's garage.

Robyn was using Edward's cell phone to take pictures on the way into Anchorage, snapping shots of one of the primary schools that had a collapsed roof. "The news says that the earthquake could be felt as far away as Fairbanks, and it has caused some fires to break out." They saw a grocery store where the glass windows were cracked and broken. "Some of Anchorage has no electricity. Some of the pictures people are sharing show broken plates and dishes, grocery stores with tons of products tossed into the aisles."

They saw homes with broken glass windows, roofs partially collapsed, a crack down the center line of one of the roadways that made Robyn feel like they could be swallowed up if it widened. "Tsunami warnings have been issued for areas located along the coast." They had to make several detours and the GPS kept rerouting them.

Signals were out, and there were no lights. Cars were lined up for gas way down the road, and Robyn was glad they wouldn't have to get gas until they were on the road home. Only two gas stations were open that they'd seen. Aftershocks could be worse than the original earthquake, so they hoped they could get out of the city as soon as they could. "Even some of the ice-covered lakes have major cracks in the ice." Robyn continued to watch the news on the cell phone. "No major aftershocks should occur, they're saying now."

"That's good news," Edward said.

"This is where you're from originally, isn't it? Anchorage, I mean," Lisa said.

"Yeah, and it wouldn't be good if my old sleuth knew I was here with Edward."

Lisa texted some more. Robyn hoped she was telling her friend to make this quick or they could have some really bad company if her family found out they were here. "Wait, that was Edward and you in your fur coats on the news?"

"Right. Which is the reason we cut our honeymoon short a day, just in case someone in my family saw the news and headed for the chalet to give us grief," Robyn said.

"I wonder if the chalet had any damage," Lisa said.

"It might have," Robyn said. "I hope not though."

They started hearing a lot of military aircraft flying over-head, surveying the damage.

They finally reached the auto body repair shop and Edward said, "I think we're here."

Billy waved them into the garage, then shut the door, and put the closed sign up. "Go inside where it's warm and I'll check out the Jeep pronto. Billy's the name. The coffeepot is fine, but it's kind of a mess in there." He shook Edward's hand. "I understand there's some bad blood between you and the missus's family. I'll get this taken care of right away, if I can, and get you on your way."

"Okay, sounds good to me." Edward stayed out there with him as Billy elevated the Jeep and they both checked out the undercarriage. Lisa and Robyn went inside to have some coffee, stay warm, and help straighten up the place. A lamp had fallen over, and magazines and books were all scattered on the floor.

"I was at college when all that went down with Edward and your brother. But I'd come home on spring break when I heard how badly injured Edward was." Lisa poured them both cups of coffee.

"I hated leaving him." Robyn added sugar and a creamer to hers. Then she made a cup of coffee for Edward.

"But you did it to protect him. I understand. You made a great sacrifice, even if he worried it was because you hated him for killing his brother."

"I didn't though. I hated my brother for trying to kill Edward. And for forcing us apart in the end. I knew my other brothers would want revenge if I stayed with Edward. And I knew if I told Edward why I had left, that I wasn't angry with him for killing my brother, he would have come after me. It would have been the death of him."

"Well, despite all that, you are finally together."

Robyn assumed she didn't know that they had the boys together. "We have two sons together."

Lisa's brows shot up. "No. Wow." Then she smiled. "He said you had kids, but I didn't know they were actually his. How old are they?"

"Nearly five."

"Ohmigod." Lisa laughed. "I bet that was a shock to Edward."

"He has already proven himself to be a great, protective dad." Robyn explained about the ice floe.

"Wow. I'm glad I don't have any kids. *Yet.* They sound like a real challenge."

"They can be. It's more than just kids that get into messes on their own. As polar bear cubs, they can get into all sorts of different trouble." Robyn tried not to glance at the clock on the wall, but she found herself looking up there despite trying not to. She left the lounge and gave Edward the cup of coffee. "Do you want me to fix you some, Billy?"

"No, thanks, I'm good."

"Alright. Thanks so much for doing this for us."

"No problem at all."

Robyn returned to the waiting room and Lisa handed Robyn's phone back to her. "Maybe you want to call your new family and let them know you're on the way home. And check and see if there has been any earthquake problems out there."

"That's a good idea." Robyn suspected Lisa also wanted to ensure they knew the conflict they could be in if any of her family discovered them here. She called Rob. "Hey, it's Robyn. We left the chalet after we had breakfast, like we planned, but we ran into some issues on the highway. The earthquake made a wreck of the road while we were trying to navigate it. We're having the Jeep checked out before we drive any further."

"Really bad sections of roads? We saw the mess on the news."

Another aftershock hit and some tools rattled around and the coffee in the coffeemaker sloshed in the carafe. Robyn and Lisa were ready to head outside! But then it subsided again.

"Right. The earthquake ripped the asphalt apart while we were on the way home. We scraped the undercarriage of the Jeep a couple of times, and we had to detour to a garage in Anchorage to check it out."

"*Hell.*"

"We're okay, so far." But she knew Rob was thinking of contingency plans, like contacting Craig and Andy to fly them out there, but she didn't even know if they could land at the airport. "I just wanted to let you know that we're on our way home as soon as the Jeep is checked out."

Edward came into the waiting area. "We're good to go."

"I was just telling Rob where we are and that we're headed

home." She handed her phone to Edward.

Edward put it on speakerphone. "Hey, Rob, we're leaving the garage now. A grizzly owns it, and he won't tell anyone we were here."

"Let me know if we need to come to your aid."

"Hopefully, we'll be fine. We're still feeling the aftershocks here." Edward climbed into the Jeep and the ladies hurried to get in. "We'll call when we're out of the city."

"Okay."

They waved at Billy, and then Edward drove off, trying to find a good road out of there that didn't have any damage.

"Turn left there," Robyn told Edward, trying to guide him out of the city. "Wait."

They paused and stared at the downed power lines crackling and sparking across the road. "Okay, back it up and turn right."

Edward backed the Jeep up and turned right and they found more power lines down. "Great."

"Well, the only good thing is that if your family is looking for you, they're going to have as much difficulty getting around the city as we are," Lisa said.

They made a little bit of progress, but then came to an overpass that had collapsed. Thankfully, no cars had been on it or underneath it, but it meant they had to detour again.

They could see buildings swaying slightly with the aftershocks. Robyn was searching for news on the earthquake to see which roads had damage. "It was a 7.0 earthquake."

"I wonder if we would have been safer staying at the chalet," Lisa said.

"They've had an earthquake at Denali National Park before. A fault line runs through it." Edward's cell rang and he answered it on his Bluetooth.

"This is Billy from the garage."

Robyn hoped he hadn't forgotten to check some crucial,

potentially dangerous problem with the Jeep.

"Take an alternate route back to White Bear," Billy warned, sounding concerned.

"Problem with the earthquake?" Edward asked. They still hadn't made it to the main highway that would take them to White Bear.

"The Conibears learned the two of you are together. A cousin of Robyn's comes in here all the time because she has a real lemon of a car. She just happened to be with one of Robyn's brothers and he smelled you had been here. Rita called me after he dropped her off at home to tell me to warn you. Some woman named Martha called Robyn's parents and tipped them off that the two of you got married and have a couple of sons. So get out of here quick, but don't take the road they'll be expecting you to take."

"Thanks, Billy. We owe you one." Edward and Billy ended the call and Edward swore under his breath.

"That's what Martha meant when she said she would get even. The hateful woman. Just because she couldn't have her way," Robyn said.

"Try to find us another way to get back," Edward said.

"I was already checking. It's a long way around. It would add another couple of hours to our trip. And there's damage on that road too."

"Enough damage to make it impassable?"

"Maybe. It's hard to tell. We were lucky we managed not to ruin the undercarriage of your Jeep the last time. And we sure don't want to get stranded way out there either," Robyn said.

"What does our normal route look like?"

She searched for reports on that one. "One collapsed exit ramp, but we wouldn't be taking that. More cracked and twisted roadways, but cars are making their way around the damage."

"If a car can manage, we can. We'll take the quickest route

home and I'll call for backup at the same time." Edward called on Bluetooth. "Hey, brother, we may have another problem. Callahan's mother is stirring up problems. She called the Conibears and informed them Robyn and I are married, and all about the kids. One of Robyn's brothers learned we were at the garage where we had the Jeep checked out. Her cousin warned us. They could be trying to run us down. We don't know that for sure though."

"Do you still have four hours to drive?"

"Yeah, we're just making it back to the highway now. The one we always take. That is if we don't have any more road damage before we get there. Some of the road is damaged going in either direction we could go, so I opt for driving the shortest route."

"Okay, I had already called Andy and Craig concerning the damage to the roads out there in case they needed to rescue you. I'll inform them of the additional trouble you're having. Hold on." Rob said, "They're headed back here on the shortest route but now the Conibears might give them some problems, Gary."

"I'll meet them halfway," Gary said.

"Did you hear that? Gary's on his way to provide you some more backup. Just keep us posted."

"Alright. There hasn't been any sign of earthquake activity out there?"

"No. We were lucky this time. The roads are good out this way. We've been monitoring the news. We thought you were still at the chalet, and we hadn't seen any issues in that direction."

"No, we'd already left by then."

"No one has told the boys. We didn't want to worry them unnecessarily."

"I'm glad for that," Robyn said. "They're doing alright?"

"Yeah. They said they were on a big adventure. They're playing a game at the tavern. I'm going to let you go so I can call our cousins back," Rob said.

"Thanks. I'll call Jeremy and Josh. They're out in this area too and see if they're having any problems with the roads. They may be closer to our location. See you and the family in a few hours. Lisa Black is with us and she's staying with her family for the holidays," Edward said.

"Okay, good show. Keep me informed."

"Will do."

At least the roads were clear in this direction. No earthquake damage that they'd seen.

But then Edward said, "I need to warn you both that we have a black pickup truck following us."

"Just now?"

"It's been following us for the last half hour."

"Nowhere to turn off," Robyn said. "They could just be going in the same direction as us. Are they gaining speed?"

"Yeah. And Billy said your brother was driving a black pickup. Could be just some other, but still, it makes me wary."

"Getting close. They might just plan to pass us, but it's good to be cautious." Edward called the Black brothers on his Bluetooth. "Hey, are you still near the chalet or Anchorage?"

"We're headed back to White Bear."

"We might have some trouble." Edward explained the situation with Robyn's family and about her in-laws being the ones who told them about it. "One of her brothers could be following us."

"Have they had any contact with Robyn?" Josh asked.

"We're turning around to meet up with you on the highway," Jeremy said, "just in case you have any problems with him."

"No, they haven't contacted me," Robyn said. "I figured they wouldn't know my phone number, but maybe my mother-in-law gave it to them. Still, if they had, why not call me? Then again, if they intend to kill Edward, they're not going to want to give us any warning."

16

Surprising her, Robyn got a call from her mother, and she could envision her narrowed blue eyes and scolding tone of voice like the last time she spoke to her after Robyn's brother had died.

"Mom?" Robyn put the call on speaker. Dare she hope that her mother had come around? She doubted it and she suspected her mother-in-law had given Robyn's phone number to her mother to stir up more trouble.

"You have a lot of nerve returning here with *him*," her mom said.

Before, when Robyn had tried to tell her mother what had really happened between Edward and her brother, her mom had cut her off, not wanting to learn the truth. Robyn had every intention of trying to tell her what had happened again. Maybe, after six years had gone by, her mother would hear her out. Even if she didn't believe Robyn, she would feel better if she could tell her mother the whole story once and for all.

"Edward's my husband, like he should have been years ago." Robyn loved her mom, her dad, her brothers, and her cousins still. They'd been good to her while she was growing up. It was the issue of her falling in love with Edward that had turned everything inside out. "I'm sure my ex-mother-in-law told you about the boys. They're Edward and my sons and could have been your grandsons but that's not happening either." Maybe she should have waited to see how her mother reacted this time, but even so, her mother hadn't been warm and welcoming with the first words she'd spoken to Robyn in six years.

"You know, Mom, none of this would ever have happened if you and Dad hadn't riled up Butch and he took it upon himself to leave Anchorage with the intention of killing Edward. And for what? Some damn territorial feud between our ancestors centuries ago?"

"So now you're blaming me for Butch's death?" Her mother scoffed.

"I am. That old dispute occurred way before any of us were born! Yes, there was a fight between the packs, and yes, the MacMathans left the territory and started White Bear. But they didn't do it because they felt they weren't justified in fighting for their territorial rights. They were way outnumbered by our family. They had no choice.

"Edward didn't want to kill Butch. He did what any man would have done in his place, protecting himself to the end. Butch wouldn't give up his pursuit. Edward tried several times to break off from the fight, but Butch believed it meant Edward was the weaker of the two bears and he thought he could finish him off. Edward did the only thing he could do and that was to finish the battle.

"Butch had badly injured Edward before he returned home. None of us even knew if he would make it. I left him because I loved him, and I didn't want you encouraging anyone else in the family to try and kill Edward next. I didn't want to lose my family members either."

"You ran off with someone from Canada," her mother

accused, as if Robyn hadn't really cared enough for Edward to stay with him.

"Right. To protect Edward and you were trying to push me into marrying an abusive ex-boyfriend. Not only that, but you hated that I was pregnant with Edward's sons. What was I supposed to do? Raise them in a hostile environment like that? No way. You were always a loving Mom until the business with Edward came up. It soured everything between us when it never should have. He held no animosity for our family."

Changing the subject, her mother said, "Your mother-in-law told me her son was killed in a hunting accident and she and her husband were trying to get custody of the boys because you were too busy trying to make a living to care for them properly."

"And of course you believe her." Robyn paused to wait for her mother's response. It wasn't forthcoming. "When they couldn't take custody of the boys because they're not even blood-related to them, she took revenge by calling you to stir things up between us."

"We know the two of you were running as bears in Denali National Park," her mother said.

Robyn figured that. "But she'd called you when? Before? After?"

"After. She...she knew you were in our area when she heard the news. She had thought you were in White Bear still. We already knew you were here."

"What were you planning to do about it? Hunt us down? Kill Edward? The boys? Me even? You loved Dad and you were able to have a family and be with the sleuth. That's all I ever wanted also."

Her mother hung up on her, but not before Robyn thought she heard a choked sob.

No one in the car said anything for a moment. Then Robyn let out her breath. "Well, that was a good talk."

Edward reached over and patted her leg. "You finally had your say at least. They don't deserve you or the boys. My aunt and uncle will be the kind of grandparents that our sons deserve."

Loving Edward, she smiled at him. "The boys will be totally spoiled. Between them, your cousins and your brother, the boys won't ever want to come home."

Edward chuckled. "Someday, your family might come around. But for now, you have us, and we love you dearly."

"Thanks, Edward. I feel the same about you."

"The truck that was following us has slowed down," Lisa said, looking out the back window. "Now, it's stopped."

Robyn glanced over the seat back. "They're turning around. I don't see anything wrong with the...oh, no, the road's cracking up back there. Drive faster." The road behind them shifted, splitting into jagged pieces with a rumble, some of the sections collapsing and others shoved up on top of the other parts of the road.

Edward drove a little further, but the part of the road that had collapsed hadn't affected the pavement in their direction. "Did you see what happened to the truck?"

"I DON'T THINK the pickup made it," Robyn said, sounding concerned.

"We're going back." Edward knew it might be one or more of Robyn's brothers and they could be itching for a fight. But if they were in trouble, he didn't want to leave them to their fate. Besides, it might not even be them and they had to come to their aid, whoever they were. "Alright, ladies?" If they had more aftershocks, it could affect them too, and he knew he needed to make sure they were in agreement.

"Absolutely," Lisa said.

"Yeah, even if it's some of my family and they were following us to cause difficulties for us, we can't leave them stranded if any of them were injured," Robyn said.

He didn't have any illusions that, if her brothers were in a bad situation, helping them out would ease the tensions between her family and his. But he had to offer assistance, no matter what the situation was.

He turned the Jeep around and drove back to the edge of the asphalt where it had cracked off. He parked and everyone got out and hurried to the edge of the road. They peered down where the truck had slammed into the earth, maybe ten feet below. There was no sign of movement in the truck and Edward moved to the right of the road where it had broken off but was only about a four-foot drop in the pavement. He stopped to help Robyn and then Lisa down. Robyn was already headed for the drop-off where the pickup's tail was in the air, the tires on the pavement, the nose of the truck slanting downward.

"I'm going down there first and see if I can help anybody out," Edward said.

Robyn was already calling Rob to tell them what was happening.

Edward handed his phone to Lisa. "You can call too and see if your cousins can come and aid us." He figured he would need Robyn to help him down below, but he wanted to be the first one to check out the situation. He hoped nobody had died.

He finally made it down to the truck, the angle of the pavement so steep, he had a time making it to the passenger door on the driver's side. Inside, he could see four men. He didn't know if the three men were Robyn's brothers or not. One of the men had a gash in his head where it had impacted with the side window. He was lying against the seat, no seatbelt on. Another was groaning in the front seat, looking dazed. The driver finally unfastened his seatbelt, but everyone appeared to be kind of out of it.

He couldn't tell what was wrong with the others, except the driver was favoring his wrist, sprained or broken, Edward wasn't sure. He grabbed the driver's door to help the man out.

"Hell," the guy said, staring up at Edward with a pissed-off look.

Edward assumed he was one of Robyn's brothers. "I take it you're kin to Robyn Conibear." Even though she was no longer a Conibear.

The guy grunted in response.

"Larson," Robyn said, her voice anxious and Edward turned to see her trying to make it down the steep pavement. She took a spill, landing on her butt, and he hurried up to help her down the rest of the way to the truck. "You'd better have been following us to congratulate us on our marriage," she said to her brother.

Larson grunted in response as he tried to climb out of the truck. The front end of the truck was crumpled against the earth. He was having such a hard time getting out of the truck, Edward watched him for a second, and noticed he was still favoring his right hand. Broken hand, fingers, wrist?

Edward smelled smoke and saw a curl of it coming out of the hood. "Fire," he warned, and hurried around to reach the other side of the truck. "Hey, let's get you out of here, now," he said to the man sitting in the passenger's seat in back. "The truck's on fire."

"I think my leg's broken." The guy was still trying to get his seatbelt unfastened.

Robyn and Larson were getting the other back door open, but Larson cried out.

"Your wrist, it's broken," Robyn said. "Try to make it up the incline, away from the truck. Edward and I will get our brothers out. What about you, Maverick?"

"I'm good. I'll help get Avery out," Maverick said.

Standing next to the back door of the truck, Larson wasn't budging. "Karl has a head injury. He's not moving. You can't carry him out of here on your own. And Avery's got a broken leg. Both Maverick and Edward will be needed to carry him out of here to safety."

Maverick was climbing out of the front seat of the truck, holding his chest, giving Edward a disgruntled look. So he was the ex-boyfriend?

"I'll help you get Avery out of the backseat," Maverick said again as Edward unfastened Avery's seatbelt.

Avery was gritting his teeth and undoubtedly feeling some pain.

"We need to make a splint for his leg, but we need to get him out of the truck right this minute," Edward said as the smoke grew thicker.

Robyn said, "Get out of the way, Larson, damn it. Lisa can help me with Karl. You can't help with your broken wrist and you're going to get us all killed."

She and Lisa finally managed to drag the unconscious man from the truck. If there hadn't been the threat of a fire and possible explosion coming, they would have left the injured men where they were so they wouldn't cause any more injuries to them. But they didn't have the luxury of time.

"Have you got anything in the truck we can use to splint Avery's leg with?" Edward asked as he and the other man tried to move Avery up the steep incline.

"A couple of rifles," Larson said.

"Were you planning on hunting for polar bear?" Robyn frowned at Larson.

"You better not have been. If you had been, we should have just left you here to fend for yourselves," Lisa said, angrily.

"I agree," Robyn said.

Larson quickly grabbed the rifles and a blanket from the truck and started to head up the incline. Robyn's brother didn't deny that he and their brothers and Robyn's ex-boyfriend had planned to hunt for bear—Edward, most likely.

As soon as they were part of the way up the incline, the truck exploded, sending flames and smoke straight up into the sky, warming the cold air and everyone hit the pavement. When they thought it was safe enough, they finally got up off the asphalt and kept moving up the incline, trying to get out of harm's way as the truck became engulfed in flames.

Larson glanced back at the truck and swore under his breath. The vehicle was most likely his and a total loss.

They finally made it to the top of the road and set Karl and Avery down on the pavement. Karl had finally regained consciousness too, thankfully, though he didn't look like he knew what was going on. Avery was groaning in pain. Edward pulled out a pocketknife and began cutting strips of fabric from the blanket to use for the splint for Avery's leg and cut a strip for Karl's head wound. He handed the one piece of fabric to Robyn. Then Edward cleared the rifles of rounds and tied strips of fabric around the rifles. Once he finished with that, Lisa and Maverick held the rifles in place for Avery's splint while Edward tied the other strips of fabric around the rifles and Avery's broken leg, making sure it was tight enough to keep his leg stable.

Edward assumed Larson had been Butch's twin brother, the bear Edward had killed in a fair fight. Larson looked older than the other men and Butch was older than Robyn and her triplet brothers by five years. Larson appeared to be in charge of the brothers this time around. Edward wondered what Maverick thought he was going to do about him and Robyn.

Even now that they were all at the top of the wrecked pavement and were no longer climbing anywhere, Maverick was having a hard time catching his breath, and Edward wondered if a broken rib had punctured a lung or if he had badly bruised ribs and it was hard for him to breathe. Though Edward normally wouldn't have wished the injuries they'd had on anyone, he felt that karma had come into play here. If it hadn't been for them all being injured, he wondered just how far they would have gone if they'd caught up to them and confronted them. Both rifles had been loaded and ready for action.

As soon as Edward finished taking care of Avery, he asked Maverick, "Did you break some ribs?"

"Yeah. And I think I have a collapsed lung." Maverick sat down next to Avery.

Lisa took off for the Jeep while Robyn had covered Karl with the rest of the cut-up blanket. Lisa soon returned with one of Edward's emergency blankets for Avery and bottles of water for everyone.

Then Robyn called her mother. Edward wondered why Larson hadn't done so, until he realized Larson was having trouble doing anything with his broken wrist.

"Hey, Mom, I sure hope you didn't send my brothers and my ex-boyfriend after us to cause us grief," Robyn said, then put the phone on speaker.

"You brought it on yourself," her mother said, and Edward felt bad for Robyn. He was certain she was upset that her mother continued to be so hateful about their circumstances.

What he hadn't expected was for Robyn to hand the phone over to Larson. "Want to talk to Mom?"

"Yeah, thanks. Hey, Mom, I suggest we let this damn grudge match go and get on with our lives," Larson said.

Edward was surprised, to an extent, but glad to hear Larson say it. Robyn's eyes filled with tears.

"After he killed Butch? How can you say that!" their mother said, irate.

"Edward, Robyn, and another woman just saved our asses. That's how."

"Lisa," Lisa told Larson.

The truck was still burning, the whole vehicle in flames now.

"He injured you?" their mom asked.

"No, damn it. We ran into trouble due to an aftershock. It's over, Mom. You can continue to hate the situation as it is or give up the damn past. You riled up Butch, causing him to try and kill the man who loved our only sister. Because of that, Butch gave up his life in pursuit of an ancient feud between the sleuths. And all for what? For no damn good reason. With Edward marrying Robyn, it proves the MacMathan sleuth has moved on. If they can bury the hatchet, we need to let it go. No good will come of continuing this fight."

They heard a helicopter coming then, and an ambulance and a couple of police cars' sirens wailing.

"We've got to go," Larson said, glancing in the direction of the emergency vehicles.

"Wait, what do you mean that they saved you?" their mom finally asked. She seemed to be so hung up on the past, that she couldn't even grasp what was going on now, or much less cared, unless Larson had called with the news that he'd gotten rid of Edward permanently.

"We'll talk about it later." Larson handed the phone back to Robyn.

Edward thought she would say something more to her mother, but she just hung up on her and pocketed the phone. To his surprise, her brothers smiled at her.

"It's over for us, as far as the vendetta against you," Larson said. "You suspected we were following you, didn't you? Instead of leaving us to try to make it out of the truck on our own before the explosion, you came to help us, risking your own necks. We won't forget that. Maverick and I could very well have been the only two to survive the accident. We might not have made it either, if we'd been trying to get my brothers out when the truck exploded. Or we might have only managed to get one of them out in time."

"You would have been killed. All of you. You wouldn't have left them to their fate." Robyn gave her brother a light hug. "Thanks for coming around." Then she gave her other brothers hugs. Not the ex-boyfriend though.

Two ambulances pulled up at the edge of the road where they couldn't go any further. The helicopter landed. Paramedics arrived to take Avery into the ambulance, though they both raised brows when they saw that rifles had been used to splint his leg. They carried Karl out on a stretcher too. Then they came back for Maverick, though he'd objected and wanted to walk out on his own, but they were afraid any more movement could cause irreparable, internal damage. They wrapped Larson's wrist to stabilize it, and then he went with his brother Karl in the helicopter. Maverick went in the other ambulance.

The whole time they were getting ready to leave, Larson was telling the police how the road suddenly shifted in front of them, and they sailed down the wrecked road until they slammed into the wall of earth. Then he told them about how his sister and brother-in-law and their friend helped them all to safety or they would have died there on their own when the truck exploded.

"Were you all going home for the holidays?" one of the policemen asked, taking notes.

"Uh, they were. We were just following them to see them safely home after all this business with the earthquake and aftershocks," Larson said. "We were fortunate they were there for us."

Robyn hugged Edward. "Thanks for helping my brothers and Maverick."

"I couldn't have done anything less with a clear conscious. As far as your family is concerned, at least your brothers seem to be willing to let things go."

"Yeah. Mom and Dad are another story." Robyn went over to the ambulance and helicopter and wished her brothers all the best.

Then the ambulances drove off and the helicopter took off.

Edward, Robyn, and Lisa piled into the Jeep and headed back home. Lisa called her cousins to tell them they didn't need their assistance.

"Josh and Jeremy were glad we're fine. They're heading back to White Bear."

"Good, and tell them thanks for trying to come to our aid," Edward said.

"I did. Well, at least something good came of all your brothers' injuries. Your other brothers weren't saying much. Do you think they agree with Larson?" Lisa asked.

"Yeah, I do. If we hadn't been there for them, they could very well have died in the truck fire." Robyn settled against her seat.

"And Maverick?" Edward asked.

"He's a wild card. He might have left my brothers to fend for themselves to save his own skin, or he might have suffered the same fate as them if we hadn't come back and saved them. How does he feel about me?" Robyn shrugged. "He was angry when I dumped him, but I don't think I mattered to him once I left town with Callahan. I think he just went along with this because the others were hell-bent on going after us."

"And the loaded rifles?" Lisa asked.

"To scare us? To shoot Edward if they were angry enough?

None of it matters now. It appears they have changed their minds and we won't have any more trouble with them. My parents won't try to send anyone else in their place to deal with us, not after my brothers tell the rest of the sleuth how we came to their aid."

"Do you think your parents will ever come around enough to see your sons and be decent grandparents?" Lisa asked.

"*I* might not be that forgiving. I'm not even sure my brothers will ever want to visit us and be their uncles either, but I'm glad that things still seemed to be resolved between us. I just hope that my brothers' injuries heal properly after we had to move them so far from the wreckage."

"They'll heal quickly and be fine," Edward reassured her.

Thankfully, there were no more aftershocks as they continued driving toward home. At least it was still daylight, and they could see what was happening. Though they had good night vision as polar bears, it was still better to be driving in daylight if the road was going to continue to break up.

"Is everyone okay?" Edward asked.

"I've never felt safer on the road during an earthquake than with you driving," Robyn said, and she meant it. "And that you were quick to act to help out my brothers."

Lisa totally agreed. "I'm just glad we weren't the ones who had the wreck. Would they have helped us out back there?"

Edward thought they would have and changed their minds about Robyn and him too.

FOR MILES, they drove without further incident and finally stopped for gas and a bathroom break at a gas station at the halfway point.

Edward had wanted to continue driving, not stopping for

anything, but everyone needed a bathroom break after all the coffee they'd had. And he wanted to fill up on gas before they went any further because there wasn't anything else for miles. He was looking at all the news on his phone and it appeared they hadn't had any earthquake rumbles out this way.

Robyn bought them cups of hot chocolate and handed him one while he filled up the tank. "Remind me to change my phone number when we get home."

"Your parents already know you're with me in White Bear again. I'm sure that if they really wanted to locate your phone number again if you got a new one, they could. Who knows. Maybe your brothers will convince your parents to turn over a new leaf. I wouldn't worry about it. How are you feeling about everything?" Edward was sure she was upset that her mother had called her, and not with conciliatory words.

"I'm annoyed that she would try to tell me off after all these years. I won't be bullied any longer by them. I ought to call my ex-mother-in-law and tell her thanks for getting ahold of my parents because we finally worked out our differences all because of her."

Edward finished his cocoa, smiled, and pulled Robyn into a hug. "You ought to. At least, you've made some inroads with your brothers."

"Excuse me, but you were coming from the direction of Anchorage, weren't you?" an older man asked them as he filled up his truck's gas tank nearby. He smelled like a wolf.

"Yes, the road was cracked up behind us. It was bad. The pickup truck following behind us had a wreck because of it," Robyn said.

"Okay, thanks. I just wasn't sure if I should continue that way or return home."

"That was the only bad part. The rest of the road was fine.

The one we took from Denali National Park was really bad also," Edward said.

"Thanks for letting me know."

"Power lines are down in some areas in Anchorage." Robyn finished her hot chocolate and threw the cup into the trash.

The old man shook his head. "I'm definitely doing this another time."

"We're you going home for Christmas?" Robyn asked.

Edward hoped the man didn't miss spending the holidays with his family. He finished filling the gas tank.

"I have family both in White Bear and...wait, you're one of the young men who serve up food at White Bear Tavern sometimes."

"Yeah, I'm Edward MacMathan. The owners are my aunt and uncle. And this is my wife, Robyn."

"Well, I'll be." The man shook his hand and then Robyn's. "Conroe Metzger. I just moved to White Bear from Anchorage, but I was going to close out my bank account there. I guess I'll wait. But I've eaten at the tavern a number of times, every time I visit White Bear, actually. It's great food and great ambience."

"Thanks. My aunt and uncle will love hearing so. Do you have family in White Bear?" Edward asked.

"Yeah, I moved close to the kids after I retired from the oil business."

"That's good news," Edward said, then saw Lisa leaving the travel center. "Hey, I'm going to head inside for a minute," he told Robyn and handed her the keys to the Jeep so she could run the engine and keep the heater going.

"Okay. We'll be waiting for you."

He told Lisa he would be right back and he hurried to use the restroom, but on the way out of the travel station, several people were talking about the earthquake and asking about the road conditions on the way to Anchorage. He told them what he knew, then hurried back to the Jeep so the ladies didn't have to wait too long for him.

"Get stuck answering questions?" Robyn asked him when he scooted into the driver's seat.

"Yeah, sorry. I was trying to get out of there as fast I could, but I needed to let everyone know what the road conditions were like, if they were headed toward Anchorage."

"We were asked the same thing," Lisa said. "Robyn was also showing them the video of what we went through. There were several travelers who right then and there decided to head back the way they had come."

"I don't blame them. That was hairy. Did anyone take any pictures of the road that broke up under Robyn's brothers' truck?" Edward got back on the road, and they had another two hours to travel before they arrived home.

"I used your phone to take some video of the road and the burning truck. I hope that was okay. We were just sitting there waiting for the rescue services and we had firsthand knowledge of more earthquake damage," Lisa said.

"Yeah, that's fine." Edward called Rob on Bluetooth to give him an update. "We're doing good. We're finally a little over halfway home." He explained about rescuing the brothers and Robyn's ex-boyfriend and how they were agreeable to let bygones be bygones. Her parents weren't changing their minds, however.

"It's a shame but it's their loss," Rob said. "That's good news about her brothers though."

"I agree. What are the kids doing?" Edward asked.

"They're both playing at the restaurant. We've been really busy, and the kids have been having a blast there."

"Okay, good," Robyn said.

"Hey, if you want another night of honeymoon bliss, everyone planned to pitch in to keep the boys busy for another night and make sure they have fun. We know you didn't plan to come in until tomorrow," Rob said.

Edward glanced at Robyn and smiled. "Thanks, Rob. I owe you."

"When our kids are that age, you can reciprocate. Let us know when you get in then."

"Sure will."

———

17

When they arrived back home, Robyn called Genevieve to let her know they'd dropped Lisa off at her cousins' house and they were now home themselves.

"Oh, good. The boys are here. They've been watching a Christmas movie. Do you want to talk to them?"

"Yeah, put them on." Robyn couldn't believe the boys were having so much fun, they hadn't really missed her. But she was glad for it.

"We had to stop the movie," Garrett said.

Robyn laughed. "You can go back and watch it. We just wanted to let you know we're home."

"Grandma said we could stay here," Bryan said.

Robyn laughed again. "Of course. Tomorrow, we'll see you at the restaurant and we'll have dinner with your uncles and grandparents for Christmas Eve. Then it's Christmas."

"Okay, can we go back and watch the movie?" Garrett asked.

"Yes. Go, have fun. See you tomorrow."

"See you," Edward said, and they ended the call as he

finished bringing in their luggage and skis. "Which means we have another honeymoon night all to ourselves."

"Even better at home. If we wake up with the munchies, we can fall out of bed, get them, and—"

"Return to bed and have some more fun."

Before they could head in the direction of their bedroom, the doorbell rang. Josh and Jeremy had arrived with the gifts Robyn had purchased for Edward's family, and Robyn was glad she and Edward hadn't gotten naked yet. She thanked them and wished them a merry Christmas.

"Thanks so much for bringing Lisa home safe and sound for Christmas," Josh said.

"She couldn't quit talking about rescuing Robyn's brothers and we're glad that the issue was resolved between you," Jeremy said.

"And just in time for Christmas." Though her parents were another story.

When the brothers left, Edward was ready for bed. He went around the house, turning off the Christmas lights. The outside ones were on a timer that would shut off automatically when it grew light out. By the time he reached the bedroom, he found Robyn in the bed already. Naked, waiting for him. Smiling.

He quickly removed his clothes, pulled the bedcovers aside to reveal her luscious nakedness, and joined her. To keep things warm until they heated each other up, he pulled the covers over them.

But it didn't take long for them to heat up with the rush of passionate kisses they shared and the friction of their bodies firing up their blood as they moved against each other, and he was soon tossing the covers aside. He had waited so long for her that he just couldn't quench his need for her. And she seemed to feel likewise, with every stroke of his skin, the manner in which she wrapped her legs around his, telling him she didn't want to let him go, that he was hers forever. Breathing in her delightful perfumed, jasmine scent, of feminine arousal, and she-bear, all made him hunger for her in the worst way. Not to mention their pheromones were engaging in their own sexual foreplay, driving them wild with desire.

He closed his mouth over hers, conquering and melding his lips with her moistened lips, but she was licking and kissing and conquering his right back. Hearts pounding, their blood hot with desire, he moved off her and began a sensual assault on her breasts, licking and teasing her already taut nipples. She sucked in her breath and ran her hands through his hair, her nails gently scratching his scalp, ratcheting up his own need to take her for his own.

Then he trailed kisses down her flat belly, his hand sweeping across her soft skin until he reached the dewy curls between her legs, and she instinctively parted her legs for him.

He brushed his thumb over her nub, and she made a ragged gasp. And then he worked up the heat. He savored every sigh, the way her body tightened with need, and how she arched against his steady strokes. He couldn't help the raw emotions swamping him, the knowledge that she was all his, after all these years of wanting.

The emotions flitting across her face reflected she felt the same way as him—the same love and need and want, the same connection they'd had before, only they were older now and had children, but the love for each other hadn't lost its beauty or strength or newness.

She moaned, clutching the bed, looking as though she was ready to fall apart, she was so near the edge of a climax. She suddenly cried out and he smiled, glad the kids weren't here. She met his smile with her own and he knew she felt the same way.

He pushed her knees further apart and centered himself on her. He took the plunge, stretching her, filling her, feeling the tumult of the orgasm she'd experienced as her inner muscles contracted around him. The raging torrent of desire had him thrusting harder, pushing for completion, knowing the end was coming.

And then he released, reveling in the feel of her as he finished, and hugged her tight, the tension in his body easing and he settled there for a moment, just luxuriating in the feel of her soft, curvy body before he moved off her. She seemed to want the moment like that, her arms wrapped around him, keeping him there.

Then he moved off her, grabbed their covers and pulled them over them, ready to snuggle with her, sleep, and repeat. "Thank you for coming home to me," he whispered against her head.

"Thank you for loving me still."

"That was a given." And then he sighed, ran his hands over her breasts, and knew it wouldn't be long before he was making love to her again.

AFTER A WILD NIGHT OF IT, either she or he started it, the next day, Robyn and Edward went to the tavern and while he helped serve meals until early closing, Robyn took videos of the fun Christmas Eve activities to show off for next year while the boys continued to play video games in the game room. She was glad that while she and Edward had been away, their uncles had taken them polar bear fishing!

Then she got a surprise call from Callahan's brother Richard. "I received the notarized birth certificates and the DNA verification that shows Edward is the boys' father. Thanks for sending them. We know you weren't able to take many of your belongings with you in the pickup. You're free to come home and move them. My brothers and I will help you. Just let us know when and we'll make it a priority to help you pack."

She was still having a difficult time believing they would let her return and not hassle her. Or even more, that they would help her. "When did you start tracking the truck?" She'd wondered about that ever since she learned a tracker had been on the truck.

"It was Dad's idea. You were taking so many trips with the boys, they were worried you were going to leave town for good. My brothers and I understand why now, but we didn't at the time. Anyway, I was supposed to monitor it, but I was busy with my job, and I had a hot date the night before you left. I slept in late, and I missed that you'd traveled so far away. Then it took me time to let Mom and Dad know it looked like you ran. And then I had to get my brothers all on the same page.

"I want you to know we did what we did because we believed our parents really were the boys' grandparents. We were pissed off at them for knowing the truth and possibly sending us into a situation where Edward's sleuth could have killed us, all for a lie. He and his people had every right to protect you and your sons. By way of an apology, we'll do anything we can to help you pack up and leave. You have our word."

"Thank you, Richard."

"You were always good to us. Callahan loved you. He would have wanted us to look out for you, and he would have been furious with us if he'd known how we had terrorized you and the boys the way we did."

"His dying words were that he wanted me to see Edward and tell him the truth about his sons. I didn't know if Edward and I could even get together again, or whether or not he was mated.

But I had to tell him about his sons, and he had the right to help raise them."

"Callahan was right. I'm glad the boys are with you and their father. It's as it should be. You've got my number. When you get into town, just let us know."

"Thanks."

They ended the call, and she was torn about returning to Yellowknife. She never wanted to go back there because of her hostile in-laws.

"Is everything alright?" Edward asked, drawing her into his arms to comfort her.

She loved him for always being so concerned about her feelings. "Yes. Richard received the paperwork you had sent to him and thanked us."

"And the tracking device?"

She explained when they had put it on, and that Richard had failed to monitor it because of work and social commitments.

"I'm surprised your in-laws hadn't been the ones to monitor it. They're no longer working, correct?"

She nodded.

"And they had all the reason in the world to keep track of you."

"I agree. But they're very controlling. I can see them making their sons do their dirty work for them."

"Do you want to return to Yellowknife and pack up your household?"

"Yeah. I do. We left in such a hurry and just didn't have the room to take as much as we would have liked to. Like our skis and kids' books and clothes I planned to replace."

"Okay, we'll fly there, hire a truck to pack it up and haul it here. We're not making that long drive out and back. And, I'll make sure we have some muscle when we go."

She prayed they didn't run into any trouble.

CHRISTMAS EVE, Robyn, Edward, and the boys drove over to Edward's cousins' house for dinner. Robyn admired the brothers for making most of the prime rib dinner, though she and the boys prepared brownies for dessert, Alicia made punch, and Genevieve threw together a green bean casserole.

The roast had all the trimmings: potatoes, carrots, and gravy. Robyn figured the guys would make great husbands when they found the right ladies for them.

When they got home that evening, they found a beautiful sign attached to the front door. Two polar bears and their cubs were featured on the sign and each of their names were engraved. A note was attached. "Oh, how lovely," Robyn said, taking the card off the sign. "It's the wedding gift from Josh and Jeremy."

"Hey, that's me," Garrett said.

Bryan laughed and pointed to his name. "And that's me!"

They headed inside to read bedside stories to the boys so they could go to sleep. Edward took a couple of turns too.

They wanted more stories read after that, but Robyn said, "Christmas is tomorrow. We have to go to bed so we can get up to open presents at your grandparents' home in the morning."

That was the end of bedtime stories and the boys eagerly agreed to go to sleep.

"Now it's time for *our* own Christmas Eve celebration," Edward said, after they slipped into bed for some loving before Ned played Santa Claus through the town.

Edward had set the alarm and when it was time, he and Robyn bundled up to take pictures of Granddad Ned dressed as

Santa Claus, calling out "ho-ho-ho!" as he rode by the house in a horse-drawn sleigh. Everyone loved it and was out watching the "show" as "Santa" drove past the tavern and shops in White Bear.

Edward was glad his uncle got to finally play Santa for his own grandchildren, though the boys were sound asleep.

18

Early the next morning, Edward and Robyn and the boys went over to his aunt and uncle's home to have Christmas. The boys were so excited to see all the gifts sitting around the Christmas tree. The boys looked like they were ready to dive into the gifts, but Alicia, Rob, and their babies arrived, and Alicia had to take the family pictures first.

All Edward's cousins were there too: Andy, Craig, and Ben. Some years, Andy and Craig had to work and they delayed Christmas for them, but today was perfect with the whole family here and sharing in the fun.

ROBYN COULDN'T BELIEVE how different it was for her and the boys living with Edward now and with his family. They'd all had a ball opening Christmas presents, and she was thrilled that everyone had loved the gifts she'd gotten for them. It was the best Christmas ever.

They were getting ready to eat Christmas dinner while Ned was carving the turkey and the boys were setting the silverware on the table. Grandma Genevieve was making sure the boys helped and they were eager to. Christmas music was playing in the background, Alicia and Rob's babies were sleeping, and Alicia was taking all the family photos, though Robyn was taking family videos also.

The boys had made Christmas cookies with Grandma the day before and had been eager to show them off to Robyn and Edward. She was so proud of them and glad their grandmother was such a good influence on them. Robyn set the bowl of potatoes and the pitcher of gravy on the table when she got a call. She pulled out her phone and thought it might be from one of her brothers wishing her a Merry Christmas. She was surprised to see the call was from her dad.

Maybe he was going to thank her for helping to save her brothers' lives. She wasn't holding her breath though.

"I'm sorry I didn't call you earlier, but we've spent the last couple of days visiting Karl at the hospital."

She had just assumed he would get checked out and then would be sent home. "Is he going to be alright?" She imagined the others would have had x-rays and their broken bones casted, well, except for Maverick, and then gone home.

"Yes, he's being released tomorrow. He's pretty pissed off that your mother wanted them to chase you down and then you ended up having to rescue them. I didn't know about it. I was working on downed power lines. Your mom didn't tell me where your brothers had gone. Though they're grown men, so it isn't like I keep track of them all the time. I would have straightened your mom out and told the boys not to go after you. You'd made your choice and we all will live with it. I was furious with her over the whole damn matter." Her father took a breath.

"You never objected...forget it." She knew her mother wore the pants in the family. Her dad would raise an objection, but once he was overridden, he would just give up. He never set her mother straight. She suspected after her brothers were all injured, her dad had finally had the gumption to tell her mother off. Or not. He was a wimp when it came to her mother. Not so with the boys though. "Forget it. It's Christmas Day and I don't want to get into this with you."

"I didn't mean to dredge up the past. All I'm trying to say is I didn't send your brothers or that ass of an ex-boyfriend of yours after you. I want to see you and my grandsons if you'll allow me to. I have to warn you that your brothers want to come too. Not Maverick. He's out of the picture."

"And Mom?" She suspected her mother wasn't interested in coming. They'd been so close at one time, the only daughter in the family, and her dad had doted on her for the same reason. Then she dated Edward, and everything was a mess after that.

Edward came over to her and wrapped his arms around her in a supportive manner. She so loved him for being aware she was talking to her family and might need his comfort. The boys were watching her, but Ned quickly took over and had the boys take glasses of water to the table for everyone.

"I suspect she'll come around. Your brothers could do nothing but praise you for all you did for them. We have you to thank for saving their lives. All the shifters in Anchorage know what you and Edward and your friend did. You're welcome to visit the city any time you like. And if you do, let me know and we'll get together. The boys said the same. Just be careful about running in your polar bear coats in Denali."

She knew he was trying for lighthearted humor, but she was still upset with her mother. "But Mom won't see us."

"She'll be the only one then and it's her loss. Do we have a deal?"

"Can you come here for New Year's Eve?"

"Hell, yeah. We'll see you for New Year's Eve then."

They ended the call and she and Edward kissed. "I take it that it was good news," Edward said.

"Dad said he didn't send my brothers after us. My mom did. If he'd known, he would have tried to convince my brothers not to go after us."

"Do you believe him?"

"Yeah. Mom has always decided things in the family. Dad just worked all the time and let her rule the household the way she saw fit. At least everyone in Anchorage knows the story. And we're welcome to visit. Which is good. I would like to take the boys there sometime to see the city and I might even get some marketing contracts if I've run out of work to do here."

"Okay, good. How is Karl doing?"

"He's still at the hospital, but they're releasing him tomorrow. Which will mean the whole family won't be celebrating Christmas until tomorrow. And my brothers are pretty banged up still, a good reminder not to listen to my mother when she's a terror and wanting them to do something they probably know in their hearts was wrong."

"I'm glad to hear he's doing okay then. And I agree about karma biting them all in the butt." Edward smiled.

"My dad and brothers want to come here for New Year's Eve."

"We'll be at the tavern for a special New Year's celebration, which means we'll be ringing in the new year there. We'll work out something on the living arrangements, so they can stay through New Year's Day, if they would like."

"Okay." She was glad things had turned around for her with the rest of her family. "Mom probably won't come." She didn't want to presume she might.

"That's okay. We'll have fun and if she comes, fine. If not, she can stew about it at home."

A WEEK LATER, Robyn was anxious about seeing her dad and her brothers at the New Year's Eve party. The boys were excited about getting to play in the playroom at the tavern. Tamara was watching them and the babies in there so Alicia would be close by and could nurse them or help with diaper changes. Not that Alicia and Tamara wouldn't have a whole lot of other help. Everyone adored the babies. Tamara had said she didn't have a date and she was happy to watch them so Rob and Alicia, and Edward and Robyn could enjoy the party.

Robyn and Edward arrived early to help decorate the tavern for New Year's. The MacMathans had closed the tavern from seven to eight that night in preparation for the party that would go on until after midnight.

The boys were even helping by setting napkins on the tables. And then everyone started arriving as the music began to play and drinks and food were set up on the buffet.

The dancing began and the boys went into the playroom to play. Edward pulled Robyn into his arms and began dancing to the music. She loved how he always seemed to know how she was feeling and took care of her. The door opened and the snow leopard brothers came in, cheering everyone.

But Edward wasn't letting Robyn go and they kept dancing.

"I couldn't love you anymore than I do, Robyn. You and the boys are the best thing that could ever have happened in my life. My new year couldn't be any better."

"I love you, Edward. I still feel I had to protect you six years ago and couldn't have stayed with you, but I'm so thrilled we're together again. You and the boys are the loves of my life."

"We've ended the year perfectly and there couldn't be any better way to begin the new year."

The door opened and he glanced at the doors. "Looks like your family is here."

Robyn turned, expecting her brothers and her dad, but her mom was with them too.

"Your mom," Edward whispered to her.

"Yes, shocker." She hesitated to go to them, then took Edward's hand and squeezed. "Ready to meet my mother and father?"

"It's too late to ask them for their permission to marry you."

Robyn chuckled. "I never needed their permission. My brothers sure look like they've been in a train wreck." It hurt her to see them like that, even though they had been on a mission to cause her and Edward trouble.

When they reached her family, her mother gave her a hug first, their eyes misty with tears. "I'm so sorry," her mom said. "We've been so foolish about all this. I...I don't know how to say how sorry I am. Will you forgive me?"

Robyn sniffled. "Mom, we were always close. I just wanted it to be the same way between us again."

"It will be. I promise."

Then her dad hugged Robyn warmly. "Glad this business is over. I'm sorry for not being there for you when you needed me the most."

She knew things would be so much better with her family now and she was so glad.

Her dad shook Edward's hand. "Welcome to the family," her dad said.

"And you, sir," Edward said, shaking his hand back. Edward turned to Karl. "How are you doing?"

"Good. Thanks for asking. And thanks for rescuing me. I don't remember a lot of what happened."

"Yeah, thanks," Avery said, walking on crutches.

Larson was still wearing a short cast on his broken wrist. "Thanks again for all your help."

"Don't mention it," Edward said.

"Can we...can we see the boys?" Robyn's mother asked.

"Right this way." Robyn and Edward led her family into the playroom. She never thought she would be showing her kids off to her family. "Mom, Dad, these are Edward and my boys— Garrett and Bryan. Boys, these are your grandparents, June and Jordan Conibear."

Her parents hugged the boys, though her sons were shy about meeting them.

Then Robyn introduced her brothers to her sons. "Your uncles, Larson, Karl, and Avery."

After that, she had her family meet Edward's family, except he did the introducing. Then the celebrating continued before it was midnight and to Robyn's surprise, her mom and dad danced, and so did Ned and Genevieve, and nearby, Robyn and Edward were in each other's arms.

It was getting close to bringing in the new year and Robyn and Edward went to get the boys so they could ring it in, but they were both sound asleep on mats near the babies' playpen where the babies were asleep also.

Robyn wrapped her arms around Edward's neck and kissed him as the countdown reached one and everyone, except for them, called out, "Happy New Year!"

They didn't cheer because they were too busy kissing and bringing in the new year right. It didn't matter about the hour, she knew when they arrived home, they would be putting the boys to bed and returning to their own bed to set off fireworks of their own.

ROBYN AND EDWARD had decided that they would fly to Yellowknife the day after New Year's Day at a family gathering for a brunch with Edward's family and hers. When they talked about their plans, Craig and Andy said they were going with them too, just in case they had any trouble, and to her surprise, her brother Larson insisted he accompany them to protect her if he needed to. Which amused all of them since he was still recovering from a broken wrist. Avery still had a casted leg and she said no to his going. Karl wanted to go, and she agreed. He hadn't had any issues after suffering the concussion in the truck accident during the earthquake.

The next morning, Robyn and the men all boarded a flight for Yellowknife, and they rented an SUV to take them to the house. Once they were there, Robyn felt a little sad about leaving the home where she'd raised her boys through their baby and toddler years. Edward noticed the ruler she'd attached to the wall and the marks she'd made for each boy as they'd grown inch by inch. He immediately looked for something to remove the ruler and take it with them. He was so sweet.

For now, she began removing the food from the cupboards and pantry and Craig and Andy began to help her. Edward pulled out all the items from drawers so they could be packed in boxes, once the packers arrived.

An hour later, the moving van arrived, and the two movers looked surprised to see all the help they would have. The men all started setting up boxes to pack what they could, and the movers began to haul out the furniture and secure it in the van. Robyn wasn't going to bother calling Richard and his brothers to ask them for help, figuring they already had enough, not to mention she still felt awkward about seeing them after the last fiasco.

But with any good bear sleuth, the word must have spread through the Yellowknife sleuth that she was at her home with a moving van. She thought maybe some of the bears had been watching her place in case there was any activity at the house.

They might have even been protecting it in case anyone had the idea of breaking and entering and stealing from her.

In any event, Richard and his brothers all showed up at the house, bringing pastries and coffee for everyone, cream, honey, and sugar too. She was grateful to them for coming, to show there were no hard feelings. At least not from them. She was sure her in-laws were another story. Even her good friend Becky Whitestone came and promised she would visit when she could. Becky was an interior designer and she was eyeing Edward's bachelor cousins with interest.

"We have room for you, whenever you would like to visit," Robyn told her.

"I would love that and as a wedding gift, if you would like, I could even give a house do-over."

Robyn smiled. "Just seeing you would be enough, but you know me. If you have any ideas, I'm all ears." She gave her friend a hug, and then continued organizing the packing effort—telling Larson in no uncertain terms, again, that he wasn't allowed to use his broken wrist in any way, while everyone was helping to pack up. She gave all the food to her brothers-in-law, and anything else she thought they could give away to other sleuth members that they didn't need—like duplicate kitchen utensils and pots and pans. With all of them working together, they were soon finished packing and she and Edward thanked Richard and his brothers and Becky for helping them and said goodbye. Callahan's brothers told her to visit anytime, but she figured that would never happen.

At the airport, she gave her own brothers hugs and thanked them before they took a different flight home, though they hoped Robyn and her family would visit the rest of the family sometime soon and they would try to make arrangements to see them in White Bear too again.

She couldn't have been more surprised to see Martha arrive

at the airport, running to catch up to them before she and Edward went through security.

Tears streaked down Martha's cheeks, and despite all that had gone on, Robyn couldn't help but be tearful to see Callahan's mother so distressed. She reached out to hug her, hoping that it was the right thing to do and that Martha wouldn't slug her for it. But the woman hugged her back. "I'm so sorry," Martha said between sobs. "I've been a witch about this whole situation. I was too ashamed to meet you at the house, but Richard warned me if I didn't do this now, we might never mend fences. I want to see the boys, and..." She sniffled and glanced at Edward. "They do favor you. I want to see you and their daddy and the boys."

Fighting tears, Robyn smiled. "Of course. Anytime. You're welcome and so are your sons."

Martha pulled something out of her oversized purse and handed an envelope to Robyn that she immediately recognized. It held her sons' birth certificates.

"Callahan told me the boys weren't his sons. I didn't believe it. Not until he dropped off their birth certificates at the house. I wasn't home, and when I saw them, I just tucked them away. I didn't want anyone to know the truth. They were...my grandsons. But I know that was selfish of me, and it doesn't matter. We love them, like they truly are our own. Please forgive me."

Robyn opened her mouth to speak, but Martha continued. "Thank you for the lovely gifts you sent for Christmas. We'll cherish them."

Then Robyn saw Arnold hurrying to catch up to them, bags of Christmas packages in hand. "I think I got them all," he said, short of breath. "Martha was in charge of stopping you before you went through security." He cast them a lopsided smile. "I don't think I've gotten this much exercise in years. We just hope you forgive us for what we intended to do and let us see you and the kids when it's convenient for you."

Robyn smiled. "You can't know how happy that makes me feel, and the boys will love seeing you again." At least if they knew they wouldn't have to live permanently with Martha and Arnold, she thought they would be happy to see them.

Then they all hugged, and Robyn and Edward said goodbye, hurrying to get through security before their plane took off without them.

She was glad she had been able to close that chapter of her life and move on. And she was thankful to everyone who helped to make it happen and that they had begun the year on better terms with both of the other sleuths.

Now it was time for them to get ready for the household goods to arrive and try to sort out everything. But Edward surprised her even more by picking up the kids and taking her to a house out in the country. He showed her the woods, a lake, and a bigger home for their family.

"Ohmigod, is it for sale?" Robyn asked. It was like the kind of dream house she'd always wanted, sitting on a picturesque, frozen lake, surrounded by woods.

"Yeah, and the asking price is right too. If you love it, we'll go from there."

"Can we see the inside?" She was so excited and so were the boys, already peering through the windows, trying to get a better look.

A car pulled up and a woman got out. "Hi, I'm Eva Wright, a relator with White Bear Reality, and you are Mr. and Mrs. MacMathan?"

"Yes. Can we see inside?" Robyn eagerly asked, smelling the woman's scent and realizing she was a polar bear too.

"You sure can. And congratulations on your marriage." Eva unlocked the lockbox and led them inside.

The kids quickly went to look for their rooms. Robyn surveyed the beautiful kitchen that would be great for big family events with an open dining and a living room just off that. A massive stone fireplace offered a perfect place for family gatherings. Picture windows looked out on the lake and a big deck stretched out from the house. She went in search of the master bedroom and she was sold. A whirlpool tub, large walk-in shower, and double sinks. A big walk-in closet was perfect for all their clothes and storage. A nice big bedroom would give them room so they could spend some quality time together when the boys were off to see the grandparents, in school, or asleep at night! And it had three extra bedrooms for guests when her family or Callahan's dropped in to see them.

Yep, this was the place for her.

"I don't know," she said to Edward, hoping he could get them to come down on the price of the house, if she acted reluctant to buy.

He smiled. "I've made an offer, contingent on you liking the place."

She smiled broadly. "Let's go for it."

"We can move your things into storage until the sale of the house goes through. Ben wants to buy our place so he can be close to the tavern since he works there, and just in case he meets the woman of his dreams."

"Have I told you how much I love you?" She wrapped her arms around Edward's neck and leaned against him to kiss him.

"As much as I love you." He kissed her right back.

THREE WEEKS LATER, Robyn, Edward and the boys had moved into their new home. Ben was already living in their old one. Being with Edward, watching him help raise the kids—she was living her dream. And the boys adored their father. Likewise, Edward couldn't have been any happier than he was now, being with her and his sons.

The bear fight that had broken them apart was in the past and all they had now was a beautiful future. Not that there wouldn't be bumps along the way. That was all part of life. But for now, as she and Edward settled on the deck in each other's arms while the boys slept, they watched the northern lights flaming across the sky, reminding her of the fun they had when they were in the hot tub at the resort on their honeymoon. Nothing could be more perfect.

"Do you want to get warmed up in the bath?" Edward asked, kissing her cold cheek.

Okay, so that could make the night even more perfect!

"Absolutely." She hurried off his lap, grabbed his hand, and pulled him into the house to enjoy some more mated bliss with the polar bear of her dreams and fantasies.

EPILOGUE

Robyn was excited about having fun with the kids and Edward and his family for Easter. The family brunch was all planned, and she didn't think anything could ruin the celebration for her, except she felt she was coming down with the flu. Next year, they planned to have the dinner at their new home on the lake, but this year, they were doing it at Ned and Genevieve's home. Alicia and Rob's babies were seven months old now and they were just starting to crawl. Garrett and Bryan were always getting down on the floor with them, and showing how it was done, which entertained everyone, including the babies. They loved the boys.

While Robyn was helping Genevieve and Alicia make the dinner: baked ham with brown sugar mustard glaze, deviled eggs, honey glazed carrots, creamy spring peas, four-cheese scalloped potatoes and asparagus and cheese tart, Rob and Edward and their cousins were making colorful Easter eggs with the boys. Ned was happy to take over babysitting duty for the babies.

Robyn had been eating way too much the last couple of weeks and it was showing. She really needed to cut back on calories and exercise more. She was getting lots done with her promo work though, videos for several businesses in town, including a pie shop where she filmed them making their scrumptious pies. And that had made her really happy.

Even Edward, Rob, and Casey's tour business had picked up a lot of new customers because of her advertising efforts for their spring tours. The tavern was experiencing even more out-of-town business, which went to show her marketing for them had really paid off. Even Jeremy and Josh had record sales after she had taken videos of their merchandise, Easter eggs, a couple of Arctic wolf pups, courtesy of one of the wolf shifter families in White Bear, a couple of white Belgian hares, Alicia and Rob's babies and Bryan and Garrett, starring as polar bear cubs. The video went viral. Not only did the brothers have a huge increase in sales for spring, but she also ended up with tons more marketing gigs. She'd even farmed some of her work out to Alicia, who happily had been helping her out.

But here it was Easter and they had so many things planned, and she really didn't feel well...like *really* didn't feel well. She hoped she wasn't coming down with the flu, especially with being around the babies. "Uhm, I'll be right back." She hurried off to the guest bathroom, luckily made it in time, and promptly threw up in the toilet.

Edward came into the bathroom to see what the matter was as she flushed the toilet and went over to the sink. "Are you okay?" He rubbed her back as she washed her face and rinsed out her mouth.

"I think I might have the flu."

"Are you sure?"

"I've been on birth control pills!" she blurted out.

He ran his hand over her belly and kissed her mouth. "It didn't help the last time."

She took a deep breath and released it. "I *have* felt tired and extra hungry. I hadn't wanted to check my weight."

He smiled. "To tell you the truth, I've noticed. Alicia and Genevieve too. If you're pregnant, I'm happy." He placed his hand on her forehead. "You're not running a fever and if you have no other symptoms than gaining weight, being tired and hungry, and having morning sickness, or in this case, early afternoon sickness, well then..." He shrugged his shoulders. "At least we still have three spare bedrooms and one can be used for a nursery."

She couldn't believe she could be pregnant. "Well, if it's true, you're shooting some determined sperm."

He chuckled. "Where there's a will, there's a way. Are you alright to eat?"

"Yeah, I feel fine now."

"Hey, I don't mean to interrupt, but I have one of these for you if you want to test it out," Alicia said, handing Robyn a pregnancy kit.

"How, why—" Robyn said.

"Genevieve and I figured you were, and we worried you were afraid to find out for sure."

Robyn loved them for being concerned and interested. She guessed she *had* been worried that she was pregnant, trying to give any other reason for the symptoms that, in the back of her mind, had reminded her of the first time she'd gotten pregnant. She'd been concerned that Edward might not be receptive to having another kid, or two, or three, and she hadn't wanted to confirm being pregnant one way or another.

If this wasn't like six years ago.

"Thanks, Alicia. I'll try it." She knew that she should try it first thing in the morning, but she suspected with the symptoms she had, she was pregnant, and the test would turn positive, especially when everybody else thought so too.

Alicia smiled and left them alone. Edward closed the door and Robyn sighed. "After this, if we're pregnant again..."

"I'll have it fixed."

Then she peed on the test strip and sure enough, two lines appeared. "We'll need to go in for a blood test, but it looks like you're going to be a papa bear again." She flushed the toilet and washed up.

"And you're going to be a mama bear again."

He hugged her gently as if he would squish the baby or babies, and then they headed into the dining room to have brunch with the family.

"Well?" Rob asked, everyone else looking eager to hear the news.

"Looks like I'm going to be a papa bear from the ground floor up this time." Edward was smiling broadly, as if this was the best news yet.

"The babies will come in the fall?" Genevieve asked.

"Uhm, yes, if I'm truly pregnant, and we have more than one. We might just have one this time."

"Or three," Ben teased, "like my brothers and me."

"And you used birth control both times?" Craig asked, looking astounded.

"Seems that it doesn't work when she's with me." Edward smiled.

Bryan and Garrett were listening to the talk and Robyn finally told them, "You may be having a baby brother or sister, or some combination thereof, about the time you start school."

"Will they go to school with us?" Garrett asked, sounding hopeful. He'd been worried no other polar bear kindergartners would be in their class.

Edward shook his head and pointed to Alicia and Rob's babies. "Remember how little they were when you first saw them? Well, the babies we have will be even smaller than that. It takes five years to get to be big boys like you."

Everyone offered them congratulations in case the news

turned out to be true, and everyone suspected it would.

Edward held Robyn's hand at the table as the family sat down to eat, the babies sitting in highchairs. He couldn't believe they were going to have babies again, and he was sure there would be more than one. But he was thrilled. This time, the family would be staying together. "I love you and the boys." He leaned down to kiss her as everyone served up the food.

She smiled up at him and sighed again. "The boys and I love you too."

They enjoyed watching the boys hunt for Easter eggs and candy after they ate, the kids racing around the house to find the hiding places while Alicia and Robyn recorded the fun. They all had a great time. After everyone in the family congratulated them again for the real possibility of them having a new baby or two, Robyn and Edward finally went home with two tired boys, and she was one tired mama bear.

The next day, she and Edward and the boys all went to see the wolf shifter doctor to learn the truth, together, as a family. She was pregnant, the babies were due in September, and she was having another set of twins. By the looks of it? Two more boys.

"Are you happy with the news?" she asked Edward.

He hugged and kissed her. "Hell, yeah. We'll have a great time. Though Garrett and Bryan will have to teach them what not to do."

"Yeah, like no riding an ice floe out to sea," Garrett said, hugging her.

"Yeah," Bryan agreed, joining in to get a hug.

Thrilled at the news, they all piled into the Jeep to drive to the theater and see an animated movie. Once again, Robyn had turned Edward's world upside down, but all for the good. And this time, he would be there for every blessed minute of it, for which they were both grateful.

ACKNOWLEDGMENTS

Thanks so much to Donna Fournier and Darla Taylor for beta reading this book! All their comments were so helpful and much appreciated starting out the new year!

ABOUT THE AUTHOR

Bestselling and award-winning author Terry Spear has written over sixty paranormal romance novels and four medieval Highland historical romances. Her first werewolf romance, *Heart of the Wolf*, was named a 2008 *Publishers Weekly*'s Best Book of the Year, and her subsequent titles have garnered high praise and hit the *USA Today* bestseller list. A retired officer of the U.S. Army Reserves, Terry lives in Spring, Texas, where she is working on her next wolf, jaguar, cougar, and bear shifter romances, continuing with her Highland medieval romances, and having fun with her young adult novels. When she's not writing, she's photographing everything that catches her eye, making teddy bears, and playing with her Havanese puppies and grandchildren. For more information, please visit www.terryspear.com, or follow her on Twitter, @TerrySpear. She is also on Facebook at http://www.facebook.com/terry.spear. And on Wordpress at: Terry Spear's Shifters http://terryspear.wordpress.com/

ALSO BY TERRY SPEAR

Adult Titles

Romantic Suspense: Deadly Fortunes, In the Dead of the Night, Relative Danger, Bound by Danger

***

The Highlanders Series: His Wild Highland Lass (novella), Vexing the Highlander (novella), Winning the Highlander's Heart, The Accidental Highland Hero, Highland Rake, Taming the Wild Highlander, The Highlander, Her Highland Hero, The Viking's Highland Lass, My Highlander

Other historical romances: Lady Caroline & the Egotistical Earl, A Ghost of a Chance at Love

***

Heart of the Wolf Series: Heart of the Wolf, Destiny of the Wolf, To Tempt the Wolf, Legend of the White Wolf, Seduced by the Wolf, Wolf Fever, Heart of the Highland Wolf, Dreaming of the Wolf, A SEAL in Wolf's Clothing, A Howl for a Highlander, A Highland Werewolf Wedding, A SEAL Wolf Christmas, Silence of the Wolf, Hero of a Highland Wolf, A Highland Wolf Christmas; SEAL Wolf Hunting; A Silver Wolf Christmas, SEAL Wolf in Too Deep, Alpha Wolf Need Not Apply, Between a Wolf and a Hard Place, SEAL Wolf Undercover, Dreaming of a White Wolf Christmas, Flight of the White Wolf, All's Fair in Love and Wolf, A Billionaire Wolf for Christmas, SEAL Wolf Surrender, Silver Town Wolf: Home for the Holidays, Night of the Billionaire Wolf, You Had Me at Wolf, Joy to the Wolves, The Wolf Wore Plaid, Jingle Bell Wolf, The Best of Both Wolves, While the Wolf's

Away, Christmas Wolf Surprise, Wolf Takes the Lead, Wolf on the Wild Side, Her Wolf for the Holidays, A Good Wolf is Hard to Find (2024), Mated for Christmas (2024)

SEAL Wolves: To Tempt the Wolf, A SEAL in Wolf's Clothing, A SEAL Wolf Christmas; SEAL Wolf Hunting, A SEAL Wolf in Too Deep, SEAL Wolf Undercover, SEAL Wolf Surrender

Silver Town Wolves: Destiny of the Wolf, Wolf Fever, Dreaming of the Wolf, Silence of the Wolf; A Silver Wolf Christmas, Between a Wolf and a Hard Place, Home for the Holidays, Jingle Bell Wolf

Wolff Family Lodge Wolves: You Had Me at Wolf, Wolf on the Wild Side, A Good Wolf is Hard to Find

Highland Wolves: Heart of the Highland Wolf, A Howl for a Highlander, A Highland Werewolf Wedding, Hero of a Highland Wolf, A Highland Wolf Christmas, The Wolf Wore Plaid, Her Wolf for the Holidays

Billionaire Wolf Series: A Billionaire in Wolf's Clothing, A Billionaire Wolf for Christmas, Night of the Billionaire Wolf, Wolf Takes the Lead

White Wolf Series: Legend of the White Wolf, Dreaming of a White Wolf Christmas, Flight of the White Wolf, While the Wolf's Away, Mated for Christmas

Red Wolf Series: Seduced by the Wolf, Joy to the Wolves, The Best of Both Wolves, Christmas Wolf Surprise

Wolf Novellas: Day of the Wolf, Seal Wolf Pursuit, Wolf to the Rescue, Night of the Wolf, United Shifter Force

***

Heart of the Jaguar Series: Savage Hunger, Jaguar Fever, Jaguar Hunt, Jaguar Pride, A Very Jaguar Christmas, You Had Me at Jaguar, The Witch and the Jaguar, Dawn of the Jaguar

***

Heart of the Cougar Series: Cougar's Mate, Call of the Cougar, Taming the Wild Cougar, Covert Cougar Christmas, a novella, Double Cougar Trouble, Cougar Undercover, Cougar Magic, Cougar Halloween Mischief, Falling for the Cougar, Cougar Christmas Calamity, Catch the Cougar (Halloween Novella), You Had Me at Cougar, Saving the White Cougar, Big Cat Magic

***

White Bear Series: Loving the White Bear, Claiming the White Bear, Bear of a Halloween

Grizzly Bear Series: Bear in Mind

***

Wolves of Old: Wolf Pack

Vampire romances: Killing the Bloodlust, Deadly Liaisons, Huntress for Hire, Forbidden Love, Deadly Liaisons, Vampire Redemption, Primal Desire

Vampire Novellas: The Siren's Lure, Vampiric Calling, Seducing the Huntress

***

Comedy Romance: Exchanging Grooms, Marriage, Las Vegas Style

***

Science Fiction: Galaxy Warrior

Young Adult Titles

The World of Fae:

The Dark Fae

The Deadly Fae

The Winged Fae

The Ancient Fae

Dragon Fae

Hawk Fae

Phantom Fae

Golden Fae

Falcon Fae

Woodland Fae

Angel Fae

***

The World of Elf:

The Shadow Elf

The Darkland Elf

Warrior Elf

***

Blood Moon Series:

Kiss of the VampireMy Book

Bite of the Vampire

The Vampire Chronicles Series:

The Vampire in My Dreams

Demon Guardian Series:

The Trouble with Demons

Demon Trouble, Too

Demon Hunter

Non-Series for Now:

Ghostly Liaisons

The Beast Within

Courtly Masquerade

Deidre's Secret

The Magic of Inherian:

The Scepter of Salvation

The Mage of Monrovia

Emerald Isle of Mists